THE LAVENDER MAFIA

JOHNNIE BARLEYKORN

Edited by Mollie A. Gill

Copyright 2020 by Gilroy Publishing

All rights reserved. This book or any portion thereof may not be reproduced or used in any manner whatsoever without the written permission of the publisher except for the use of brief quotations in a book review.

Printed in the United States of America

email: johnniebarleykorn@gmail.com

Find us on Facebook: 12-Step Survival Guide

ISBN13: 978-1-6794-5283-3

Disclaimer: Names and identifying information have been changed to protect the privacy of individuals mentioned in this book. All characters are fictitious and composites.

For all the devout clergy in the world who stay loyal to the teachings of Jesus Christ.

You serpents, you brood of vipers, how are you to escape being sentenced to Hell?
    Matthew 23:33

Chapter 1

Bishop Louis Cesare, a tall, lean man with thin lips and a beak for a nose, sat comfortably in the back of his Cadillac sedan. He enjoyed being chauffeured and had not driven for years. Approaching sixty years of age, he sported a full head of gray hair, his dull, green eyes hidden behind thick gold-rimmed glasses, some would say distinguished looking. Others closer to him observed a dismal spirit, a man not very fond of his flock, or those he referred to as the sheep, "the mindless sheep."

The bishop straightened up in his seat and glared out the window. "Goodness me, Father, can't you drive a little faster? I have a busy schedule today."

"I'm already exceeding the speed limit, Your Excellency, and it doesn't seem proper for a bishop to get a speeding ticket. The police are quite aggressive on this interstate."

"Yes, I know. I've traveled this highway a thousand times. Look, I understand you are new, but let me tell you something, Father. Things will go much better if you simply take my direction without hesitating. That is how my servants best serve."

"Of course, Your Excellency, but with all due respect, it's my license on the line."

"This is a good Catholic county and most of the officers are baptized. Plus, the local police chief is a Catholic deacon. None of my drivers ever got a ticket and none of them ever will. Now, do you understand?"

"Yes, Your Excellency."

"As you said before, it would not be proper for a bishop to get a speeding ticket. And the police have already been told as much, so you were right without even knowing it. Just keep it under ninety so we don't draw attention from the public, but the police know my Caddy and wouldn't dare stop us. It's a time-honored policy. Just get us to the soup kitchen before the photographers leave."

The Bishop leaned back in his seat, stretched out his legs and let out a big sigh. "There is nothing more depressing than a soup kitchen with all those soiled indigents and emaciated drug addicts. This visit will be rather brief so have the car standing by."

Bishop Cesare had been a bishop for almost fifteen years and had risen through the ranks quickly, becoming an auxiliary bishop in his late forties and subsequently a diocesan bishop, quite a powerful one. His contacts in the magisterium of the church were stellar. He was part of a formidable network but was tired of this current role and had his sights on archbishop, a spot that might be opening up soon. Ah, archbishop. More prestige, bigger budgets, more properties, and best of all, the absolute rule of two large beach houses.

It was almost lunchtime and a crowd had formed in front of the soup kitchen, centered in a seedy part of the city.

"Pull around the back. I don't want those people pawing at me."

The car veered down a side alley and stopped abruptly near a green dumpster. "Is this okay, Your Excellency?"

"Yes, it will do. Now go in and tell the staff I'm here, and I will need one of those dreadful aprons and a pair of those horrid plastic gloves. Once the photographers are ready, come back and alert me, then stay at the car. Do not leave under any circumstances. If I come out here and you're not at your post, it will be your first and last day as my driver. Are we clear, Father Paul?"

"Yes, sir."

After five minutes, Father Paul returned. "They're ready for you, Your Excellency."

"Okay, remember what I said, be ready for an abrupt departure."

With the best grin he could muster, Bishop Cesare entered the kitchen area and greeted the crew. "God bless all of you for the fine work you do for these disadvantaged people. What are we serving today?"

A worker pointed to the steaming silver trays. "It's beef stew Bishop, made with real beef and vegetables, not some processed stuff out of a can. We try and put out the best quality for our clients. We believe it is most nutritious, and many of them need all the nutrients they can get. If you're able to stay for lunch, I'm sure you'll find it most satisfactory, even more than satisfactory." The other workers chuckled.

"I'd love to stay, but unfortunately my schedule does not allow it. After you hand me my apron, I will assist with the serving but not before I give my blessing. Please open the doors so we can get started. I can't tell you what an honor it is to be a servant for Christ."

After fifteen minutes of spooning out the stew and mashed potatoes, and posing for numerous photographs, the bishop tossed off his apron, threw it on the countertop, and was out the door with a quick smile and wave.

"Let's get out of here, Father. I have a standing Thursday lunchtime reservation at The French Table, my regular booth near the window. Their cordon bleu is exquisite. I trust you know where it is?"

"Yes, Your Excellency."

"Beef stew my ass."

"I'm sorry, Your Excellency. What did you say?"

"Never mind, it's nothing. And make a note to have Monsignor Sabatini review the budget for the soup kitchen and be prepared to discuss it with me, likely opportunities for cost savings."

Across town, Peter Matson, owner of Matson's Floral, slammed the cooler door. "Where the heck is the baby's Breath? I always keep it in that corner bucket."

"I don't know," said his wife, Erica. "You did the order last week, didn't you? Did you order it?"

"Maybe, or maybe I screwed it up, or maybe the wholesaler did. But I can't worry about that now. I need baby's breath for Bishop Cesare's order, and I need it now."

"Really?" said Erica. "He can't do without baby's breath for one day? With that huge bouquet and all the other flowers? He probably won't even notice."

"Oh, he'll notice, trust me he will notice. He was adamant his order be just so when he gave us the business. I remember his rep telling me if I want to keep the business it has to be perfect. And he said the bishop always wants baby's breath flowers because they represent purity, and who am I to argue? This daily delivery is an extremely lucrative piece of business. Tell the driver to stop at Franklin's and get some baby's breath and not to mention a word to them about the bishop's daily order."

"Okay. I'll tell him to just stick it in the middle before delivering."

"Not quite," said Peter Matson. "Tell him to bring it back here. I'll arrange it and deliver it myself. I am not taking any chances. This account is paying half of Kim's college tuition."

In the meantime, things were a little hectic back at the chancery. "Where are the bishop's flowers? They're usually here by now."

"Don't worry, Alice," said Gil Rodgers. "They're on their way. I just called."

"Okay great. Thank goodness the bishop had to be out this morning, or it might've gotten ugly. They're supposed to be here by 9:30."

"Yeah, big deal, so today it will be 10:30. He doesn't have to know. Plus, in any event, they will be even fresher than normal."

Alice laughed and said, "Don't be surprised if he notices."

"It wouldn't surprise me in the least. He notices everything. Don't you think it's a little odd for a bishop to be ordering fresh flowers for his residence every day? I mean once in a while, sure, but every day? If you ask me, that's a little light in the loafers."

"What's that supposed to mean?"

"Never mind," said Gil.

"Gil, you had better watch your snide remarks. The walls around here have ears. One misstep and you're gone. You have a good setup here. Although I will concede some of it is a bit over the top, but with all the remodeling and upgrading the bishop has done, it makes things easy for a maintenance man, no old wiring or plumbing to deal with."

"Yeah, you're right, Alice. I need to keep my mouth shut, but some things I see just don't sit right with me."

"No one is perfect, Gil, including the bishop. If you're going to work here at the chancery you have to have discretion, or you won't last. With a handicapped child and Dusty's health problems, you need to keep your thoughts to yourself."

Father Paul, a handsome man with delicate features and bright blue eyes, pulled on the interstate and merged. Having just turned thirty-six, he was most pleased with his new role as the bishop's driver and personal assistant after working for years as an assistant pastor in large parishes. Driving the hierarchy of the church was a proven path to a cushy career in the pastorate. If you demonstrated your loyalty and prudence, you could establish yourself as part of the team, the network.

Growing up in a middle-class, Catholic family, Paul George had never been particularly devout. His father, Hermann, had become a union representative after working for years in the sanitation department and was still very active. He had developed a reputation as a zealous union man, which didn't always leave much time for his son Paul, an only child. His mother, Colleen, admired her husband's work. She worked long hours in retailing and regularly felt frustrated at Walmart's abuse of their employees and the failed attempts at unionization. The family life was reasonably good, and everyone shared a similar ideology.

His parents went to church semi-regularly and supported some of the tenants of the faith, but were most sympathetic to the Catholic Worker's Movement, social justice issues. The priest at their local parish was not especially orthodox, so his parents found him more acceptable than many of the more conservative priests that had been customary in days past. And even though his parents were not especially devout, they still felt it was well worth the investment of over $16,000 a year to send Paul to the local Christian Brother's Academy, an all-boys school which was the only reasonable alternative to the local public school which had recently installed metal detectors and was infested with drugs.

Paul had found much to like about the academy as he was bright and a deep thinker. He especially liked art, literature, and philosophy. Realizing he was getting a good education and considering the sacrifice his parents were making, Paul tried to tolerate the more traditional Catholic teachings. How could anyone even believe this stuff about demons and Hell? It was right out of the middle ages. Harry Potter seemed tame compared to these supernatural, or more accurately, superstitious beliefs. Honoring the bone fragments of saints and calling them relics? Every religion has its peculiar features, but there did seem to be some good aspects to it. He decided to take what he wanted and leave the rest.

Paul was befriended by one of the Christian Brothers, Leon. It evolved into a very special bond and the connection continued until this day. It was Leon who would teach him about liberation theology and direct him to Georgetown University to continue his studies. Thankfully, at Georgetown, Catholic orthodoxy was virtually non-existent, and he became more interested in a vocation. The church needed an overhaul, too many antiquated ideas. It could best be accomplished from the inside. Paul loved the elaborate artwork and pageantry of the church, and especially the vibrant, colorful, vestments the priests got to wear. He could never envision himself married with children, this seemed like an attractive career path with like-minded people.

"Father Paul, since I do not have a meeting scheduled today, you will be dining with me, but you can't count on this as being routine. It will typically depend on my itinerary. Also, often very sensitive matters are discussed at my restaurant stops and until I know I can trust you implicitly, it will take time, you may have to grab something nearby when I have a meeting."

"Of course, Your Excellency, but it will be an honor to dine with you today."

"Obviously, but eating alone is just dreadful. Drop me at the front door and then park the car."

Father Paul stopped the car, got out, and opened the rear door for the bishop who abruptly strutted into The French Table. "Good afternoon, Your Excellency, your table is ready and so is your server."

"Yes, thank you, but it's quite chilly. Can you lower the air-conditioning?"

"Yes, of course, Bishop Cesare."

"Oh, never mind, by the time it warms up I will be like an ice cube." Just then Father Paul entered. "Father Paul, go to the car and get my sweater."

After being seated, the bishop picked up his XR Gold, Apple iPhone. "Get a photo from the soup kitchen up on Facebook and Instagram as soon as possible. And make sure I'm not blinking and there's no glare on my glasses. It needs to be a clear, clean photo showing me serving the people. Also, contact that photographer from *The Star-Ledger* and ask when they're going to do a write-up. Tell him I can be available for a phone interview this afternoon. I want a report on my desk today citing relevant data for our soup kitchen, the number of meals served, and volunteer hours, etc. Also, I want a list of all the ancillary services we provide, like toiletries, winter jackets, backpack giveaways and so on. That needs to be on my desk by 2:00 p.m."

The bishop put his phone into his jacket pocket and smiled contentedly. "Order what you like, Father, you are my guest today."

"Thank you, Your Excellency."

"And please, you can stop referring to me in such a formal fashion. 'Bishop Cesare' will do for now. Perhaps in time, we will develop a more familiar and friendly relationship. That has been the case with most of my drivers. You come to me highly recommended. It seems we share a similar ideology. That is crucial to a good working relationship and a very attractive quality in a young man, I might add."

"Thank you, Bishop Cesare, I feel that it is time for the church to change and get in line with the modern culture. We need to be more inclusive and tolerant."

"Exactly, Father. I think we're going to be just fine together. Maybe more than just fine." The bishop motioned to the server who made his way over, pleasantly calculating the forthcoming tip.

"Good afternoon, Bishop. A Perrier with lime?"

"Yes, thank you."

"And what can I get for you, Father?"

"An iced tea with lemon please."

The owner of the restaurant approached. "Good afternoon, Your Excellency."

"Hello, Alex. Alex, I would like to introduce you to my new driver. As you can see, he is well-suited to be linking up with me. Meet Father Paul. Alex is someone you can rely on, Father, you have my word on that."

"How nice, good to meet you, Alex."

"The feeling is mutual."

After the meal and exceptional service, the bishop stole an admiring glance at his new driver. Life is good. "Father, when we leave here I wish to be taken back to the chancery. I need to take care of some church matters, then have my 3:00 p.m. nap. Later, I will be presiding at the five o'clock mass at the cathedral. Now go and pull the car around."

Gil Rodgers arrived home to find his wife asleep at the kitchen table. "Dusty, you look weak, why don't you go lay down? I'll make dinner."

"Thanks, Gil, I don't know what I'd do without you. Billy is sleeping, but he sure is a handful. Thank God my chemo treatments are almost over. I hope I get my energy back. Maybe I can go back to work soon."

"Don't even think about that yet," said Gil. "Take some time and rest up. There's no rush. Taking care of Billy is enough, and it'll be good if you two can spend some time together, at least temporarily. We'll be okay on one income for a while."

"I appreciate you, Gil, and I'm grateful you have decent health insurance."

Father Paul was assisting Bishop Caesar to prepare for mass. "Where is the sacristan? There is a wrinkle in my alb."

"I don't believe he's readily available," Father Paul said. "Once you put your stole on, it will barely be noticeable."

"Barely noticeable is still noticeable! I need you to find the sacristan so I can get a proper alb." The bishop glanced at the clock. "Oh never mind, I'll just have to endure it. It's pitiable the things I have to tolerate around here. From now on, it will be your responsibility to guarantee my vestments are impeccable. I want you to meet with the sacristan regularly to ensure I don't have any more humiliating incidents."

The bishop made his way into the church with two altar servers and Father Paul assisting. The church was packed as it was a holy day of obligation. As the bishop eyed the congregation, he felt pleased with the sermon he had prepared. After the gospel reading, the bishop began his homily.

"Today we have the parable of The Good Samaritan, a message most relevant to our modern age. It's noteworthy that Jesus uses a Samaritan in His parable because the Jewish people, who comprised the majority of Jesus's audience, despised the Samaritans, who had intermarried and worshipped idols. But it was a Samaritan who helped the man on the side of the road, expecting nothing in return. Many others passed by, including a priest, and ignored this person who was in obvious need.

"So that brings us to a piece I recently read in *The New York Times*. A woman, who lives in a border town in New Mexico, was driving on a two-lane highway and saw three men, obviously immigrants, who were clearly distraught, not far from the roadside. She promptly stopped her car and assisted them. They had not had any food or water for two days. She drove to the nearest gas station, and as she was attending to their needs, a border patrol officer, who was observing the situation, decided to investigate. It resulted in this woman being arrested and detained. She spent three hours in a holding cell, a woman whose only crime was compassion.

"It was not clear from the article what the final outcome was, if charges were dropped, perhaps that's what happened, and that's what should've happened, but the point is the woman was persecuted for an act of justice.

"I wonder how many of you would have kept on driving. I wonder how many of you would have picked up the dirty, disheveled immigrant.

"You need to look at yourselves and examine your racism, the enmity you have in your hearts against people who don't look like you, people who have different cultural backgrounds or sexual orientations. You are living a very comfortable lifestyle and have no idea what it's like to be oppressed, to have to leave your homeland with only the shirt on your back. You want to close the doors of our country to the less fortunate who only want a better life for their families. Why? Why don't you want these people here?

"You don't want to pay higher taxes to provide basic necessities for these underprivileged people. You don't want them in school with your children, and you don't want them standing in line at the grocery store. God forbid they should be buying groceries with some form of assistance program.

"You want to keep your pristine neighborhoods and country club lifestyles. That is not the message of the gospel. Jesus calls us to give of ourselves. To see Jesus in every person. As you do to the least of my brothers, so you do unto me."

The bishop continued along the same lines, chastising the mostly upper-middle-class congregation for their lack of sympathy. More than a few in the assembly did not appreciate the tone and felt it was more complicated than just compassion. The bishop had anticipated this and as he judged the demeanor of the gathering, he was happy he had prepared a "beat-down" to preempt the critics.

"Perhaps you think this homily is too harsh or political. I think we need harsher homilies in the modern church to prompt many of you to search your hearts and find the darkness. Any issue that concerns fairness, justice, and, of course, racism, is surely appropriate. If you are upset, don't blame me, you can blame our Lord and Savior, Jesus Christ. It's His parable."

After mass, Father Paul was assisting with the bishop's vestments.

"That was an excellent homily."

"Thank you, and I think you did a commendable job today, Father. I believe you will make a fine attendant for me. Plus, you are cuter than my last driver."

JOHNNIE BARLEYKORN

Chapter 2

"You are too young to make a decision like this."

"Dad, it's just a decision to pursue a vocation. If I decide to go to the seminary, I'm not deciding to be a priest. I'm simply deciding to take time to discern a vocation."

"The priesthood is a very difficult and lonely life. You have so much potential. Why wouldn't you want to do something more lucrative?"

"Maybe it's because I think God is calling me."

"Calling you? Do you really believe that stuff?"

"Yeah, I do. I can't explain it, Dad, but there is something there, and that's what the whole process of discernment is about, determining the nature of that force."

"So you think that is the best life for you, Jack? I just don't see it, and after all, I'm your father, that must count for something."

"Of course I'm interested in your opinion, Dad, but do you believe God calls men to the priesthood?"

"Well, I guess, I never really thought about it much."

"I think that is typical," said Jack. "Most Catholics don't think about their faith much. I think if you have faith it should be a real force in your life that guides and directs your actions. I don't want to be one of those people who go to church on Sunday for an hour and lives the rest of the week never considering what God wants. You and Mom raised me in the faith, but do you really believe in God?"

"Sure I do. I believe in God. I'm not an atheist."

"Do you ask God to guide and direct your life?"

"Well, if I'm being honest, I can't say I have done that recently, or maybe ever."

"Why not?"

"I just haven't felt the need. God knows I'm a good person."

"Yes, of course, Dad, and you've always been a good father to Beth and me, but you ought to consider making your faith real. It can only make it better. One of the best pieces of advice I ever got was when Mom told me, before I make decisions, ask myself, 'Is what I am about to do pleasing to God?' That's an example of what I mean by making your faith real."

"That's fine, Jack, but you know I'm not a deep thinker like your mother. All I'm saying is, I think you're too young to go to the seminary. Why not wait? Go to college or do something else first, maybe look at the military. Why rush into it?"

"I get the feeling you don't want me to join the priesthood."

"Well, Jack, with all the problems the church has been having, and all the sex scandals, the priesthood doesn't have the prestige it once had."

"I don't care about prestige, Dad. And the scandals are irrelevant. Actually, it makes me think maybe the church needs more men like me. Men who are not signing up for a comfortable life of leisure. It's obvious the church has more than its share of effeminate priests, although many of them may be good priests, some clearly have not been."

"Exactly, you wouldn't fit in."

"I'm not trying to fit in. Maybe the church needs some misfits - a different breed of men to help get the church back on solid ground."

"And you think you can do that? You're just one man, so maybe you'll have one parish, big deal. What impact could you possibly have on the massive Catholic Church?"

"It's not what I can do, Dad. It's what God can do with one priest's vocation. And I'm not expecting to cause major shifts in the church. I simply want to do my part. The rest is up to God."

"I just think you are being naïve. I admire your good intentions, but I think there's so much more you can do. If you had not given up football, you would've been the starting quarterback last fall, God knows they needed a decent quarterback. Right now you would probably be getting a scholarship."

"The coach was a profane lunatic who had no respect for academics. How someone like that gets hired to work with young people is beyond me, just insane. High school sports have gotten completely out of balance, with all these off-season "volunteer" practices and emphasis on winning. There's nothing wholesome about sports at my high school, or probably any school for that matter. Why would I want to put my time and energy into something so unhinged?"

"I guess I have to respect your position, Jack, because I really don't have an argument, other than it would have been nice to get scholarship money."

"Yeah, and then I go sell my soul to a college program and deal with a different more deranged coach who doesn't care about me or my studies. They will own me just because I play football. No thanks. Unlike the rest of the culture, I just don't think sports are that important. Plus, God will provide."

"Okay, Jack. I admire your faith. I can't say I understand, but your thinking does have a humility and honor about it."

"Thanks, Dad. I hope so. Humility means I'm on the right track." Jack went over and gave his dad a hug. "Goodnight, Dad. Love you, Dad."

Jack, who was of average height, with a boxer-like physique, and dark black hair with matching thick eyebrows, had always felt a subtle urge, a calling perhaps, to become a priest. In his mid-teens, he had heard a visiting missionary priest give a homily about the lack of vocations in the modern church. The priest said, "God is still calling men to the priesthood. God has always called them, and he is still calling them. They are just not listening! I ask every man in this congregation, are you taking time to listen? Are you ever taking a moment to ponder and consider the possibility God could be calling you?"

The priest's voice gained volume. "Every young man and woman, every decent Catholic, needs to search their hearts, and discern their vocation. Of course, God isn't calling everyone to religious life, but He is calling some of you. If He is calling you will want to answer. There's nothing more exciting and fulfilling than to walk with God.

"You all could benefit from aligning yourself with God's will. You fight and resist it, seeing it as an undesirable path, but I can tell you it is the path to the greatest peace, not the materialistic, self-indulgent lives so many of you seem preoccupied with, including, unfortunately, many of my fellow clergy.

"Jesus says in the book of Matthew, Chapter 6, 'when you fast.' So in those days, it was *when* you fast. You get the impression it was a routine practice. But now, almost no one fasts and on the few days when we're supposed to fast, many aren't even able to do that and find lame excuses and rationalizations for disqualifying themselves.

"I know some of you don't want to hear this, but the Catholic Church puts too much emphasis on food. I realize many of these fundraisers benefit the parishes, but I think we need more emphasis on fasting and less on eating. Years ago, the church seemed to value spiritual exercises. We were all required to fast from midnight until morning mass when communion was received. It reminded us of the solemnity of the sacrament. Now the fast is only an hour before receiving, and half of you aren't even practicing that. Let me read you this quote from St. Athanasius who lived in the third century. Here is what he said about fasting." He picked up a paper off the lectern. "'It heals diseases. It strengthens the body by eliminating excess fluids. It frightens away devils. It purges the mind of unclean thought. It clarifies the intellect. It purifies the heart. It sanctifies the body. And finally, it leads a person to the throne of God. To fast is to banquet with angels.'

"So there you have it, you can banquet with angels. We need to make time for spiritual exercises. Take time to exercise your spirit and strengthen it. A strong, healthy spirit is what will enhance your life, not more pierogies or potato pancakes. Romans 8:13 says, 'For if you live according to the flesh you will die, but if by the Spirit you put to death the deeds of the body, you will live.' Work on your spirit and put to death the deeds of the body."

Jack loved the homily, it was rare to hear a homily about vocations even though there was a priest shortage, and he definitely felt some sort of calling, but no one seemed to understand, except his mother, Mollie.

If God really did exist, if Jesus really died on the cross and rose from the dead, if He was the son of God, and all of this was true, why would anyone want to do the minimum? Why not put more into it? Why not put everything into it? What could be more fascinating than God and spirituality? At least that's how Jack saw it.

The visiting priest had been the only one who ever gave a homily like this. Live by the spirit, what a concept. It made sense. A fundamental truth, yet no one was doing it. It made sense that by denying yourself things and suffering physically, mortification, you could strengthen your spirit; the real power is with the spirit. Jack felt inspired. These are the kinds of things people need to be hearing about from the pulpit. I think that's what I want to do.

The next morning, Jack entered the kitchen to the aroma of hot oatmeal, one of his favorites. He liked to add a dash of cinnamon. His friend Hector usually picked him up. Jack tried to avoid the bus, too much juvenile behavior. He ate quickly, rinsed his bowl, and left it in the sink. A few minutes later, Hector pulled up in an older model Chevy Blazer.

"Thanks for the oatmeal, Bye, Mom."

"Hi, Hector, how's it going?"

"Good, now that I finally got a date for the prom. I was almost at the point of desperation. I asked Jennifer yesterday morning after band practice, and she said, 'yes.'"

Jack laughed. "I knew you could do it. I'm proud of you Hector, you just needed to get up the courage."

"You were right again, Jack. I guess you're going with Nora, right?"

"Yes, of course."

"You're so lucky. She's so nice and friends with everyone. She's like the perfect girl, popular and nice."

"Yeah, she's great. But we're more like friends."

"What are you crazy? Friends?"

"I have other things on my mind right now. Plus, she isn't Catholic."

"Who cares? As a Catholic myself I could easily overlook that, at least in her case."

"If two people are going to unite, they should share the same ideology," Jack said. "Ideology provides the foundation for all decision making and provides a road map. If people have different road maps, there could be conflict."

"Wow, Jack, that is so deep. Where do you get this stuff?"

"I don't know, probably from talking to my mom. She is so wise. But, it's just common sense."

They pulled up in front of the school and parked. There was one group of seniors who congregated in the front, another group, mostly weed smokers, were in the rear parking lot, behind a utility building.

Hearing the first bell, many started to stroll inside. Jack walked into the main lobby and made eye contact with the Navy recruiter who had set up a table. He had seen him many times before, but today something seemed different. His uniform was sparkling, very impressive, so squared away. As he walked to his locker, Jack began to ponder military life. He had considered it before but had never really thought it through. Now was the time to thoroughly examine things. Dad doesn't want me to jump into the priesthood, and the military sure would help with college money. Going to the seminary is not free, at least not the undergraduate degree. Mom always says gathering more information is a good approach, as more facts come in decisions get easier.

Jack decided he would stop and see the recruiter during his study period this afternoon. He wanted to see what the Navy had to offer, maybe even talk to the other branches. It was 1:45 p.m. He excitedly headed for the recruiter.

"Good afternoon, I'm Chief Petty Officer Wilson. What can I do for you?"

"I'm interested in what kind of jobs might be available, or how this all works."

"Sure, what's your name?"

"Jack McCreesh, I'm a senior here."

"And you have decent grades?"

"Yes, more than decent."

"Ok great, so what made you stop today? What interests you about the United States Navy?"

"I'm not really sure. I thought I should consider the military as an option, and serving one's country is surely a good thing, and I'm not going to lie, college money is a huge attraction. I have a little sister who will be going to college too."

"Of course. If you enlist full-time for four years," CPO Wilson said, "you'll qualify for the G.I. Bill, which will basically pay your tuition, including room and board, at any state university. It's the primary benefit upon completion, but there are many others as well. But most men feel it's the discipline and life experience they gain that is even more valuable than the college money."

Discipline. Jack loved that word, so many good things seemed to revolve around discipline, and he remembered being told the word "disciple" was the root word. It felt right. He started to daydream and saw himself in uniform. Quickly snapping out of it, he asked if he could have information. He wanted to take it back to the study hall and pour over it.

"When will you be back?"

"Next Tuesday."

"Okay, I'll probably want to talk to you more. Thank you, Chief Petty Officer."

Jack went back to the study hall and opened the folder. The ships looked so impressive on the massive seas. He scanned the job listings. Navy corpsman jumped off the page. Wow, so cool, just the name, how you say it with a silent "P." He knew it was the Navy's counterpart to the Army medic. What a great way to serve, to be of service to the men in our great military. He looked forward to researching more on YouTube. He texted his mom at work.

Hi Mom, I really need to talk to you. Will you be around tomorrow morning?
Sure Jack, going to the grocery store 1ˢᵗ thing, then home all day
Thanks Mom!
Ur welcome. be up early and help me bring in the groceries, lol
Sure Mom. I will help

Later that evening Jack was having ice cream with Nora.
"I'm so excited about the prom, Jack."
"Yeah, me too. It will be the last major event of our senior year, the last time we'll get to be with all our friends."
"I hesitate to ask you this, Jack, but did you commit to going to the seminary?"
"No, I'm thinking of other options."
"That's great news. So maybe we will be able to keep seeing each other."
"I'm not sure," Jack said. "I'm taking a look at the military, first the Navy."
"The Navy? You would probably go far away."
"Nora, you're a great person, and you know there's nothing I wouldn't do for you, but we're too young to be making any kind of plans. You know what they say, 'Man plans, and God laughs.' I think it's best to maybe go our separate ways for a while. What will be, will be."
"I don't like hearing it, but I know you're right." Nora grinned and took a spoon full of ice cream. "I'm only seventeen, but I've never met another boy like you, Jack. You're different, loyal and dependable. I'll be local Jack. I signed up for the nursing program at the community college, so whatever you end up doing, I hope I can see you from time to time."
"Nursing. How interesting. Good for you, Nora. I know you'll be a great nurse, and of course, no matter where life leads us, I want to stay friends."

JOHNNIE BARLEYKORN

Chapter 3

Bishop Cesare's neo-Gothic mansion, adorned with thick oriental carpets and priceless antiques, made for comfortable surroundings. With its beautiful grounds located in a nice center-city neighborhood, an unobstructed view of the river, and in close proximity to all the major attractions, real estate experts appraised it at 5.2 million.

Bishop Cesare shared the mansion, which had several private suites and full-time staff, with three other hand-picked priests, one of whom was always his driver/adjutant.

Some thought it was bad form for the bishop to live like a medieval monarch, but Bishop Cesare would merely point out that these residences were built many years ago, and he was simply residing there. In addition, there were many practical uses for the large residences, including diocesan offices and hosting guests and fundraisers. It didn't square with a Christian life of simplicity and austerity, but in all fairness, diocesan bishops do not take a vow of poverty.

Bishop Cesare was drinking his coffee in the library after being served a hearty breakfast by his housekeeper. He also employed a chef who could prepare food to the bishop's satisfaction, for the most part.

The bishop picked up the latest copy of *The Catholic Beacon*, the bi-weekly diocesan newspaper. He wanted to ensure he was portrayed as a busy and caring prelate out amongst the people, down in the trenches. The photos from the soup kitchen were not quite what he was hoping. It should have included a closeup, but they were mostly group photos, pan shots. Looking at the pictures in the diocesan paper always left him feeling dissatisfied. It was newsprint. He had been told a photo could only look so sharp in a newspaper, yet he felt there was room for improvement.

His housekeeper came in. "Your Excellency, they just called from the chancery. Monsignor Sabatini has arrived for your 10:00 a.m. appointment."

"He's early."

"Yes, Your Excellency. He always comes a few minutes early. Do you want him to come to the residence or do you wish to meet him at the chancery office?"

"At the office, at the appointed time. Tell them I'm on my way. Get me my cape."

Stopping to check himself in the mirror, he was satisfied with his appearance, regal but not too gaudy. A bald, portly man with rectangular black-rimmed glasses, Monsignor Joseph Sabatini was the Vicar General for the Diocese, second in command. His job was overseeing day-to-day operations, temporal affairs the church called it, things like finances and employment issues.

Taking a short cut through the formal gardens, the bishop was soon on the elevator to the third floor. Nodding briefly at the office receptionist he turned towards his guest. "Good morning, Monsignor Sabatini. How was your golf game yesterday?"

"As bad as usual, Your Excellency, nothing like a game of golf to ruin a nice walk in nature."

"True, I've had some long, hot days on the course also. Our vocations tournament is next month, maybe you can take some time and practice."

"Yes, Your Excellency, but it won't do any good."

The bishop chuckled and motioned for the monsignor to have a seat in one of the sturdy stuffed leather chairs adjacent to his huge mahogany desk. "I want to talk to you about the tournament and other items, but first, do you have the latest numbers on the appeal?"

The Bishop's Annual Appeal was the major fundraiser for the diocese. It had started thirty years ago simply as an appeal, at a time when the church claimed they needed a sort of helping hand, due to poor financial status. It was decided an "appeal" to the flock was in order, a one-time solicitation to boost the diocese's finances. The *one-time* bishop's appeal went so well, it soon morphed into The Bishop's *Annual* Appeal. The goal this year was 7.5 million, an eight percent increase over last year.

"It's not going well, Your Excellency. It looks like only twenty percent of the parishes will meet their goal."

"That is outrageous, absolutely unacceptable."

"I agree, Your Excellency. I'm afraid the grand jury report had a negative impact."

"Absurd," said the bishop. "Most of those incidents, some only allegations, happened decades ago."

"Yes, but not all," said the Monsignor. "But I believe it was the coverup that was most troubling to people, the somewhat lackluster response of the diocese."

"There was no coverup, Monsignor. It was appropriate and not lackluster, not in the least. Priests were removed, sent to treatment, counseled and in some cases law-enforcement was even notified. What more can be expected? This is all just a media witch-hunt."

"Of course, Your Excellency. I shouldn't use the word coverup. I apologize, foolish of me, reading too many newspapers. In reality, the church did a commendable job."

"Well, whatever happened, the overwhelming majority of it was not under my administration," the bishop whined. "It's so unfair I'm being punished for this. People have no idea what a bishop has to endure."

"Do you think eight percent over last year was too much to expect, Your Excellency? Considering the current climate."

"No, absolutely not, not at all," said the bishop. "Our financial obligations have not decreased due to the 'climate' as you put it. They have continued to increase, therefore so must our revenues. It has nothing to do with the temperature. We must have sufficient revenues to sustain our mission. You need to inform the pastors everything must be done to meet their parish goal. So tell me, Monsignor, what's your plan to address our predicament?"

"We will be showing the video at all the masses this weekend, every parish."

"That should help. I worked so hard on it, getting it just perfect. It was exhausting, but I soldiered through and was quite pleased with the end result. Everyone was captivated with my presentation."

"Yes, as was I, Your Excellency."

"Well perhaps the video will give us an essential boost, but we need to exert tension on these pastors, lean on them a bit."

"Everything within reason is being done, Your Excellency."

"Apparently it is not working, Monsignor. Perhaps other measures need to be considered, that are not so reasonable."

"What did you have in mind, Your Excellency?"

"I don't have all the answers, Monsignor. This comes under your purview. I can't do everything around here. But perhaps you can start by reminding these pastors they will be expected to make up any shortfall with parish funds, just like we've done in the past."

"But, Your Excellency, things are different this year. Most of the parishes are also feeling the effects of the grand jury report. Their bank balances are down as well. Maybe we could be more lenient this year. This scandal will pass."

"Absolutely not. Once we start letting them miss their goal, they will expect it every year. I assure you, Monsignor, we will get the funds," the bishop said. "It's not my fault we have to dip into the parishes' bank accounts. It's the parishioners who are not contributing their fair share, and if they can be so easily deceived by the media, clearly, they are deficient in their faith."

"Perhaps we could consider cost-cutting, Your Excellency. Maybe we could put some of the chancery and residence renovations on hold. All the remodeling might not look good."

"I wholeheartedly disagree. It's only a tiny fraction of the overall budget. I can't concern myself with how things look, or what every misinformed parishioner thinks, that's no way to manage a diocese. Plus, I've told you before, I will oversee the finances for the residence and chancery. You need to focus on other areas, and yes, I believe there are opportunities for savings, but first, let's discuss the vocations golf tournament."

The annual vocations golf tournament, which had been held for the past ten years and started as a sort of afterthought, had become quite a little revenue generator, most pleasing to the bishop. At $300 per player, and spots for 168 players, crammed onto a 27-hole layout, the proceeds were looking good even before the first tee shot. Not to mention the hole sponsorships at $750 per clip, and additional sponsorships, closet to the pin, longest drive, and various other signage and promotional pieces, including a printed program, all available for a price. Prizes were donated, and the country club provided a discounted rate since it was the church. And it was only $2,000 if you wanted to be in the bishop's foursome.

"How is the tournament coming along?"

"Quite well, Your Excellency. It's almost sold out, and we have half the hole sponsorships filled."

"Only half? We need all those filled. It's only three weeks away. Have our people contact our vendors, cleaning companies, landscaping, insurance companies, etc. Actually, I want you to print a list of the vendors we do business with, from top to bottom. In other words, have a list generated telling us who we spend the most money with. These companies need to be contacted and advised if they wish to stay in our good graces, they need to support the vocations golf outing. Vocations ensure our future viability, and the revenues these companies receive from us, I might add."

"Yes, of course, Your Excellency. Outstanding idea."

"Now getting back to cost-cutting. I have some thoughts."

Father Paul was enjoying a morning respite in his suite. He would be driving the bishop this afternoon. Looking around at the carved mahogany in his room and the mini kitchen and beautiful bath, with elaborate ornamental fixtures, he felt quite content. Easy access to the gym and an indoor lap pool were an added bonus. Exercise was part of his routine. This was like living in a mansion. Not many people get to live in a mansion with full maid service. He might only be here a year or two before he was assigned to a parish, but he was confident, if he played his cards right, he would be allotted a desirable assignment which also included maid service.

His cell phone rang.

"Hi, Leon, I'm so happy you called. How are things at the Christian Brothers?"

"Okay, but I wish I could see you more. Maybe you could join our faculty or come back as a student."

Father Paul laughed. "I miss you too, Leon, but with my new assignment, I'm only thirty minutes away. We should be able to see each other a lot more."

"Yes, exactly, that's why I'm calling. When can I see you?"

"Maybe this weekend. I'm still trying to get a feel for this place. I have a private suite with a private entrance, so if you want to come and spend the weekend with me, it should be okay. Most of the staff is off on weekends including the maid. We would just have to be discrete."

"Interesting, I could plan a weekend," said Leon. "And once school is out, I could come more often. Do you think the bishop would mind?"

"No, I don't. He already told me I was permitted to have visitors to my suite. He has frequent visitors as well."

"Oh really. How is the bishop, Paul? I mean, to work with and be in close contact with?"

"He's fine. A little demanding but I respect his orderliness. He wants to do things right. It's admirable. We get along well. He's really a fine man and rather distinguished-looking, a nice aura about him, quite striking I might add, so intelligent, studied at the Pontifical Ecclesiastical Society in Rome, has a doctorate in both Canon Law and Theology."

"Wow, impressive. How is your suite?"

"It's gorgeous, I love it. I'm savoring every moment."

"You know I have to ask. What would be the accommodations if I'm able to come?"

"Well my suite is a one-bedroom, there's a sofa, but my bed is a king-size, so you would have options."

Downstairs Gil Rodgers was mopping the banquet room. Alice always liked the pine scent.

"It's looking good, Gil."

"Good morning, Allie, do you know the bishop's schedule today? I always feel better knowing his whereabouts."

"He's meeting with the vicar general right now."

Gil stood erect with the mop. "Oh, that should be interesting. I wish I could hear that discussion. Maybe I could put some bugs in his office."

Alice grinned. "Gil, let it go. It has nothing to do with you. It's just going to aggravate you."

"I can't help it. Did you hear about the bronze window frames? Replacing every window in this mansion with bronze window frames? Do you have any idea what that costs? It's easily $2,000 per frame, and there are 80 windows in this mansion, not including the outbuildings. And do we really need to replace the walkways with heated stones? Heated stones? Who even thinks about the temperature of their feet when they're walking somewhere? Someone who is overly concerned with their comfort, that's who."

"Gil, I can't say I disagree, but we have no control over these things. It's just how life is. It's our nature. It's very easy to become slaves to our desires, obsessed with ease and comfort. It happens to many celebrities and can make you miserable. Christianity is giving of yourself, but you don't see much of that around here. Pray for him, Gil."

"I'll have to think about that one. There are others at the top of my prayer list, and he would be at the bottom if he even makes the list at all. Did you hear about the spiral staircase?"

"No, I missed that one."

"Well thank goodness it's not going to happen, but the architect told me the bishop wanted a spiral staircase, just off the parlor as you enter, but it wasn't practical."

"Wasn't practical?" Alice said. "Since when does that matter?"

Gil laughed. "Yeah, especially after he spent $50,000 on an elevator. Why would he even be thinking about a spiral staircase? And he spent all that money on the gym. He should have taken the stairs for exercise and did without the gym, and elevator for that matter."

"Let it go, Gil."

"Before I give you my ideas for trimming expenses, do you have any suggestions?"

"No, Your Excellency, other than what we discussed, but given time to think further I'm certain I'd have a notion or two."

"Please, work on it. In the meantime, I have some ideas," the bishop said. "First off, I want you to look at the soup kitchen. They are serving fresh foods. Using a wholesaler would save a lot of money. They serve over two thousand meals a week."

"Perhaps, Your Excellency, but the soup kitchen prides itself on quality."

"Need I remind you, Monsignor, pride comes before the fall."

"Yes, of course, what I mean is they want it to be good for the homeless," the Monsignor said.

"Wholesale food is fine, good quality and the same nutritional content."

"Yes, Your Excellency, but a lot of it is processed and stored for long periods. It's not fresh."

"It's fine, they will never notice," said the bishop. "And it will be less strain on the volunteers, simply heat it up. There will be no further discussion. Also, I want you to contact the food wholesalers we use for the schools and set up a meeting. We're going to offer our business exclusively to one vendor if they're willing to give us a ten percent across-the-board discount."

"I'm not sure that will leave them with much of a profit margin, Your Excellency."

"Their profit margins are not my concern. They are free to decline, but I expect you to follow my directives. My mission is to select one vendor, the one who offers the most generous discount, is that understood?"

"Yes, Your Excellency."

"And of course, in lieu of a discount perhaps they could offer cash incentives."

The Monsignor opened his mouth like he was going to say something but then simply nodded his head.

"Okay fine, now what about the health insurance? The bill we are paying is shocking. The teacher's contract is forthcoming. It's essential we look at higher deductibles and co-pays."

"Certainly, Your Excellency, but keep in mind the deductibles are already quite high, we raised them three years ago. Our teachers need a living wage."

"And they have it," the bishop said. "They all have sufficient food and shelter. They don't look undernourished to me. Several could afford to exercise more prudence. They knew when they signed up, they were working for a church. It's a vocation. Sacrifices are part and parcel when one is serving mother church."

The Monsignor felt tension in his forehead, always the first sign of stress. He dare not say a word, but it was unreasonable to ask the teachers to take more cuts, and he would bear the brunt of the pushback as the bishop stayed comfortably behind the scenes. Even the soup kitchen plan left a bad taste in his mouth. He tried to think of some alternative cost savings. As thoughts passed through his mind, he knew they would all be shot down by the bishop. They just did not see things in the same light. He decided to keep quiet and follow the directives. Plus, no one ever saw the diocesan books, so why even worry about it.

Peter Matson was preparing to lock up after a long day at the flower shop when the phone rang. "Mr. Matson, it's Frank Collins from the bishop's office, I trust I didn't catch you at a bad time."

"No, not at all," said Peter. "I hope everything is satisfactory with the floral delivery."

"Yes fine, just beautiful. The reason I'm calling is the bishop was wondering if you would be interested in supporting our vocations golf tournament this year. Are you familiar with the outing?"

"Sort of, but I'm not a golfer."

"I understand, but this year we have made arrangements for non-golfers to attend, dinner only. The bishop has a seat open at his table. The suggested donation is $1,000. Should I put you down?"

"When is it?"

"It's May 12th."

"Oh, the Friday before Mother's Day. I don't think that works for me."

"So, should I tell the bishop you won't be able to join him for dinner?"

"Uhm, no. Ah, wait, it's only dinner. Of course, I can. What was I thinking?"

"Wonderful, the bishop will be delighted. I'll send you the information. You can make the check payable to 'Bishop Louis Cesare.'"

"Hey Erica, you're not going to believe this. I just got a call from one of the bishop's henchmen. We will be donating $1,000 for the golf tournament so I can have dinner with the bishop. I can't freakin' believe it."

"Take it easy," Erica said. "Business is good, we can afford it, plus it's deductible."

"Yeah, I know. I just don't like the way they do things. Now I know why they call them the 'Lavender Mafia.' Lavender, I never really liked lavender."

Bishop Cesare

Chapter 4

It was a cool April morning. Some extra sleep would have been nice but hearing his cell phone beeping, Jack was glad to be getting up to help his mom and have a talk. Just after he finished his cereal, he heard the car zoom up the driveway and went out to help.

"Hi, Mom, let me get that for you."

"Get the other case of water too, and grab the stuff in the back seat. Thanks, Jack."

As they were putting the groceries away, Jack was trying to decide how to start the conversation, when his mom simply said, "Is what you are thinking about pleasing to God, Jack?"

"I think so, Mom. I'm thinking about joining the Navy as a Navy corpsman."

"Okay, so that's obviously a yes. And what about the seminary?"

"It can wait, Mom. It will give me four years to serve my country and ponder my vocation. In the meantime, I'm sure I could do a lot of good in the Navy. Dad will be more comfortable if I wait. And the money for college, they will pay for my college and leave more money for you and Dad to spend on Beth."

"You don't need to feel responsible for Beth's college, Jack."

"Yeah, Mom, I know. It's not like that. It's just another positive. And I feel happy when I think about it, Mom. I can see myself in uniform, helping the men."

"Well, I can't say I see anything wrong with it. And if there's happiness in your heart, that's good too. God speaks to us through our hearts, but we also must use our minds. Let's pray and let things unfold. If it's meant to be, you'll know it, just take a couple of weeks before you sign anything, so we can ask for guidance. What does Dad think?"

"I haven't talked to him yet. I wanted to talk to you first, Mom."

"Well as a former Marine, I think we both know the answer."

Jack laughed. "Yes, Mom, Dad will be onboard."

"I am going to miss you, Jack," Mollie said.

"Same here, Mom. But thank you for raising me right, and for teaching me the faith. I still think I have a calling, but the church seems so lame. Why don't the priests talk about the afterlife? And they never mention the Devil. They need to teach the people they have an enemy."

"Okay, Jack. If you might be going away, it's time we had a talk. The laundry can wait. I know we've discussed some of these things, but I need to make sure you understand the big picture. Let me get a cup of coffee and we can go into the den - this might be a while. Turn off your cell phone."

Mollie McCreesh was a strong, principled woman. With her bright blonde hair and trim physique, she embodied positive energy. Growing up in a devout Catholic family, she knew the faith. Her parents had lived it in a way that was attractive. There was no whining or complaining. It was a sense of doing your best with a good attitude. Mollie was exposed to the true benefits of living a Christian life. Her dad always told her, "Make your faith real in your life. It will give you the best life by far," and, "Walking in faith is a lonely road. Follow the narrow path, because the way is broad and wide that leads to destruction."

They went into the den, a small room located just off the living room. A large Bible was prominently displayed on a sturdy oak coffee table. Mollie began.

"Jack, the church is in a sorry state. It's been in deteriorating for the past fifty years."

"How can that even happen, Mom?"

"It's simple, Jack. The church is under attack by the forces of darkness. Whether the people responsible are aware of it, I can't say, most have just been deceived, but the pastorate has become weak and fearful, and those who are more orthodox are not held in high regard, persecuted even.

"There have been all these seemingly small changes which have completely watered down the faith and emasculated the church. It's nothing like the bold, confident church of my childhood. It is a very different church, one that has been cowed by the media, a media which is also being controlled by dark forces. Even abortion is not vigorously opposed by the bishops."

"Why doesn't somebody do something? Don't they see what's happening? Don't they believe in Satan?"

"Not so much. Once you stop believing in the Devil, you are completely exposed. The first thing the Devil needed to achieve was to get people to stop believing in him, and the supernatural, mysterious spiritual warfare taking place around us. If you have an enemy who is trying to destroy you, and you don't believe in him, it's much easier for the demon to reign."

"How could these priests be so careless, Mom? Didn't they learn anything in the seminary?"

"Oh, yes, they learned a lot, they surely did - a lot of liberal bilge." Mollie took a sip of her coffee and sighed. "You see, Jack, and you'll need to be ready if you ever go to the seminary, the faith has been undermined everywhere, even in most seminaries. The Devil has succeeded in portraying belief in him as a form of archaic superstition, something only a fool could believe. In other words, if you really believe this stuff, you are a simpleton who probably also believes in the Easter Bunny and the Tooth Fairy. But Jesus repeatedly talked about the Devil, and it is all spelled out in the *Catechism of the Catholic Church*."

"How can they be Catholics and not believe?" Jack asked. "That makes no sense."

"Precisely. I'm determined my kids are going to know about the Devil and his devious ways and I'm not ashamed to talk about it. It's my job as your parent, maybe my most important job."

"It all started in the Garden of Eden," Jack said. "If there's no Devil, that means there's no Hell, and if there's no Hell, then Jesus didn't have to die on the cross. So then what's the point?"

"Exactly, Jack. The church is afraid to talk about Satan, and they don't discuss the afterlife, another basic tenant of the faith. We're all going to church every week, well not all, maybe 30 percent, but many of us are practicing the faith. But in the end, Jack, what is the goal?"

"To get to Heaven."

"Yes, I want our family to all make it to Heaven! It should be the guiding force of our lives, yet the church does not mention it. Or if they do, it's probably some pablum about all of us going to Heaven. There is even a bishop on the internet spreading blather about 'a reasonable expectation all men will be saved.'"

"But that's not what Jesus said in the gospels."

"Precisely, Jack."

"How could we ever have gotten to this stage, Mom?"

"The forces of darkness have been very successful portraying religion as weak and narrow-minded. We see regular attacks on Christianity in our culture, especially Catholicism, which should tell you something about the veracity of the faith. Catholicism is not popular in the entertainment industry, for example. It impedes their hedonism. Hollywood hates the church. Catholicism is the demon's number one target. Anti-Catholic bigotry is the last form of acceptable prejudice in our society."

Jack's father came in. "I'm opening the pool this weekend, Jack. Do you think you can help me tomorrow?"

"Sure, Dad."

"I'm going out to the shed and get all the pool stuff organized. That way, we won't waste time looking for parts. What's going on?"

"We're just talking about the faith, Pat."

"Oh, I'd rather spend hours looking for a skimmer basket than listen to this."

Jack smiled. "No problem, Dad."

"But we will be going to church in the morning, so don't forget," Mollie said.

"I won't, but I'm sure you'd remind me. And that coffee smells good. Save me a cup."

He put on his hat and sweatshirt and went out.

Jack's father, Patrick McCreesh, sometimes tried to slack off on his church attendance but Mollie was having none of it. "I am not going to be one of those wives who goes to church to pray for her husband. I expect you to be there right beside me and setting the proper example for the children," and so he did.

Mollie took another sip out of her mug and continued. "You see, Jack, no one wants to be viewed as too 'religious.' It's more acceptable, even more cool, to say you are 'spiritual but not religious.' Everyone wants to be seen as 'spiritual' because it means you are an advanced, open-minded, transcendent super-soul and not some pig-headed, intolerant, religious freak who is living in the dark ages.

"You can't be irreligious and spiritual at the same time. Most of these people who say they are 'spiritual' are simply lazy. Devout practices require effort. And since there's no moral code to follow, they can do whatever they want, whenever they want. And since there's no Heaven or Hell, what difference does it make?

"The Ten Commandments are simple and will give you a good life but if you're not 'religious' you can simply ignore them. Some see it as freedom, but really, it's a deception. Sin hurts the sinner. For example, sex outside a committed relationship, dare I say marriage, hurts the participants but also leaves many children in its wake who grow up without fathers. The jails are full of them, but the so-called 'spiritual people' don't live for the spirit at all. They live for the flesh, self-indulgent lives, not a path to joy and peace, not at all.

"The whole 'I'm so spiritual' meme is just another lie from the dark side. It's simple. Jesus either died on the cross and rose from the dead, or He didn't. Do you really think Christianity would have survived and spread all over the world if it wasn't authentic? The evidence is all around us. Seek and you shall find, but most are too busy posting their selfies on Facebook to even consider the fundamental truth of their own beings. Jesus was either the Son of God, or He was a crazy person going around claiming to be the son of a deity and fooling people with magic. Many are being deceived and the modern church is anemic."

Jack put his feet up and stretched out on the couch. "Yeah, I was thinking in history class how communist countries always try to snuff out Christianity. It makes sense. They want the government to be the god people worship. But if God wasn't real, if Christianity was a fraud, why would they fear it?"

"Right, Jack. And it was Pope John Paul II who defeated the Soviet Union through the faith of courageous Polish Catholics, but you'll never read it in your secular history books. The communists even tried to assassinate him, and according to his own testimony, he was saved by The Blessed Mother.

"Most have no faith. That's the real issue. The media has done a great job making Catholics feel embarrassed by the basic tenants of their faith."

Jack got up and picked up a globe that was on a small desk and laid back down.

"I believe the gospels, Mom." Jack started examining the globe. "Wow, I never realized how close Poland is to Russia."

"Remember Jack, if you ever go into the seminary it won't be an easy road for you. You will always be in the minority, but that's true for all Christians who try to live their faith. If you're feeling oppressed it means you're on the right path."

"It sounds discouraging, Mom."

"That's because it is, but don't worry. God is in charge, Jack. We simply need to stay faithful and do our part."

"How would a young priest even begin?" Jack asked.

"Start your day by asking for guidance from the Holy Spirit. And remember, all the apostles, except Saint John, died a martyr's death, some quite horrific, and these were the men closest to Jesus. Preach boldly to your parishioners, Jack. Their souls are yearning for truth. They will love you for it, of course, not everyone. There will be those who will persecute you for speaking truth. They can't allow it. Don't worry about them. Focus on those who have not yet hardened their hearts. Be patient, Jack. Most have never learned the faith. You always need to be teaching when you're preaching, hitting the hard issues.

"When I was teaching the 8th Grade CCD class, I was shocked, that after seven years of schooling they knew nothing about the Devil or the afterlife. They were fascinated when I started to talk about Purgatory. One kid even said, 'We're learning things we never learned before.'"

She picked up a glossy covered religious ed book off the bookshelf and held it up. "This textbook they gave me didn't even have the word 'Devil' in it, and no mention of Hell or Purgatory."

"Really, Mom? What was in it?" Jack got up to replace the globe and sat down.

"It had some good things, stories of saints, Jesus's life, and Bible stories, but it was all scrambled with no continuity. Kind of like a jumble of nothing, designed to leave one uninspired. The theme was mostly 'be a good person, be nice' something we're always hearing from the pulpit. It's worth noting the word 'nice' comes from a Latin word meaning ignorant or stupid. Plus, kindness and charity should be obvious to anyone who studies the faith. It's worth an occasional mention, but sadly it's the basis for most homilies, lukewarm ones I might add.

"I didn't use the book a lot, which seemed to annoy the nun who ran the program. She didn't like me going off script, a nun who didn't wear her habit. She told my class she stopped wearing it because she didn't want to give the impression she was better than everyone else. I saw it as another Catholic who had been cowed by the media."

"The media is everywhere'" Jack said. "How could a priest even begin to combat it?"

"Tell the congregation to stop sitting in front of screens all day. It's going to leave them feeling restless and dissatisfied. They're not going to find what they're looking for there. They need to open their Bibles and learn the faith."

"Do you think they would?"

"No, but I would keep preaching it. Those who are sincerely seeking need guidance. But since most are already addicted to TV and social media, where the Devil reigns, I'd challenge them to consider new material. For example, YouTube has very interesting videos about people who claim to have experienced the afterlife. Let me show you what I mean."

She turned on the TV and activated the Roku, then clicked on YouTube, and searched "Hell." A plethora of videos displayed, people who had visions of Hell and other supernatural occurrences. "I'm not saying I accept everything I see here. One always needs to ask for discernment but watching these reminds me of the afterlife, keeps it in the forefront of my mind. I think that's helpful. It's one of the places people are talking about it like it's real. Everyone wants to go to Heaven, but no one wants to die.

"Challenge people to research the afterlife, Jack. Not sure if it would work, but a priest needs to be a man of prayer. If he is, he will be an effective homilist. Just get out of the way, and let God speak through you. A holy priest stands in the person of Christ, in Latin, it's *in persona Christi*, so you don't have to stress. Pray, Jack. Don't worry, pray."

Chapter 5

It was a breezy, sunny, spring day at Treetop Pines Country Club, and the parking lot was virtually filled as the bishop's black Cadillac sped up the winding entrance road. As a member of this club, the bishop was quite familiar with the setting. The car dropped him at a golf cart that had been standing by, and his golf bag was briskly removed from the trunk and placed on the rear passenger side. He would be paired with Monsignor Sabatini. Father Paul would not be playing golf but driving the refreshments cart. No one needed to tell him to make frequent stops at the bishop's group. At that very moment, inside the clubhouse, the catering crew was putting a bottle of Four Roses Single Barrel bourbon on the bishop's table, his favorite, but he would drink Crown Royal in a pinch.

The bishop stepped out wearing large sunglasses, black golf slacks, and a gleaming white Nike golf shirt. A black, tweed, newsboy style golf cap had been requested from the pro shop just moments ago and would be arriving at the 10th tee in a few minutes, the bishop's assigned starting hole for the shotgun tournament, everyone starting simultaneously. The format was captain and his crew, choose the best shot of the foursome and everyone proceed from there.

It was still twenty minutes until the shotgun start and the bishop was mingling making sure to touch base with all the major players and the well-monied. The law firm that represented the diocese, including defending sex abuse scandals, was there, happy to sponsor a hole and two seats at the bishop's dinner table. A large financial services firm responsible for the numerous investment accounts the diocese maintained, some funded via huge endowments few even knew about, were happy as well to have a chance to show their loyalty.

After the bishop had directed the vendors be contacted, the hole sponsorships had filled right up, and the tournament was on track to take in well over $100,000. Ostensibly to assist seminarians, and some of the money would be spent on that, but there was no oversite or accountability, so how much was a mystery. Most didn't even take a moment to ponder it and think about where the money went, after all, it was the church.

Golfers had made their way from nine different counties in the diocese. With 168 players packed onto 27 holes, play would be slow, but the refreshment carts would ease things a bit. Several players, including a few priests, would be quite drunk when the round was over.

The shotgun sounded and the golfers began. Playing for many years, the bishop and monsignor were decent golfers, but the bishop made sure to have at least one "ringer" in his group every year. It made the round more enjoyable, a stellar player to carry the rest. As they headed down the fairway of the tenth hole, a long par four, play had already started to back up. There was a wait.

"This might be a good time to discuss that letter you wanted to talk to me about, Monsignor," the bishop said. "What is the gist of it?"

"We have a report that Father Kenneth fondled a sophomore boy, supposedly happened in the band room."

"Oh no, not him again. When did this happen?"

"About two months ago."

"Has the media gotten wind of this?"

"No, Your Excellency, but Bishop Rahmney has already said he will accept his transfer."

"Okay fine. Arrange the paperwork."

"What about the family, Your Excellency?"

"Send them the standard letter, you know, the one about how the circumstances are unclear, but we are sorry for any pain that may have resulted, and how the church is taking steps, blah, blah. That one. It usually does the trick. Most of these parents are not really wanting to broadcast it anyway, but if need be, I'll meet with them and give them the traditional spiel, that usually works, but if not, our attorneys will handle it."

Back at the bishop's mansion, Gil Rodgers was waxing the floor he had mopped two days ago when Alice came in.

"The bishop said his bathroom sink is draining slowly, might be clogging up."

"Ok, I'll check it. I'm almost done."

"Good, Gil, but don't stress, you can take a breath. He's out all day. Today is the vocation's golf outing. He won't be having his dinner here tonight, a long day golfing and a peaceful afternoon for us."

"Thank God, Alice. I've been feeling the strain lately. Billy needs a new wheelchair. Insurance only covers half. You wouldn't believe how much they cost, but he is growing out of his old one. It's getting uncomfortable for him. And I thought we were covered with all the chemo treatments, but I forgot about the deductible. So now I've got to come up with $2,000. I hope they'll take payments."

"They will, Gil. Take it easy. God knows about your wife's cancer and your son's handicaps. Since the bishop is out today, why don't you take a few minutes and go into the chapel and pray? Pray for strength to face your problems. Stay in the day, Gil, don't worry about tomorrow. That's what Jesus tells us in the book of Matthew. You have what you need for today, food and shelter. And if it makes you feel better, I'll make sure you always have a place to live. Since Otis died, I'm in that big house all by myself. I wouldn't mind some company."

"Thanks, Alice. I really hope it doesn't come to that, but having a friend like you sure does help. You really are a good person, Alice."

"Oh, I don't know, Gil. I try, maybe more than some, but a selfish life is an unhappy life."

"Maybe someone needs to tell our fearless leader."

Alice chuckled, "Yes, Gil, many are deceived, but it's a fundamental truth, in giving we receive."

"You make it sound so simple."

"It is, Gil."

Across town, Father Kenneth Bertram was coming out of the movies with his new friend, Fabio, an altar boy who had just turned fifteen.

"Did you like the movie, buddy?"

"It was okay, I mostly like the special effects, but the older Star Wars movies are still the best, the first three."

"Yes, I agree," Father Kenneth said. "You're such a smart boy, Fabio."

"Not really. I mean, I don't do good in school."

"Oh, don't' fret, Fabio. It's not unusual for young people to feel challenged in school. I can help you with that. I see a young man with a very powerful, inquisitive mind. God gives every human being a strong, healthy mind, unbelievable the power of a human mind. You just need to learn how to relax and tap into it, to stop worrying so much."

"That's so cool," Fabio said. "Sounds like me, I think that's my problem. How do you do that?"

"I can teach you. It will just take some time and effort. We can start working together, meeting at the rectory. You can begin by bringing all your homework assignments, relieve the stress."

"That would be great. I gotta' paper due but don't know how to start. Mostly I don't even do homework. A lot of kids are always organized. They seem happy. Maybe I can be like that."

"Yes, no doubt, I will be your guide. Just trust me. Your homework is going to be awesome going forward."

"Wow, thanks, I feel better already."

"My pleasure, Fabio. I want to help, and you really like Star Wars, don't you?"

"Yeah, I love it."

"How would you like me to buy you the complete box set. You can buy the whole series on Amazon."

"The whole series? Every episode? That's a lot of money!"

"Don't worry about it. I know how much you like it. I'll tell you what, tomorrow is Saturday. Go home and organize all your schoolwork and bring it to the rectory tomorrow afternoon, say 2:00 p.m. I'll get that all cleared up for you. Then we can go on my Amazon Prime account and order you the Star Wars box set, two-day delivery. You can pick it out, just click on it and it's yours. How does that sound?"

"Really, Father? It sounds unbelievable. I'll definitely be there."

"Excellent, Fabio, and in the meantime, may the force be with you."

The golfing was done, and after hot showers in the deluxe locker room, everyone was feeling chipper drinking cocktails and enjoying hors d'oeuvres. After the cocktail hour, it was time for dinner and prizes. The bishop gave the invocation and dinner began. A lively banter filled the room. After the meal, while coffee was being served, the bishop, who was now formally dressed in his jacket and collar, took to the microphone.

"I am just overwhelmed with what I see here today. I feel so blessed. I am a blessed bishop to be among a group of faithful who are standing boldly and supporting vocations, edifying the church, the church, our hope, our only hope, our future. God is pleased with each and every one of you. For many years we saw a decline in vocations. Now we are seeing an uptick, small perhaps but an uptick, nonetheless. I believe this signifies a major shift, early tremors before the quake. I sense the Holy Spirit is presently moving more men to this path. It gives one cause to be optimistic, to be hopeful, to have faith.

"The Bible tells us in the Book of Hebrews, 'faith is the substance of things hoped for, the evidence of things not seen.' So we should have faith, faith in our future because even though we shouldn't require evidence, we have evidence, evidence in our ten seminarians who are present tonight."

The bishop paused for effect, prompting a round of applause.

"Stand up men, stand up and let everyone see who you are. You are surrounded by people who love the church and love you for giving your life to it. I challenge you, men, to go forth, go forth with apostolic boldness and share the message of the gospel.

"The funds raised tonight will go to support the Society of St. Peter the Apostle, representing a beautiful charism, which in addition to assisting locally with vocations and strengthening our present seminarians, also assists in building seminaries and novitiate houses in developing countries, which in turn may provide future priests for our parishes.

"Recently, there have been countless media assaults on our faith. Some deserved but most of it slanderous, but we priests will continue to suit up and show up because we have the assurance from our Lord that the gates of Hell will not prevail against our church.

"So while some in the media are attacking us and ignoring all the good we do, we in the chancery are working harder than ever to redouble our efforts to offer spiritual support and access to social services, to the needy, the single mom, the drug addict, the homeless, and our immigrant refugee brothers.

"My dear people, our faith requires sacrifice, sacrifice from the faithful. If we are not willing to sacrifice, we cannot expect to have victory, to triumph.

"Which leads me to the appeal, The Bishop's Annual Appeal. Money is often a delicate subject, but the church cannot wage war without proper funding. So far, the numbers are not looking good. I am not going to go into a long diatribe, I'm just going to ask some of you, many who have been extraordinarily blessed, to reconsider your commitment, and to remember, it is in giving that you receive. Renewal begins when efforts to do with less are made. All of you can make do with less, discipline yourselves. It will make you stronger spiritually.

"Help us to sustain our mission. Jesus said, 'Sell your belongings and give alms. For where your treasure is, there also will your heart be.' Help us to clothe the naked and feed the hungry. Recently, I had the opportunity to go to our soup kitchen and serve the poor, and what a great honor it was indeed. Whoever experiences poverty in person will discover the true greatness of God. These beautiful people have a simple faith. I saw it in their eyes. It reminded me that a person can be dirt poor, but rich in mercy and piety, truly authentic riches, unlike the materialism running amok in our culture, more false gods, more false promises. And I would like to finish with a quote from Socrates, 'He is richest who is content with least.' Give more, be happy with less, and you will be among the richest."

Wanting to work on the sink while the bishop was away, Gil decided he would get right to it and took the elevator up to the bishop's quarters. Employees were permitted to use the elevator, but no one could ride with the bishop. If he was on it, you would have to wait until it came back, so most just used the stairs. It was awkward if the elevator stopped when the bishop was on it; he, or one of his lackeys, would simply gesture for you not to enter.

Gil made his way with his plumbing tools and walked through the bedroom. The housekeeper had already made up the bishop's huge canopy bed. Everything was neat and orderly. He was anticipating an easy fix and was an old hand at this type of thing. With his assorted tools and gadgets, he had never met a clog he couldn't defeat. After running the water and seeing the problem, he decided he would start with his long, thin, plastic drain cleaning tool, the Zip-It. Sticking it in, he was pleased to see it immediately unclogged the drain, and he removed the hair attached to its jagged edges. He wiped it off and laid it on the sink. As he was cleaning the sink, he knocked the Zip-It it to the floor. Kneeling down to retrieve it, he saw a small cardboard flap sticking out from under the vanity, apparently missed by the housekeeper's vacuum. Curiously, he slid it out and examined it. *What the heck is this doing here, in a bishop's residence?*

After a frantic day at the flower shop, Peter Matson, who had just endured the bishop's speech, was looking for an opportunity to exit but knew he needed to wait for another hour to make it look good. He decided to try and make some small talk. There was a man sitting next to him, a dark complexion, strikingly handsome. He seemed to have an accent, didn't really fit in with the others at the table, and younger than the other men.

"My name is Peter Matson, owner of Matson Floral."

"It's a pleasure to meet you, Peter. I love your floral arrangements, and so does the bishop."

"Oh, you are familiar with them?"

"Yes, I have seen them at the residence. I am a friend and supporter of the bishop. My name is Alex, Alex Montalvo. Your flowers are beautiful. I admire your work."

Father Kenneth was tired of looking at porn on the internet. Not kiddie porn, that didn't interest him. Young men in their teens were his target, and there were plenty of perfectly legal sites. Yet it always made him feel more empty, more lonely, but he still stayed on for hours, getting more and more depressed. Abruptly, he decided to take a break and look for Star Wars gifts on Amazon.

Looking at all the merchandise, he was pondering what to buy for Fabio after the box set, the next lure. He felt a pang of conscience. *I really need to stop meeting with boys.* The incidents in the band room had just blown over. Thankfully, the parents didn't know the full story, but he really wanted to stop. He slouched in his chair and stared at the ceiling.

The hell with it, just this last time. It looks like they'll be transferring me out of state anyway, and Fabio really loves Star Wars. Plus, they'll probably send me to that rehab again.

He remembered when Fabio's mother, who had just moved into the neighborhood, came to the office to join the church. It was mid-morning and he could smell a faint odor of alcohol. He checked her eyes, dull and tired, an overall washed-out look. Yes, she was a drinker, no doubt. Completing the paperwork, it excited him to see there was no meddling father in the picture. An ideal situation, an alcoholic mother and an absent father. And Fabio, who was fourteen at the time, was just so needy and vulnerable, obviously lonely and lacking love and nurturing. A single mom preoccupied with drinking made it all so easy and Fabio a fine-looking boy. This was not something he could pass up; it didn't happen every day. It's not my fault these parents aren't doing their job.

He decided to order a Star Wars T-shirt. Let's see, adult small should be good.

Having just served the bishop's foursome refreshments, Father Paul parked in the shade and called his parent's residence. His father, Hermann George, answered.

"Hi, Paul, glad you called."

"Thanks, Dad. I just had a moment. I haven't called in a while. How's the union work going?"

"It's going well, but we need more funds to hire protestors so we can hit the streets. We're trying to get our donors to open their wallets again."

"Can't you use union funds?"

"Yes, we do. But that's for our rank and file who are laid off and want to pick up a few bucks, but if you really want a decent demonstration, you need more than just the rank and file. Our efforts are no longer just union issues, but the larger issues in society as well. Social justice affects everyone."

"Yes, of course, Dad. So what's your next objective?"

"Well, there's a conservative group scheduled to protest at the border. Their theme will be lawfulness, the rule of law, constitution, etc. We're going down to counter-protest and support the immigrants. These people simply want a better life and once they're here, we gain even more support, political support, if you catch my drift."

"Yes, I get it. Good for you, Dad. I hope it goes well."

"Oh, it will," Hermann said. "You might want to pay attention to the news. We're going to put KKK hats on a few of our people and plant them in the crowd of conservatives. We'll plant some others waving rebel flags, wearing rebel hats, t-shirts, whatever. The media will eat it up. It will totally undermine them and paint them with a broad brush. We call it a false-flag attack. It's very effective."

"Wow, that's brilliant, outstanding, Dad."

Feeling rather lightheaded, Bishop Cesare stretched out across the rear seat of his Cadillac. Other than having to deal with a prime rib that was a bit overdone, the day had gone well, and it was always a positive when the weather cooperated. That last drink was a bit strong, but good, nevertheless. Maybe one or two more before bed. Tomorrow was a light schedule.

"Father Paul, what did you think of my talk?"

"Very good, Your Excellency, most effective. You are an excellent speaker, Your Excellency."

"Thank you, I thought I did quite well, bearing in mind I had almost no time to prepare."

The bishop, feeling a bit drunk continued.

"And I told you to stop calling me, Your Excellency. Actually, I want you to start calling me Louie, I mean when we are alone, but not in public of course."

"Yes, certainly," said Father Paul, "if that is your wish."

"It is, and I have another wish, Paul."

"Of course, Louie, what is it?"

"I feel like I strained my shoulder today. I would like you to rub some ointment on it before I retire for the evening."

"Yes, certainly."

"Fine, you can meet me in the hot tub for a nightcap first."

Hearing the rectory doorbell chime, Father Kenneth felt a pang of excitement and anticipation. He's right on time. Dressed in freshly pressed blue jeans and a bright pink Titleist golf shirt, the priest walked hastily to the door.

"Well, hello, Fabio. I see you brought your homework." He gave him a quick hug. "Come sit here on the couch. Let's see what you've got."

"This is what I'm stuck on," Fabio said, "or just not doing I guess."

"Yes, I see. This will be a breeze. I don't see any math or algebra."

"I'm really good at math, Father. I don't even have to study. It's all the other stuff. I don't like writing or English, stuff like that."

"Wow, you didn't tell me you were a math wizard. You only have to be good at one thing to succeed in life, Fabio. Having high math aptitude is such a blessing, so many opportunities for someone like you. I see a bright future for you."

"Really, Father. Bright future? For me?"

"Yes, yes. And honestly, I'm relieved you didn't bring me your algebra homework, never my strong suit, but writing, English, social studies, right up my alley. We complement each other perfectly. We make a great team."

Fabio smiled.

"Let's do some homework first," Father Kenneth said. "Maybe not all of it today, but some or whatever is pressing, then we can order the box set. How does that sound?"

"Great, Father."

"Okay, fine. First, I want to teach you some relaxation techniques. An anxious worried mind lacks focus and concentration. You might remember, I was explaining this concept to you after the movie. So we are going to start with a back rub, like a massage, to calm your mind, relieve the tension. Okay?"

"Okay, Father."

"Take your shirt off. It will work better. And please, call me Uncle Kenny."

Chapter 6

Sunday mornings were a happy time for Mollie McCreesh, a time for the whole family to be together. First, morning mass, then a large Sunday dinner. She was carrying on the traditions of her parents and grandparents. Sunday was her favorite day of the week.

However, recently she had been coming out of morning mass more and more frustrated. This did not happen years ago, but as the homilies became more lukewarm and syrupy, she became more weary and was losing her patience. The new priest who came last year was a kind man, but it was clear he would not be tackling the hard issues, speaking boldly. The militant church, that is what the church on Earth is called, and Mollie was all about militancy. Fighting, fighting against what was happening in society and the decline in morals and values. Yet the church ignored it.

The homilies were always directed at the people in the pews, calling them to be better Christians, more Christlike. She wanted to scream, "Yeah, okay we got that, but we're the ones in church today, the 30 percent who come every week. Maybe we're not the problem." But, of course, Catholic guilt is renowned, so let's keep piling on the congregation every week, self-reflection, relentless self-examination, just what I need, more guilt.

She felt these sermons belonged in the 1950s. They never took a stand against abortion, the greatest evil of our age. They ignored the decline of the culture, the rot on television and the garbage coming out of Hollywood. It was infuriating to see the pope hobnobbing with movie stars and pop idols. Too many of these higher-ups, star-struck bishops and cardinals, were overly eager to be seen with celebrities and attending their galas; what kind of message did that send? They should be condemning these people and doing it boldly. The rubbish they were shoving in the face of our children daily, it was pure evil, attacking traditional values and the family and elevating everything that is dark, sexual promiscuity, all sorts of twisted self-indulgence. She felt it was sinister, yet the church just sat by as a sort of disinterested spectator, watching but ignoring, as if it was none of their business when it was exactly their business, the business of morals and virtues.

THE LAVENDER MAFIA

Mollie had been trying to be more tolerant. She didn't want to come out of church every week complaining about the lame homilies or lack of reverence. It was not her nature to be attacking and criticizing priests.

But she was fed up by the lack of reverence. Whatever happened to reverence? She would sometimes just need to close her eyes. Ushers, who were supposed to be setting an example, dressed in t-shirts and baggy gym shorts as they took up the collection. Eucharistic ministers (who were not even necessary, but, of course, we have to rush through the mass) wearing sneakers, children who were disruptive and parents who seemed to enjoy the attention, the cell phones going off, not to mention the loud talking right after mass, etc. It was getting worse every week, and the priest never preached about reverence. Casualness, sloppiness really, ruled the day. Yet Mollie was not going to leave. The sacraments were still valid, so if there was discomfort involved it was okay, all part of the Christian walk.

But today was not going to be a good day. Walking into the church, Mollie spied a massive flat-screen TV, just to the right of the altar and within a few feet of the sacristy. It was almost too much. Then it occurred to her. We're going to have to watch a stupid, fluffy video about the bishop's appeal. First off, it was exasperating to see a huge television, a tool of the dark side, in church. Do we really need to watch a senseless video instead of hearing commentary on the gospels?

It reminded her of the plastic people on the videos at The United Way dinners she was forced to attend by her employer. Afterward, employees would be pressured to donate. She was outraged when she saw the exorbitant salaries of the upper management of The United Way in the newspaper. The church was becoming more and more like The United Way and less and less sacramental.

She sat and stewed, envisioning herself standing up and screaming, "This is outrageous, I can't take it anymore." But that was not an option, and maybe the priest felt the same way. It was obviously marching orders from the chancery. The video droned on with pie charts, interviews with young seminarians, and a drug addict who was given housing. So the church is using some of the money to help people. Hooray. Let's all pat each other on the back. And that bishop, just not seeing much humility there, typical jabber.

She peevishly listened to the bishop's taped remarks. "We as Catholics do not have the privilege of compromising our moral values with our pre-existing beliefs and stereotypes. We must continue to advocate for the less fortunate and needy, regardless of race, color or creed, those on the margins of society."

The preachy, condescending tone was maddening.

Walking out of the church with a knot in her stomach, Mollie let out a huge sigh.

"Don't start, Mollie. It's too early for one of your rants. No offense, but you know I'm not that interested in church stuff. Why do you get so worked up?"

"Because I have faith. I believe the church is God's house, and He is present in a very special way, and you see a lot of behavior that is improper, offensive even, but you're right, Pat. Let's go have a nice dinner."

"Okay, Mollie. I'll carve and help with the dishes."

While waiting for dinner, Jack was falling in love with the Navy. With each YouTube video he watched, his desire burned brighter. The uniforms were so cool. He was hoping to work with Marines, the men who had it the hardest and suffered the most. They deserved good medical care. Jack was excited knowing he would learn about first aid and emergency medical. It was a perfect fit.

With the aroma of roast beef still in the air, Patrick and Jack helped with the dishes while Beth went to clean her room; it always needed it and her mother required it.

"Hey, Dad, after I clean my room will you help me with my homework?"

"Sure, Beth."

After they left, Jack was helping his Mom load the dishwasher.

"Does it really bother you to see a TV in church, Mom?"

"Yes, Jack it does."

"Why?"

"Television is one of Satan's favorite tools. It does not belong near the altar."

"But there are some good things on television, Mom."

Mollie chuckled. "Some? Maybe five percent. Even *EWTN* is not what it once was since Mother Angelica is gone, more diluted faith, cowardly even. Sure you'll see shows on *The History Channel* and *Discovery* with titles like, "Who Was Jesus?" or "Finding

Jesus." But these are basically covert hit pieces designed to undermine your faith. If you watch, they will plant doubts in your mind. Your faith will be weaker. That's the goal.

"Some guy with a British accent usually narrates. I guess it's supposed to make it more credible. People need to be warned from the pulpit, but we never are. It wouldn't surprise me if some priests are being influenced by these shows. Based on their homilies, a lot of them are clearly watching too much TV."

"Don't you think they need to know what's going on in the world, Mom?"

"Yes, but If they really want to know what's going on they should read the Bible, they won't acquire wisdom by watching television, a dark, distorted view of the world."

"It is distorted, Mom. It almost seems the meteorologists give weather forecasts in a way that's designed to agitate us. Every single solitary piece of weather that is not a perfect, sunny 70-degree day is treated as Armageddon, and rain is bad, even though if it didn't rain we would all die."

Mollie smiled and closed the dishwasher door. "Exactly Jack, a television does not belong near the sacristy. Show the video in the basement after. Maybe not too many people will watch, but who cares? Do we really need to be treated like children? Like after all these years, we don't know what the appeal is for? It's ludicrous, intolerable, offensive even."

"Don't sugarcoat it, Mom."

"Okay, Jack." Mollie grinned and sat down at the kitchen table. "But it's not only the TV, it's everything. It's sad to see the church becoming more worldly. I almost want to leave.

"It's like everything bothers me. It all seems backward. Take the music for example. Right now, we have a missalette that has three hundred songs in it. Then there's the Gather Hymnal with another five hundred songs. After that, of course, we need a music supplement because we don't have enough songs already. Then they pick obscure songs that are chosen once every ten years, and you need to be a music major with an operatic voice to sing.

"How are people supposed to sing a song they hardly ever hear with notes all over the scale? It's almost like they want to make it hard for people to sing. Something is not right. I mean, I like to sing. I want to sing! They make it so hard. Why not just have a reasonable number of songs, the traditional ones people love and maybe some others that are easy to sing and people can remember?

"And then they keep changing the acclamations and responsorial psalms. Once you become confident you can sing with a little passion, they change them, to a completely different melody that's all over the place. It's baffling. It's almost as if there are forces at work trying to keep the mass dispassionate. Maybe I am overly preoccupied with dark forces in the church, but I'd be interested to trace this. Who is responsible for making these idiotic decisions about music? There is a music ministry in each parish, but I suspect they're being influenced by some higher-ups in the church."

"I can see why you get aggravated, Mom. I think you're right. Something is amiss. I'll bet most people don't even pay attention to this stuff."

"I agree, but they should. God and church, Jack. God must be first. Seek ye first the kingdom of God."

After asking permission to leave the lunchroom, Jack walked briskly down to the main corridor.

"Good afternoon, Chief Petty Officer. Could I talk to you for a minute?"

"Absolutely, Jack, and are we still on for tonight, 7:00 pm?"

"Yes, sir. I wanted to tell you I decided on the corpsman job. Are there openings?"

"Yes, Jack, and you may qualify for an enlistment bonus of $20,000 if you meet everything. I mean, you said your grades are good, you look fit and healthy. You need to meet the physical requirements, 50 push-ups, 10 pull-ups, things like that, and I'm thinking you'll do well on our ASVAB, so assuming you meet the qualifications, I think we could hook you up with corpsman. There's a need currently, Jack, so you're hitting us at the right time."

"Okay great. Then I think I'm going to sign up. Can I pick whether to go with the Navy or Marines?"

"I can't guarantee it, Jack. Most want the Navy because Marine life, especially with the infantry, is harsh. To tell you the truth, that is where the need is right now, more with the Marines."

"Well, I'm interested in going with the Marines. My dad was a Marine, but any corpsman job would be great. I just want you to come and talk to my parents before I sign."

"Of course, Jack, we want your parents onboard."

Later that evening, Chief Petty Officer Wilson pulled up in a gold Chevrolet Malibu with United States government tags. Jack was watching and excitedly opened the door.

"Hello, Chief Petty Officer, please come in. I'd like you to meet my mom and dad, Mollie and Patrick McCreesh."

"My pleasure. Your son has made a very good impression and I pulled his transcripts. You must be very proud."

"We are, so proud," Mollie said.

"To be honest, there's a shortage of men like Jack in the millennial generation. Jack is the kind of man we're looking for."

"Thank you, Chief Petty Officer," Patrick said. "I served in the Marines. I think we can cut right to the chase. My wife and I have been talking about this. I always hoped Jack would join the military, so we're behind him 100 percent if he decides to join. It's his decision."

"Thank you," said CPO Wilson, "That's good to know."

"Yes, I agree with my husband," Mollie said, "but could you go over the benefits and tell us a little bit about yourself. I'm curious and want to know more, especially about college money."

"First off, we're paying a $20,000 enlistment bonus now for a corpsman, upon completion of training, which could be set aside for college," CPO Wilson said. "In addition, the GI Bill will pay a four-year education at a state school, including expenses. You can also take classes while you're in the Navy, although it can depend on the deployment, and schools will give you college credits for training and experience. There are other benefits, such as extra points on civil service tests, lifetime access to the Veteran's healthcare system, and pension and retirement benefits."

"We bought this house with a VA loan," Patrick said.

CPO Wilson nodded and continued. "As far as my personal experience, I came from a difficult family background, much different than what I see here. I was a yeoman working administration for my first four years and was out to sea quite a bit, until later when I was stationed in a barracks and obtained an associate degree. Soon, I'm finishing up an eight-year hitch. I haven't decided if I'll reenlist or not, but I'm very happy with what the Navy has done for me and the options I have presently."

"It's so exciting," Mollie said. "Maybe we should hear from Jack."

Jack laughed, "I've been listening, and I like everything, all of it. And I was ready to sign before I even knew about the bonus, so now it's even better."

"Let me ask you, Jack, on a scale of one to ten, as far as enlisting, ten means you 100 percent want to, and one means go away and don't come back, where are you?"

"I'm a ten," Jack said.

The next day Hector and Jack were riding to school.

"How did it go with the recruiter last night, Jack?"

"Good I guess because I'm signing up."

"Wow, Jack. You are a beast, a Navy corpsman, man you got guts."

"Not really, Hector. There are a lot of people doing it. I think it will be fun."

"Fun? You're like a medic. You might find yourself in combat dodging bullets and applying tourniquets. My dad was explaining it to me. It's not something I'd sign up for, but good on you, Jack."

"Was your dad a medic?"

"No, Jack, a doctor. He became a doctor in the Army. It was a long time ago, but he knows all about medics and corpsman. He said they're respected by everyone and most of them were really good people, kind of like you, Jack."

"Thanks, Hector, I love what your Dad said."

"So are you still going to college, Hector?"

"Yeah, even though my dad could pay without blinking an eye, he wants me to go ROTC. He thinks I need more discipline. He's probably right." Hector chuckled, "Of course, I'd rather not do it. He says you're a good example for me. So thanks a lot, Jack."

"My pleasure, Hector. A little ROTC never hurt anyone, what branch?"

"Not sure yet. Probably Navy."

"Oh, that's great," Jack said. "If our paths cross later, I'll have to salute you. I hope we're never stationed together. That could get really annoying after a while."

"Don't worry, Jack, I'd be nice about it. Just make it crisp so I don't have to correct you."

"Ok sure, Hector, got it. What a pal. Hey, do you want to go to my sister's track meet with me after school? I could pick you up."

Jack was texting Nora.

Hey Nora, wanna go to the track meet with me lata? gotta pick up Beth
Love to Jack.
Ok, Hector is coming too. Pick you up after school.

They pulled up to the stadium and easily found a spot, not too many attended the meets. Beth was participating in the long jump, 100-meter dash, and 400-meter team relay. She was a fast runner and loved to fly.

When she was a freshman on the high school field hockey team, she had beaten a senior star in a dash down the field at a field hockey camp. The coach did this every year, promising free camp tuition, two hundred dollars, to anyone who could beat the senior star. In twenty years of races, no one had ever beaten the senior before, that is until Beth came along. The coach, who was making a lot of money off the camp, in the end, did not give Beth free tuition as promised, but some cheap bracelet. Beth lost some respect for the coach that day, Coach Fritz, who would later be her varsity field hockey coach.

But today was about track. Beth came in second in the long jump and lost to an all-scholastic senior in the 100-meter dash in a photo finish. Jack was loving it and cheering her on. He loved his little sister. Then came the 400-meter team relay. Beth, who was the anchor, ran the last leg. Her team was in great shape, well ahead. Beth had her hand out waiting for the baton. She was bursting with adrenaline and could not wait to get it and bust out the last leg, but then the pass went poorly; she dropped the baton. She spied the opposing runner pass her. Grabbing it off the ground she exploded with a fiery burst of speed, it was doable, she was gaining ground. *I'm going to catch her*, and Beth would indeed catch her but not until just after the finish line. *Oh well, I tried my best.*

While Beth was coming off the track, Jack heard the coach going into a profanity-laced tirade berating his little sister for dropping the baton. The meet was over, and it had cost them the win. The coach was red in the face. He could see Beth was on the verge of tears. It was too much.

"Hector, come with me." Nora followed behind.

Jack walked up to the coach and got right in his face. "What gives you the right to talk like that? Do you eat with that mouth?"

"What are you talking about," the coach said.

"I am talking about your foul mouth which can be heard all over the stadium. Is that how you motivate athletes? Is that how you speak to a young woman? What the heck is wrong with you?"

"Who are you?"

"I'm Jack McCreesh. Beth's my sister. She is your best runner, and this is how you speak to her?"

"Oh, I get it." The coach said. "Listen, McCreesh, mind your own business this is competitive sports. Things get a little heated sometimes."

Beth piped in. "It's okay, Jack. It's not a big deal."

"Yeah listen to your sister," the coach said. "It's just words, words you hear at school every day. Suck it up, buttercup."

Hector had noticed Jack clenching his fists. He knew about Jack's righteous temper. Just as Jack lunged at the coach, Hector grabbed him in a bear hug.

"Come on, Jack, he's not worth it."

It took a second, but Jack composed himself and walked away with Hector and Nora.

"It's okay, Jack," Nora said. "Take a breath. That coach is an imbecile."

Walking to the locker room the coach turned to his assistant. "What's up with that McCreesh kid, spazzing because I dropped a few f-bombs? All the coaches do it."

"Who knows?" the assistant said. "But I think the family is like major Catholics or something, kinda weird."

In the meantime, across town, at her job at the Social Security Administration, Mollie was in a similar conflict. She worked in an office where profanity was rampant. Men who worked in nearby cubicles would yell out the f-bomb, whenever they felt like it, if the computer was slow, like it should never ever be slow, and every program they used, there were several, should always be operating smoothly and seamlessly or they would throw a little tantrum, like a two-year-old, but with profane adult language. She realized it was the culture of the office. These things had a way of taking root and then spreading. It was really the management's fault, after all, they allowed it.

She had complained before, but it never did any good. Maybe things would get better for a day or two, but her fellow employees would not focus on their own inappropriate behavior, but on who ratted. That was not allowed.

A few months prior, a new hire, Tammy, reserved and professional, had made the mistake of being honest and forthright when the section chief asked her about the colleagues in her work area. She naively mentioned the profanity and afternoon naps two of them took at their desks. The section chief foolishly did not keep the source of her information confidential, and after the offending employees were reprimanded, they were overheard to remark, "snitches get stitches." Odd to hear at a federal office but maybe not at a federal prison.

Mollie had comforted the distraught woman who half the office immediately turned on. "Don't let anyone run you off. You did nothing wrong. They need to look at themselves. You have at least one friend here, Tammy. If you need anything, anything at all, come see me."

The behavior did not change. The men literally shouted curses from their desks, like whiny little brats. They sounded like little babies. Mollie loathed victimhood.

Today Mollie reached her breaking point. She heard a man yelling at his computer. "You gotta be f**king kidding me, come on, what the f**k?"

It was too much. She yelled out, "Wah, wah, wah. Poor baby." The man, whose name was Sam, said, "Did you say something, McCreesh?"

"Yeah, I did. I don't feel I should have to listen to your foul mouth all day. And if you're having a problem with your computer, maybe you should just deal with it, like a mature adult, instead of a petulant, spoiled child and disrupt everyone else. Do you really expect your computer to work perfectly all the time?"

"What's wrong with you, McCreesh? You really need to work on your temper."

"Yes, my temper is the problem, my temper, but you don't have to listen to me cursing or crying every time my computer acts up, do you?"

"Why don't you put on your iPod and mind your business?"

"I would, but even a cranked-up iPod can't drown out your vulgar mouth."

The supervisor came out, "That's enough."

Later, her friend Stephanie approached as she was turning off her computer. "Hey, Mollie, are you okay? I heard you were flipping out this morning."

"Flipping out? Really? The world is a crazy place, Stephanie, just nuts. That's all I can say."

Sam, the profane co-worker, was walking to his car with his buddy. "You should've seen McCreesh spazzing today, just because I cursed. She's a strange woman. I think she's like really Catholic or something, it's weird."

Chapter 7

Jack tossed and turned. Navy basic training was in one week. He really needed to stop watching all those YouTube videos, too much information.

Yes, they screamed at you when you got off the bus, but it wasn't the Marine Corps. They were going to apply a little pressure, but he could handle the physical training, so it would be mostly mental.

"Good morning, Jack. How did you sleep?"

"Not so good, Mom, a lot of anxious thoughts."

"What are you worried about?"

"Not sure, everything I guess like the training and meeting all the new people."

"Jack, wait until you get there, then deal with it. You are completely capable of handling whatever comes along. Stressing about it now is just pointless. You can't deal with it until you get there, but if you want to keep thinking about it, see yourself as facing everything with courage. You are training and preparing, working out, so feel good about that. Thousands have gone through this training before, Jack. All these people were not smarter than you."

"Yeah, you're right, Mom," Jack said. "I like what you said. The heck with it, I'll just face things when I get there."

"Exactly, and with that in mind, I think you should stop worrying and start thinking about who you're going to help at boot camp. I want you to prepare as best you can so you can help the next person. You're in good shape and you've had lots of experience with team sports. This will all work to your advantage, and you won't need any help with the academic portion. Plus, I'm sure the Navy is going to want to see you succeed after all the investment they're making, likely lots of help available."

"Yeah. I feel better after talking to you, as usual. And like you always say, when you're overly worried or anxious, you're not trusting in God."

"Amen, Jack. It's not always easy to discern God's will, but if He is calling you to the priesthood, it seems reasonable you can take a hitch with the Navy as a corpsman, take time and ponder, while you serve your country. It will only make you a better priest. There's nothing to worry about. A Navy corpsman dedicated to his job is a life pleasing to God."

"Yeah, I need to approach this with an attitude of service and helpfulness."

Several days later, Jack was walking with Nora. "I can't believe it, Jack. Everything went by so fast, first the prom then graduation and now you're leaving for the Navy tomorrow. I'm going to miss you, Jack, but I think you'll do really good. Plus, you'll look great in uniform, just like you did in your tuxedo."

Jack smiled. "Thanks, Nora, but everyone looks good in a tuxedo. I thought you looked great too, in your gown. I'm going to miss everyone, but this is a great adventure. Who knows where it will take me? The places and things I'll see, maybe even be on some foreign land or out on the ocean, could be anything. Whatever it is, I know it will force me to grow, although it may not always be easy. Are you still going to nursing school?"

"Yeah, at the community college. My parents thought it would be a smart move, more affordable. It's twelve months, kind of intense, but there are jobs when you graduate. It's in my heart to be a nurse."

"That's a good sign, sort of how I feel about the Navy, and sometimes about the priesthood. It's just that the priesthood is so permanent. You'll be a great nurse, Nora."

"Whatever you do, Jack, I hope we can always keep in touch and at least stay friends. None of my other friends are like you."

Jack picked up his buzzing cell phone. "What's up, Hector?"

"Just wanted to say goodbye, brother and wish you luck. Who knows when I'll see you again, but I know you'll be a great corpsman, just keep your head down."

"I will," said Jack. "It's a natural response when bullets are flying, but odds are I won't see action."

"But you never know," said Hector. "War could break out at any time, and there are probably troops deployed in hot spots the government doesn't even tell us about."

"You're a smart one, Hector. You should never join the military unless you're prepared for the worst. To join the military for all the benefits and college money, and then complain when you actually have to go in harm's way is lame. Everyone knows once you put on a uniform it could get hazardous. All throughout history men have died for our country, Hector. I hope I'm not going to be one of them, but at least it would be a noble way to go out, like hundreds of thousands before me."

"You say some of the strangest things, Jack. Do you really believe that stuff?"

"I believe in the afterlife. Once you believe in the afterlife, it gives you a whole different perspective."

Riding to the airport Jack was anxious but hopeful. He kept looking at the clock in the car as his mom and dad made small talk.

They pulled up in front of the recruiting center at the local shopping mall. It was awkward. Even though they had been aware, and prepared months for this day, no one was ready for the uncomfortable feelings. His dad felt like he wanted a drink. His mom felt like she just wanted to squeeze the stuffing out of him and not let go. Jack was already feeling homesick, but they soon said their goodbyes, knowing it was necessary and inevitable.

His first flight was only 25 minutes to Pittsburgh where he would catch the next plane to Chicago.

Returning home, Mollie and Patrick McCreesh found Beth sitting at the kitchen table looking at a field hockey camp flyer.

"You should have woken me," Beth said. "I would've gone with you."

"Jack said to let you sleep," Mollie said. "I guess you guys had a long talk last night, he felt like that was your goodbye."

"Yeah, Mom we did, and I was in a deep sleep, so maybe I needed it. I've been looking at this field hockey camp stuff. I'm not sure what to do."

"I think you should work it," said Patrick. "If you get more playing time your senior year, you might get some scholarship money."

"Well, some extra money would be nice, but don't do it just for the money," Mollie said. "If your heart isn't in it, it's not worth it."

"I love field hockey, Mom. I just don't care for Coach Fritz. Maybe if I played more, I'd have a better attitude. Plus, we all work this camp for free and the coach gets all the money."

"Hmm, not sure what I think about that," said Mollie.

"And you're the fastest sprinter on the team," said Patrick. "The fastest are always the best athletes, Beth. It's annoying you didn't play more, but if you don't work her camp, you know she won't start you senior year, no matter how good you are. She plays favorites. I really don't understand her thinking though. It's like she has some twisted agenda."

"Well, I guess I'll sign up since I don't really have anything else going on and most of my friends are on the team. Will you give rides, Dad, on your way to work?"

"Sure, Beth."

Arriving in Chicago, Jack had already made a few friends on the plane. After landing, they were directed to the USO where they were given further instructions and some light refreshments. Soon, he was sitting in a large open area with numerous other recruits from all over the country. There was a nervous tension in the room. Everyone was talking about the same YouTube videos about arriving at boot camp. They all knew the first 24 hours would be a challenge with little sleep and a lot of standing in line. One boy was upset about the head-shaving that awaited him. Jack thought it a bit weak but kept his thoughts to himself. If you are going to worry about your hair, you are already off to a bad start.

After completing some forms they grabbed their gear and lined up for the 45-minute bus ride to the training installation. During the first 20 minutes, there was a video by a Navy officer giving an overview. Several recruits slept through it. Jack was determined to stay awake and pay attention. After all, the main theme of what he saw on YouTube was to listen to directions. If you did that you were less likely to get screamed at. After the video, the bus fell into an eerie, ominous silence. Jack saw the sign, Naval Station Great Lakes. There was no turning back now.

Mollie McCreesh was coming out of Confession. Every month or two she liked to go on Saturday afternoon and then sit in church for 30 minutes before mass and pray for the children and her deceased relatives, especially her mom and dad. It was believed that Confession made prayers even more powerful.

She grabbed a quiet spot in the rear of the church. After she said her penance, she prayed for Jack at basic training. It always made her feel better to pray, lifted anxiety. Just as she was entering a peaceful state, three women came in and sat in the very last row, three rows behind her. They began talking, whispering, loud whispering. It sounded like gossip, clearly saying disreputable things about others. She had experienced this before. They come early and blabber on in the back.

What was with these people who go to church early to gossip? Gossiping in a church, just reprehensible. There was only one reason to go to church early, and that was to pray and meditate, not to gossip or read the bulletin. It was annoying. She was tempted to say something, or at least shush them, but this was the modern church. Then the gossip finally died down. Silence is golden.

Then an older man entered and spoke to the women.

"Did you see that new bakery across the street? They're charging $3.49 for a brownie. I wanted to get a brownie, but I am not going to pay $3.49 for one brownie. Since my wife passed away, I hardly ever get to have a good brownie. It's outrageous. I can't afford that."

"I know," said one of the women. "A medium coffee is $2.75. It's a rip-off. You should try Price Chopper's brownies."

"I tried them," the man said. "They're not moist enough. Plus you gotta buy a whole tray."

"My neighbor has a good brownie recipe," the other woman said.

"I don't want to be bothered baking, too messy. I just want to find a place where I can get one freaking moist brownie. I don't think that's too much to ask."

Mollie couldn't take it anymore. Figuring a confrontation was not appropriate, she decided to move up to the front. Loud whispering. How stupid is *loud* whispering? And why are so many Catholics preoccupied with food? Too many church events revolved around food. We need to hear more about fasting, but that will never happen. And maybe something about gossip, or just sin in general. And forget about praying after mass, it was like you were walking out of a high school basketball game, with all the chatter and giggling, so different from the deferential days of her youth.

What happened to reverence for God? Sheesh. She settled in down front, much better but she could still hear them, barely. A thought came to her, "judge not lest you be judged." *Okay, God, but you really need to do something about the sad state of your church.*

Thirty minutes later, she was gritting her teeth listening to the homily. There had been a shooting on the west coast this past week. The shooter apparently targeted Hispanics. After the first two sentences out of the priest's mouth, she knew what was coming. Here we go again; he is going to lecture us about what some madman did 3000 miles away.

The priest preached on. "Why can't we just accept people the way they are, regardless of race? Why can't we just love our fellow man and not give into racism?" Mollie sat and stewed. "We?" Why can't *we* accept people? Infuriating. I didn't shoot anyone and never would. I don't have a racist bone in my body, yet I have to come here and listen to you deluded, social justice warrior priests, lecture me about my prejudice and how *we* need to examine our racism! She thought about getting up and walking out. She wanted to stand up and scream, "You are watching too much cable news, Father! Turn off the television. Open up your Bible! Get on your knees and pray to the Holy Spirit. You are being deceived - you fool!"

We? Collective guilt, a tool of the dark side to dispirit and divide. The church had fallen into the trap of always employing collective guilt. Whenever there was some tragedy or some outrageous, diabolical crime, the church always felt the need to blame us, the ones (the minority of Catholics no less), who decided to actually show up for mass! Yet, here it was again, collective guilt versus personal responsibility. It would include blather like, "We are all responsible for what happened in California," or "We all need to look at our role in this," or "We all need to examine our racism." No, Father, *we* all are not responsible, just some mentally ill, reprobate in California, that's it! And here's a newsflash, Father – we're not all racists. She looked around at the congregation, perhaps a lot of lukewarm Catholics, many she knew for years. Racism was not the vibe she was getting. But what could you do except tolerate the priest's pablum?

I could just see myself trying to explain to this priest how I don't feel racism is an issue for me. He would probably sit there smirking, thinking I was in denial or just didn't understand my passive-aggressive, subconscious racism, due to white privilege.

She clenched her jaw and remained silent.

While Mollie was at church, Patrick picked up the landline.
"Hi, Dad!"

"Jack, it's great to hear from you! How are you? How's Navy boot camp?"

"It's fine, Dad. We just got off the bus a half-hour ago. We get three minutes to use the phone. So far, I'm fine. Everyone was tense coming in, but I think we all feel better just getting here. Mostly we'll be getting our gear, our hair cut, stuff like that, but I don't think we get to sleep until tomorrow night. Is Mom around?"

"No, Jack. She's at church."

Jack smiled. "Praying for me, no doubt."

"No doubt, Jack. I'll tell her you called. She'll be so happy to hear you made it."

"Good, Dad. But I don't think I'll be able to call again for a few weeks. And I'll be mailing a package with all my personal stuff, so you can expect that in a week or two. But don't worry, Dad, I'm fine. I feel at peace. Some guys here don't. They keep saying things like, 'What was I thinking?' It's kind of funny. It will take some getting used to, but I think I'm here with a good group."

Two days later, Beth was sitting in the bleachers waiting for the field hockey camp to start.

Her friend Jen came walking up. "Hi, Beth, I wasn't sure if I was going to see you here."

"I decided I'd give it one last shot, but if I knew it was going to be this hot, I think I would've just gotten a summer job at a place with air conditioning and made some money. The only one making money here is Coach Fritz."

Jen laughed. "At least we get free lunch, but who wants to eat hot dogs every day for two weeks."

"It's the cheapest lunch, that's why. Do the math, Jen, 75 players at $200 each. It's a nice summer job for a teacher, two weeks and $15,000. Plus, she is still getting her teacher's salary."

Jen chuckled. "Gym teacher. What a job! Hand out the kickball and sit and watch."

"Yeah, and that's pretty much what she'll be doing here, hand out the turf ball and sit and watch, but at least we get to work with the kids. It's fun teaching them."

Chapter 8

"I have some good news for you, Your Excellency," said Monsignor Sabatini. "We just received a contribution of 1.5 million dollars directed to The Bishop's Appeal. That should go a long way in helping make up any shortfall."

"All well and good, but do not make this public until the very last minute. Pressure still needs to be put on these parishes to make their goal. This windfall, which we can't count on every year, does not absolve them of their responsibility to the chancery."

"Of course not, Your Excellency."

"And I just saw where St. Mary Czestochowa took in over $100,000 at their church picnic," the bishop said, "a staggering amount of money for a small parish. Do you really think they need all that money? What in heaven's name will they do with it, Monsignor?"

"I believe the church is in need of some renovations, Your Excellency, including a new roof."

"I was just there earlier this year," the bishop said. "It looked fine. Maybe they need a roof, the rest is probably frivolous. How much can a new roof cost anyway? Some of these parish picnics are taking in obscene amounts of money. Don't you think it's time we reconsidered this policy of allowing parishes to keep all of that money and not give a cut to the chancery?"

"Perhaps, Your Excellency, but this policy goes back over one hundred years. It has always been a way for a parish to sustain itself with an event that brings energy and unity to the church community. The parishioners feel edified by volunteering, and cooking over hot stoves, knowing that it will help support their parish and take some pressure off the priest."

"Pressure off the priest? They don't know what pressure is compared to running a diocese. They wouldn't last one day in my shoes. We need to reassess this church picnic issue, Monsignor."

"Yes, Your Excellency."

Bishop Cesare picked up an alumni magazine off his desk and held it up.

"I should have joined the Holy Cross Order. I had my chance when I was there. Do you know, Monsignor, the chancellor of Notre

Dame, the good Reverend Jenkins, makes almost a million dollars a year? Not bad for a humble priest. And here I am a bishop of this huge understaffed diocese, and I have to make do with a salary slightly better than a country pastor. Oh, what I couldn't do with a million dollars every year.

"And while I struggle to get 7 million for the annual appeal, Father Jenkins is sitting on billions. Do you know Notre Dame has an endowment of over 14 billion, Monsignor? That is billion with a 'B.' Could you imagine sitting on 14 billion dollars and watching it grow *tax-free* every year? And even though you're sitting on all that money, you get to charge these cash-strapped Catholic students $70,000 a year and keep raising it, as long as there are more applications than spots open, many more. And the parents and students are happy to participate, and never object to the fleecing. Ah, the Catholic University, what a system! I wish I could go back and do it all over again. Even the professors there are paid five times my salary and all they have to do is a lecture or two a day."

"Well, it is Notre Dame, after all, Your Excellency."

"Yes, of course, one of the most lucrative, but you would be surprised how many of these Catholic colleges have huge endowments and gorgeous salaries. They just throw up new buildings without blinking while I struggle to upgrade my residence under all this painful scrutiny. And I can't just raise tuitions."

The bishop grabbed his reading glasses and looked at the appeal numbers. "So where did this 1.5 million come from anyway?"

"The will of a Mr. Charles Burnside. He was a bachelor, no family."

"Yes, I am well familiar with Mr. Burnside, also an alumnus of Notre Dame. Thankfully, the greedy bastards didn't get their hands on it."

Fabio came out of the rectory feeling bewildered and anxious, maybe it was the cupcakes, too many cupcakes. It seemed like some good things were happening, but it was unsettling. He felt ashamed but was happy to have a full stomach for a change. Having all his homework done, was something new too, so that was good, but it was troubling what had happened in Father Ken's house. The massage had started out good, relaxing and peaceful, scented candles and soft music, but then something had gone terribly wrong. He knew it wasn't right, but father said to keep it a secret or they both could get in trouble. People wouldn't understand their special relationship.

Maybe I shouldn't feel bad. I didn't do anything wrong, did I? I didn't mean to. It was only a few minutes, and he's a priest so he must know. He tried to put it out of his mind and focus on the good stuff.

He couldn't believe the size of Father's residence, all those rooms, and only one person living there. It seemed like a castle. The living room, with its huge flat-screen TV, was bigger than the apartment he lived in, not to mention the massive kitchen with the granite countertops. The large fridge-freezer was loaded, snacks, beverages, a variety of frozen dinners, and three different flavors of ice cream. Then there was a pantry crammed with more stuff, including a selection of Tasty Cakes, his favorite, and he was allowed to eat whatever he wanted.

He was looking forward to returning in two days to pick up his Star Wars box set. Father Ken said he also had ordered another special Star Wars gift but wouldn't say what it was. He pulled $40 out of his pocket and looked at it. *Wow, what am I going to do with all this money?*

Inside the rectory, Father Kenneth poured himself a brandy. He didn't have anything until the 10:00 a.m. mass tomorrow. He could have a few stiff drinks this evening. His mind was racing. He wanted to slow it down with some alcohol. Putting his drink down on the coffee table, he saw the brochure. That freaking brochure for the behavioral modification rehab, behavioral health, emotional issues, addiction and compulsive behavior, preventative and restorative care for clergy. Ugh. *Another inpatient program, but it probably won't be that long. The relapse program was shorter.*

The counselors at this place were tough. Confrontation, making you consider the impact on the victims, the long-term damage. It was not pleasant, but he was a good actor and knew what they wanted to hear. Plus, the food was decent. *I actually wouldn't mind going if I thought they could cure me. It would be worth it. Really though, it's just a waste of time but a good place to hide out and lay low until things quiet down.*

Deciding he'd better get his sermon ready for tomorrow before he got too drunk, he went on a website where he could grab a Catholic homily pertinent to the Sunday reading. He had purchased a one-year subscription. Print it out, read it over, edit a little, and that was that, too easy.

The next day Father awoke feeling a little shaky. He had drunk a whole bottle again the prior evening. This was becoming a habit. As he tied his shoes, he noticed the unsteadiness. He hoped the altar wine would settle his nerves before Communion. He planned on filling the chalice to the top.

As he got up to give the homily, the air conditioning was not working properly, and he was still feeling woozy from the booze. He decided to keep it brief and skip over portions of the edited pre-printed homily.

"Dear Friends, today we gather in union with Christ, our savior, our salvation. The Word made flesh. We must embrace the Word, and make it part of our being, unite with The Lord, and nourish and renew our spirit. Today the reading calls us to reconsider our relationship with Jesus, to go deeper, to give of ourselves completely, holding nothing back.

"I ask you today, was Jesus the Son of God? Do you truly believe? Are you ready to surrender? But how often, as you go about your daily life, do you consider His role, His hopes, His desires for your life? It is He who suffered for us on the cross. Yet, every time you sin, you drive another nail into the cross, causing our Lord to suffer again, more agony. Some of you are living a life of sin and succumbing to improper urges. You live as if He is not present among us. Vanity of vanities, all is vanity.

"His kingdom is a gift. There is reason to be buoyant. The kingdom has been given, given by God's love for man, through the sacrifice of His Son. Much has been given, much is expected. What kind of life are you living? The message of Jesus brings us hope and comfort, and most of all unity, unity in Christ. Jesus challenges us to love.

"We must shatter the mold, break the inertia, and crush the wickedness in our lives. We must permit God to be our director. Our mentor. Our guide. Our father. Pause, contemplate, give thanks and enter into spiritual union with our God.

"Yet, your hearts have become hardened by the deceitfulness of sin. Sin is a demon lurking at the door. Sin must not be permitted to take route over your mortal bodies and evolve into depraved habits. Do not allow yourself to become a slave to sin. Do not let it reign over your life, sin that displeases God, sin that is always prowling, plotting, and acting.

"The door is open, only you can close it, by hardening your hearts. Learn to love as Christ did. Follow the example we have been so freely given, submitting to divine providence, giving everything, trusting, holding nothing back.

"Today, friends, I ask that you reject temptation and let the flame of Jesus's love burn radiantly in your hearts. Flee from corrupt passions and turn to Christ. He will give you a peace that surpasses all understanding. Look at those areas of your life preventing your soul from burning brightly. Turn away from sin, sin that displeases God. Sin is a cunning and relentless adversary, a great deceiver, always pressing forward. Do not be deceived. Stay alert and watchful. Persevere with diligence and earnestness. Put on Christ, and free yourself from the condemning power of sin."

The next morning, Gil Rodgers was doing some mortar patching on the front steps when he saw the Matson's Flower truck pull up to the rear of the residence. Gil had gone to high school with Peter Matson. They played baseball together, so whenever he was around, he would help with the flower delivery.

"Hi, Pete. Let me give you a hand."

"Thanks, Gil, appreciated as always."

After they had loaded the flowers and were chatting near the truck, an olive-skinned man, wearing dark sunglasses came out of the back of the mansion and briskly walked past. They watched discreetly as they saw him get into a late model black BMW coupe, with light tints, a shadowy figure.

"I wonder who that was?" said Gil.

"I think I know him. I met him at the vocation's dinner. His name is Alex Montalvo, a friend and supporter of the bishop."

"Supporter? That's weird. It's not the first time I've seen him creeping around here. I wonder just what kind of support he gives the bishop."

"I was thinking the same thing when I met him at the dinner," said Peter. "He just seemed different than the others at the table, chic and sophisticated, mysterious even. I was wondering if he was the bishop's boyfriend."

"Bishop's boyfriend? Wow. Hmm. I probably should be shocked, but I've been noticing things. I'm a little surprised to hear

THE LAVENDER MAFIA

those words coupled, but I feel like a light is going off in my head. I feel like it explains some things, some things I can't really talk about right now, but the fog is lifting."

"I think I know what that fog is all about," Peter said. "Let me fill you in on something, on the down-low. There is a gay network in the hierarchy of the church. I'm close to my pastor. He is an old-fashioned, orthodox priest. He told me about this group, not just locally, but positioned all throughout the hierarchy of the church, they call them the 'Lavender Mafia.'"

"The Lavender Mafia? How can that be? Why doesn't he say something?"

"He said he tried years ago, made some reports, but he was the one who was punished. He said they're very powerful and not to be messed with. It's deep, Gil. If you want to continue working for the diocese, you best learn to look the other way."

"I don't know, Pete, that's not my nature. That's not how I was raised."

"Well, don't say I didn't warn you. And one more thing, the conservative priests have a nickname for our bishop."

"A nickname?"

"Yeah, they call him 'Louise.'"

Surfing the internet, viewing all the attractions, Father Paul was looking forward to his trip to Italy as part of the bishop's contingent, a nine-day Taste of Italy excursion scheduled three weeks hence. He was hoping Leon, from The Christian Brothers, would still be able to make it. Leon, who still worked at the high school, was starting his summer break soon. It was all looking promising. As the bishop's driver, Paul and a fellow traveler (his choice) would be able to tour at 50 percent off.

The local travel agency had already comped two tickets for the bishop, as long as they could use his image in the half-page ads they would run in *The Catholic Beacon*. There was a large elderly Italian American population in the diocese and the agency was confident the spots would fill up quickly.

Father Paul texted Leon.
Could you take a call now?
Yes, give me a min so I can get to a good spot. I w/c you.

"Sup, Leon?"

"I just wanted to get to a quiet spot. People around here just need to learn to mind their own business. I really need a getaway, Paul."

"Okay, great, so you're definitely going?"

"Absolutely, I would not miss it."

"That's wonderful, Leon. I'm so excited. I was just looking at the tour details, seeing the history and architecture of ancient Rome. This is like a dream come true. The Tower of Pisa, Tuscan wine, The Coliseum, I get goosebumps just thinking about it."

"Oh my, Paul. This will be epic. You and me in Rome."

"We will be sharing a room, Leon. But it's a huge suite so it won't be close quarters."

Leon laughed. "Well, either way, I'm planning on staying close to you the entire time."

An hour later, relaxing in his suite, Father Paul was flipping through the channels. The announcer on CNN said, "Coming back, after the break, battle at the border."

Wow, Dad. Is that your people down there? He waited through the commercials.

"Today at the border there was a clash between alt right-wing extremists and supporters of the migrants and undocumented workers. We have some video for you. As you can see, there are a number of racist symbols, KKK attire, and rebel flags. Today we have Representative Noah Collins, of New Mexico, as our guest. Representative Collins, what is your assessment of this border conflict?"

"I think it's pretty obvious. They're a lot of angry people, mostly white people, who don't want these people of color to have the same opportunities they had. Their great-grandparents came here as immigrants, but now they have no compassion for others who want to have a better life. Their ancestors came from oppression and persecution, half-starved, yet they have no concern for these unfortunate people, who only want the same opportunities for their grandchildren that these angry right-wing extremists were given years ago. It's just cold and callous."

"Well stated, Representative Collins. What do you make of the racial hate symbols that are clearly visible on one side?"

"I think it's reprehensible. I thought we were so past that, no more Jim Crow, but as you can see, the evil of racism is alive and well in the United States. And they don't even try hiding it. They're proud of it, even putting it on display like a badge of honor. Really, it's sickening."

Father Paul stretched out on his recliner and cracked a Heineken. "Wow, Dad. Perfect, just perfect. Go, Dad."

Meanwhile, Gil and Alice were chatting near the formal gardens.

"Alice, I have to tell you something. I have to tell someone, and I don't want to stress out my wife. This is a bit stunning, but I need to tell you what I found in the bishop's bathroom."

"I might not be as stunned as you think but try me."

"I found the flap from a box of condoms under the vanity."

"Under the vanity? What were you doing under the vanity?" Alice asked.

"I wasn't doing anything. I saw it sticking out, a cardboard flap. It's not like I was snooping around, but did you hear what I said? Condoms, Alice, in the bishop's bathroom."

"Yes, I've heard rumors over the years, Gil. I just keep my mouth shut."

"So, do you think there's hanky-panky going on?"

"I try not to think of it, but yes, I do."

"Wow, Alice. We need to do something."

"Like what? Think about it, Gil. There's nothing you can do, and if you do try and do something, you'll just end up losing your job and the hanky-panky will continue long after you're gone."

"Jeepers Alice, someone else basically told me the same thing earlier today. This is unbelievable!"

"Monsignor, I need you to have a staff member call the travel agency and verify the details of my trip."

"Of course, Your Excellency."

"First off, I want you to ensure, I have two first-class seats. I filled half that plane for them, it's the least they can do. Plus, they already agreed to it, as well as a car."

"A car, Your Excellency?"

"Yes, a sedan. A roomy sedan. Father Paul will drive. I will not be taking the bus with all the pilgrims. It will take forever for everyone to get their luggage and board the bus. And make arrangements for the proper baggage to be delivered to my suite, including my guest's. I have better things to do than be standing around an airport. One last thing, ensure my guest and I have adjoining suites, that was the agreement. Nothing less is acceptable."

The next morning, after dropping his wife at the doctor's office, Gil Rodgers arrived at work extra early. Getting out of his car, he noticed a man in the distance. He spied Alex Montalvo get in his BMW and make a beeline off the property.

What's that guy doing leaving the property at 7:30 a.m.? This is disgraceful, but what can I do? Alice and Pete might be right.

How do you report a bishop? Can you go to the cardinal? Maybe he is part of the mafia too, maybe go right to the pope, but the pope isn't going to read it. Who will end up reading it? And what can I put in the letter? I have no proof except a condom box flap that I threw out, but even if I did keep it, it's not much in the way of evidence. I need to take my time with this, be smart about this, not do anything until Billy gets his wheelchair and Dusty is sure she had her last chemo treatment. For now, I am going to keep my eyes open and my mouth shut.

Chapter 9

"Get the freak up! Out of bed right now, little darlings!"

The Chief Petty Officer came up to Jack's bunk and screamed, "Get up off that rack, boy!"

Jack realized he wasn't dreaming. It was another early morning at Navy Boot Camp. The barracks was lined on both sides with metal bunk beds, or "racks" as they were known, with shared bathroom facilities. There was no privacy and little storage area. It was all designed to prepare someone to live on a ship. Each barracks was named after a boat and nautical themes abounded. Majestic buildings and flawless landscaping on the grounds completed the picture. Jack loved the orderliness and tidiness of it all.

The first week of boot camp had been tedious, P-days, processing days. Waiting in line to get shots, dental work, and all the other medical processing was boring and, of course, a head shaving. Everyone was outfitted in their "Smurfs," dark blue sweats and gold t-shirts, navy colors. Sneakers, New Balance, one style and color, white with blue stripes, were also provided. After the first forty hours without sleep, (they said it was to get everyone on the same sleep schedule) things had settled down considerably.

But now it was week two, and this was the real start of the training; the intensity was picking up. Chief Petty Officers (CPOs) seemed to be everywhere you turned giving directions and scolding. Some were louder than others, but they all seemed to bleed Navy blue.

"Okay, ladies, you got fifteen minutes to hit the head, and do what you gotta' do but shaving better be one of them. If any jackass has beard stubble on his chin, like those two fools yesterday, there will be extra PT for everybody. Do you understand?"

"Yes, Chief!" They all said in unison.

They hurried into the lavatories. There was not much talking as everyone was focused on being efficient and getting back quickly in order to have time to get their rack ready for inspection.

Fixing his rack, Foster's hands were shaking. "McCreesh, I can't get this. How do you do that?"

"Here, Foster. Let me help you. You have to crease it, fold, and then put it under, see?"

"Yeah, I see, but I still don't know how you're doing that."

"It just takes a little practice, Foster. I'll show you later but don't worry, you're good for inspection. I got you, Foster."

"Thanks, McCreesh. I'm tired of getting yelled at, but I think I'm getting immune to it."

Having been invited to the CCD teacher appreciation dinner, Mollie sat down at a table of eight. She knew most casually, but not well. It was order off the menu, and the church was treating. A woman sitting next to her was already contemplating cheesecake for dessert. It resulted in considerable chatter.

"Yes, the cheesecake here is pretty good but not as good as Carmen's Bistro."

"Carmen's isn't bad, but you really ought to try my grandmother's strawberry Oreo cheesecake. It's made with fresh strawberries from her garden, and she doesn't allow pesticides. The strawberries are organic, just scrumptious."

"That sounds delicious, but for the best cheesecake ever you need to go to Café Roma in Queens. It's only available on Wednesdays."

"What kind of a place serves cheesecake only on Wednesdays?"

"It's a small family run bakery. You can only get it on a Wednesday, and you have to order at least one month in advance."

"Wow, do you have the number?"

"I think I can get it, but it won't do you any good. You have to know someone to get on the list. My aunt got two whole cakes last spring and she put a large slice aside for me. It was perfect, can't even describe it, out of this world. I can't wait until I get another slice in November."

"So your aunt has a cheesecake connection for this place?"

"Yes, but she's limited to two purchases a year and her cakes are pretty much spoken for. My aunt and I are close, so after she takes care of her family, she puts aside a slice for me, but I'm the only one outside of the immediate family. It has caused some friction with my other cousins."

"Do you think I could get a bite of your piece, like a smidgen?"

Mollie started rubbing her neck. She decided to excuse herself until the unattainable cheesecake summit ended. Five minutes later, she returned relieved the conversation had shifted.

The server took the orders. One person asked if the cheesecake was fresh or frozen. Mollie was grateful it didn't trigger another rant.

After the server left, a woman mentioned The Grammy Awards ceremony she had viewed the previous evening, others who watched chimed in. A man said he was amazed at how good Madonna looked for her age. A few of the women agreed, all with high praise. Another man, with an oversized cell phone, pulled up the photo of Madonna, scantily clad, and excitedly passed it around to a chorus of approving "oohs" and "aahs."

That was it, last straw. After pretending to see something on her phone, she simply stood up and said, "I'm so sorry, but I have to go." She found the server and canceled her order.

Getting into her car, she slammed the door. Really? Madonna? Madonna in a black, leather 'who knows what,' but it didn't leave much to the imagination. And we're going to pass it around at a dinner for religious ed teachers and drool over it? Pathetic. "I hope the flippin' cheesecake is rancid."

Jack was seated on the floor next to Foster. It was week two, day one. An impassioned, female CPO, the Lead Recruit Division Commander (RDC) began.

"Good morning, I'm RDC Jackson. Are you all delighted to be here this morning?"

"Yes, Chief," they all screamed.

"Yes, of course you are, and you should be. You should be proud to be part of the greatest armed forces the world has ever seen, the United States Military, and the greatest naval force on Earth. Being accepted into this organization is the greatest thing that has ever happened to you. Isn't' that a fact? Isn't that true?"

"Yes, Chief!"

"Of course it is. But now you have to prove yourselves and demonstrate you are worthy to wear a uniform that carries enormous pride and tradition, that of a Navy sailor. In the next several weeks you'll have the opportunity to demonstrate your determination and desire to be part of this great naval force, but no one is guaranteed a spot. You must earn it. Did you hear what I said? You have to earn it!"

"Yes, Chief!"

"That's right, you need to work for it. You'll not be coddled or disrespected, but you will be held to a high standard. Do what you are told and be prepared to give 110 percent. Now, before we get started, I need a show of hands. Anyone present who did not volunteer for this, please raise your hand."

There were no hands.

"Okay, good. So who we have here are a bunch of patriotic Americans who chose to do this, who went through a long process and jumped through many hoops to get here, and you should feel good, since some did not make it through the screening process and are home in mommy's basement playing video games, but you're lucky because you're here, but I need to make something clear. You signed up for this! Didn't you? You wanted to do this, you wanted to be a recruit! You chose this, didn't you?"

"Yes, Chief!"

"You're so lucky to be here, aren't you?"

"Yes, Chief!"

"Good, now this should be obvious since you wanted to be here, but regretfully some recruits arrive with negative attitudes and feel the need to complain which is just verbalizing their negative mindset. It's pathetic and has no place in the Navy! A whiny, weak mind has no place at recruit training, does it?"

"No, Chief!"

"I don't want to hear any complaining or grumbling. We're going to mold and shape you into sailors, which means there will be discomfort. Pain is part of the process. If I hear anyone griping, there will be extra PT for everyone. Complaining is for weak-minded civilians, not for Navy recruits. You are no longer a civilian, leave the belly-aching behind. Do you understand?"

"Yes, Chief!"

"And I mean complaining about anything. I have no tolerance for it, none. And that includes grumbling about the chow, the weather, your rack, your rack mate, or your fresh, off-the-hook New Balance sneakers. It's all weak. To me, it sounds like whining little babies. I have zero tolerance for it. It does not belong here. It's a cancer. Do you understand me? There will be no complaining here. Zero whining. Are we clear on that?"

"Yes, Chief!"

Several weeks later, just before hitting the rack, Jack's rack mate, Foster, was stressing.

"McCreesh, I don't think I'm going to make it. I should've prepared more."

"You can do it, Foster. Remember what the drill instructor said, it's 98 % mental and 2 % physical. You might not be in top shape, but that's what the training is for, to improve. Don't focus on where you're at now but where you can go. Just do it. Chances are they won't send you home if you're making the effort, only if you give up and give in to discouragement."

"I don't want to be held back," said Foster.

"I don't think you will be," said Jack, "but so what if you are? It's only for your benefit, to give you more time to make it."

"Yeah, you're right. I got nothing else."

"Foster, I'll try and help you, but I can't do it for you. Pay attention to what they tell us. Remember, the open side of the pillow has to be on the right."

"Why can't I remember this stuff?"

"You will, Foster. It will get easier, I promise."

"Next week we got to do that run, 1.5 miles in fourteen minutes," Foster said. "I'm not there yet."

"You don't need to be there yet, it's next week, and your times are improving. Cut back on your food intake this week, Foster. Give it all you've got. Dropping a few pounds might make the difference. Plus, I'm going to run right alongside you. You're going to make it if I have to drag you. I am not going to corpsman school without my buddy."

Foster had grown up in rural West Virginia and had no family support to speak of. His father disappeared in his youth and his mother, who was currently in jail, had a long rap sheet due to meth addiction. Foster was a strong, husky, kind-hearted man with a ruddy complexion, sandy brown hair, and sad blue eyes. He liked to say he wasn't sure if Foster was his real last name, or they just gave that to him as he moved from one foster home to another. He always wanted to play football, be a linebacker, but the frequent moves prevented him from participating in team sports. It never worked out.

He usually managed to do decent in school, and when he realized he could qualify for the military, he did not hesitate. He couldn't believe he would get a $20,000 signing bonus for corpsman, that is once he completed all the training, and met all the physical requirements. Presently, he could do six pull-ups and needed to get to ten but had started at three. He had to keep striving. Foster loved the notion of corpsman, and it was quite a coincidence he ended up on the same rack as Jack. Corpsmen were a special breed, and after a few weeks, Jack and Foster felt bonded within the ranks of recruits. Yes, they were part of the team, but they were also a team, a team of two, two corpsmen.

A week later Jack was on the phone with his mom.
"Hi, Mom, I miss you, Mom."
"Hi, Jack, of course, you miss your mom."
Jack smiled. "It's going good. We're really getting into a good routine and learning so much. It would be fun if the pace was more reasonable and there weren't so many petty officers everywhere you turn."
"It sounds like you're dealing with it," Mollie said. "That's how you do it."
"You should have heard our lead trainer, Mom. She gave a great talk about whining. She warned against anyone being negative or complaining, reminded me so much of you. You always told Beth and me, 'No complaining in this house. America has enough complainers. We don't need anymore. Those spots are taken.'"
Mollie chuckled. "Yeah, Jack, my workplace is saturated with complainers, professional whiners. It's an art form, especially when you embellish it with profanity. Let me guess, some are still complaining anyway.'"
"Yeah, but not within an earshot of the chiefs. It's more like grumbling under their breath, not openly complaining. Like you always said, it's human nature. Isn't there a Bible verse about it?"
"Half of the Old Testament is about the Israelites complaining," Mollie said. "Which did not usually work out well for them, but the quote I like is in Philippians, Chapter 2. It says, 'Do everything without grumbling or questioning.'"
"Everything? That almost sounds un-American."
"Yes, Jack. Funny but true. Complaining dominates the culture. God is not pleased."

"We can run together, Foster. Sometimes just having someone beside you helps. I'll get you at a good pace."
"Okay, what I'm doing is not working, it's worth a try."

The next day the run began, all the recruits were participating. Halfway through, Foster was fading. "Come on, Foster. Get the lead out, you can do it. Embrace it. Don't let up."

While breathing heavily he said, "I can't do it, McCreesh."

"But you are doing it! We're on pace, just keep going. I'll stay with you, Foster. I'm not going without you. You have no choice."

Foster was huffing and puffing. "No, McCreesh, I don't want to hold you back. Go on and finish."

"Foster, we're doing it. Relax, keep jogging. Stay with the group."

It was the last quarter mile. "Dig deep, Foster," Jack said. "You can always do more than your mind is telling you. It will be so worth it."

Foster was gasping for air but staying with the others, barely. They crossed the finish line together at the tail end of other recruits with 20 seconds to spare.

Foster collapsed on the floor wheezing. He whispered, "thanks, McCreesh."

Jack grinned, "No problem, Foster. I told you it was all mental."

Later that night, everyone was relieved as the recruits relaxed in the barracks. They had made it through the hardest part. The last event would be the "Battleship" exercise the following week, simulating firefighting and essential teamwork aboard a ship.

"Ok, Foster. Remember, tomorrow is inspection. Let's see your bunk."

"Thanks, I forgot."

"That's why we're doing this. I'm going to teach you how to stay proactive, instead of always reacting, and in a rush. It will help you in corpsman school. Now, this isn't folded right. It needs to be at a right angle and a three-fold."

"Oh yeah, thanks, McCreesh. How can you do that so fast?"

"I practiced one day for an hour. Proactivity, that's what I'm talking about. Wow, look at these boots," Jack said. "That is awesome, Foster. Did you shine these?"

"Yeah, I like shinning boots, making them sparkle."

"I can almost see my reflection," Jack said. "Maybe you can give me some tips on shoe shining. I still gotta' do mine."

"Just good old-fashioned elbow grease, McCreesh, but next time I'm waxing them I'll show you my skills."

Beth disappointedly looked at the starting lineup posted at the last practice of the summer. *I knew she wouldn't start me. I should have gotten a summer job. This is just a waste of time.* Beth knew she deserved to start. She had scored more goals than anyone during the summer practices. The assistant coach was a big fan and had even told Beth she would try and lobby for her. Coach Fritz was known to play favorites, but no one could ever figure out just what her agenda was.

Fritz was starting five freshmen this year. Of course, it was a talented group, but they were only thirteen and fourteen-year-olds, needed time to develop and mature. If they were as good as Beth, which they weren't, shouldn't the senior get the nod? That's how it used to be. That's what her dad told her. Seniors were always given priority years ago. It just made sense. They had worked hard, let them play and the others would get their turn.

But that was not how Coach Fritz saw it. She wasn't thinking of the players. She was thinking of herself. If she started playing these freshmen now, maybe they could win her a state championship in two or three years. It had been almost twenty-five years since her last and only one, and Coach Fritz had become increasingly frustrated and annoyed watching her fierce rivals winning state titles.

Even though a solid senior player could expect to get some decent scholarship money, and the great experience of participating at the varsity level, Coach Fritz was more about the praise she would get when she won a second state title. She was a young coach the last time, now she was in the twilight of her career. She used to be fit and trim and run laps with the team. Now she was thirty pounds overweight.

Beth wasn't the only senior who was benched to let the talented freshmen play. Funny thing, some of the more successful coaches, the ones who *were* winning state titles, played their seniors along with subbing and even starting freshmen, realizing a successful team should have balance.

In spite of routinely taking the turf ball off the senior players in practice, and being the fastest sprinter on the team, Beth did not play much her junior year, much to her family's dismay, especially her dad. He had been especially aggravated after a Division II college coach, who had seen Beth play for only 20 minutes (after a forward twisted her ankle) asked to set up a meeting with Beth at the school.

It was going to be another long season. Beth decided she would talk with her dad later.

Jack had just gotten back from shaving; inspection was in five minutes.

"Damn, Foster. I forgot to do my boots."

"Give me them bad boys, McCreesh, I got you."

"You only got a few minutes," Jack said nervously. "They're really grimy."

"Shut up and just hand them over, McCreesh. I got time cuz' you helped me last night."

Foster grabbed them and spit on them. It was crude, but Jack was in no position to object. In two minutes they were handed back glistening in the morning sunlight.

"Wow. How the heck did you do that, Foster?"

"Growing up in the hollers of West Virginia," Foster said, "you just know stuff."

Chapter 10

Mollie had fallen asleep on the plane to the humming of the jet engines.

"Can we talk about field hockey now, Dad?"

"Sure, Beth."

"I'm thinking about quitting. The coach obviously doesn't like me, Dad. It's awkward. Plus, they think field hockey is the only thing in life. They made such a big deal about me coming on this trip. I'm only missing one practice. Fritz was so mean about it, after all, my brother is graduating Navy Boot Camp, and I'm basically a sub."

"It does seem extreme," Patrick said. "So if you quit, what would you do?"

"Get a job and make some money for college."

"With Jack joining the Navy, Mom and I are in a better position to help. I'll tell you what, Beth, just give it a few more weeks. Like Mom always says, it's good to let things unfold. Quitting stuff is not something I take lightly, but perhaps that's my crazy Marine training. Maybe I've been putting too much pressure on you about the whole scholarship thing, but if in a few weeks nothing has changed, I promise to support whatever you decide."

It was the Captain's Ceremony, and the recruits were lined up. Tears streamed down Foster's face as his RDC handed him the new ball cap that said, "Sailor," signifying his successful completion of Navy Boot Camp. Formal graduation was tomorrow, but right now, as *Anchors Aweigh* played, he was overwhelmed with emotion. This was the greatest thing that had ever happened to him.

After the ceremony ended, he found Jack. "McCreesh, I can't thank you enough. This means so much. You're like a brother to me, the brother I never had."

He gave him a big bear hug.

"Take it easy, Foster. You got a lot stronger here. You're like a freaking bull now."

Foster laughed, "Thanks, McCreesh, I feel great. I've never felt like this before, like I belong, like I'm part of something. You really helped me."

"You did it, Foster. You did it on your own. Give yourself credit. I simply helped you to believe in yourself, something your parents should've done, so you should really give *yourself* credit, foster homes to completing Navy Boot Camp. Now on to corpsman school."

"Yeah, McCreesh. I'm really nervous about it."

"Were you nervous about boot camp?"

Foster laughed, "Yes, terrified."

"Ok, it's the same thing with corpsman school. You'll be fine. I'm going to make sure of it. Plus, there's always the next thing in life, the next thing to worry about. After you finish corpsman school you might worry about getting to the fleet. It's just life, so enjoy the moment. You earned it. We have graduation tomorrow and get to see our families."

"I don't have any family coming," Foster said. "My mom's still in jail, not that she would've come anyway."

"You can hang with my clan, Foster, go out to eat with us," Jack said. "My mom wanted to meet you anyway."

"Meet me?"

"Yeah, I told her all about you."

"Wow," Foster said. "That's different."

"The three of us are at the airport, Jack. We're so excited to see you. We'll be checking in later this afternoon. You can count on us being there tomorrow, first thing. We're so excited I am so proud of you, Jack."

"Thanks, Mom. And can my buddy Foster go out to eat with us tomorrow?"

"Foster? The one you told me about, the other corpsman prospect?"

"Yeah, Mom. He doesn't have family coming."

"Absolutely, Jack. I want him with us. I really want to meet him. It will be an honor to meet him."

"Ok, Mom. Remember, you have to pick up your tickets at the Recruit Family Welcome Center."

The next day all the families crammed into the huge drill hall. Once the crowd settled in, a Navy band took the floor playing patriotic songs and marches. The appropriate hymn for each branch was played, and veterans present were asked to stand during their branch's song. Mollie was so proud when Patrick stood, thinking about her husband (and Jack) made her misty. Beth hugged her dad just as the *Marines' Hymn* ended.

After the music subsided, the new class of sailors paraded into thunderous applause. They looked grand marching in their dress whites, men and women alike, all looking proud and patriotic, standing straight and marching in formation as more military music played. There were speeches and awards and soon it was over. The families rushed onto the floor to greet their sailors. Beth was the first one to hug Jack. As she embraced him, Mollie noticed a man standing aimlessly nearby. Jack can wait, she thought.

"You must be Foster."

"Yes, are you McCreesh's mom?"

"I sure am. I'm so proud of you, Foster." She gave him a sturdy, sustained hug. "Thanks so much for helping, Jack. It means so much!"

"Helping Jack?" Foster said, "but I didn't do anything."

"Oh, yes, you did! Trust me, I know my son. I could never thank you enough, Foster." She finally released him

Then Beth followed with another generous hug.

"I'm Beth. Good job, Foster. Jack thinks the world of you."

Then it was dad.

"Thank you for your service, sailor. I'm a Marine and love all corpsman, including future ones." Patrick smiled, patted Foster on the back, and said, "Always remember, there's nothing a Marine won't do for his corpsman, and there's nothing a corpsman won't do for his Marine."

Foster was overwhelmed with emotion, so much positivity coming at him, love and kindness. This must be what it's like to have a family. Tears streamed down again. *I don't know why I keep crying.*

After a long wait, the group sat down to eat. Patrick said, "I hope you boys are hungry. I'm buying, don't hold back. That was a great ceremony. Memories of my time as a USMC grunt were flooding in."

"I don't know what it is about the military," Mollie said, "but I kept getting choked up, thinking about the tradition, all the men who died, giving their lives, in often horrific ways. We don't think of our veterans enough, about what they've done for us, their sacrifices, especially the ones who are no longer with us. They don't even teach history properly anymore, but it doesn't change the facts, so many suffered for our freedom."

After eating, they were saying goodbyes. Patrick said, "You boys deserve a lot of credit, signing on to be corpsmen. It's not for the faint-hearted. They save a lot of lives but also have one of the highest casualty rates, a rare breed a Navy corpsman. No single rating in the Navy is more decorated for valor than the hospital corpsman."

The boys would be shipping out tomorrow for Fort Sam.

The new sailors landed at the airport and in fifteen minutes were at Fort Sam, Houston, Texas. They found their quarters and went to bed early. Things would begin first thing in the morning.

The next day an officer was speaking. "Welcome to Navy Corpsman School. Here you will learn various aspects of emergency and primary care. You will be trained as basic emergency medical technicians, and learn basic life support, basic field medical care, and essential first-aid procedures. There are many options for a Navy corpsman, you can end up on a battlefield, in a hospital, or on a ship."

Later that day, after the evening meal, Foster was sitting in the rec room all alone reading a letter from his mother. He began recalling his childhood, bad memories. Why wouldn't she come out of the bathroom? She would be in there for hours smoking that stuff. It was so cruel. She could have at least made me some macaroni and cheese, but I had to do it myself. And my father, I barely even remember him. How can parents be so lame?

Jack approached with a casual strut carrying a shiny blue Monster Energy Drink.

"Here I got this for you. How ya' doing, buddy?"

"Okay, I guess. I got this letter from my mom."

He handed it to Jack. Jack noticed the return address was from the Beckley County Correctional Facility.

Dear Richie,

I can't tell you how proud I am of you graduating Navy boot camp. I keep telling all the girls here about you and showing everyone the picture with your uniform. This place is dreary, so it really brightens up my cell. My cellie likes it too.

I know I have not been a good mom Richie, but I am going to a program here and this time I think it's going to be different. I really want it this time. I want to stay sober and see my son when I can. I have had enough of this life. It's time for a change.

You are an inspiration to me. I am so proud of you Richie.

*Love,
Mom*

"That's a great letter, Foster. It sounds like your mom is really ready to turn it around."

"You might not think it was so great if you read a version of that letter fifty times before, like I have, beginning when I was like nine years old. I always hope she will stay sober, but I keep my expectations low. I can't worry about her. It kills me when I think of my mom. It gets my worrying thoughts churning, so I've learned to set it aside. My career is something I can control, but I have no control over her meth habit, and obviously, neither does she. Meth was big back where I come from. I saw it get ahold of a lot of good people, it's sinister. No, McCreesh, I can't see my mom getting sober anytime soon, but now that I have a bank account, never did before, I'm going to send some money to the jail, put some real money on my mom's books. That is something I can do, after all, she's my mom."

The training was hard, combat trauma training, lifelike with grotesque realism, including missing limbs. Both men did well, but Jack had been more nervous than Foster. Foster was not fazed by medical training, whether it was drawing blood or giving shots. He had a calmness about him like he was always in a zone and right where he belonged. Jack was happy to see him thriving and was fascinated by how Foster did everything with ease and cheerfulness.

Beth had not been seeing much playing time, but now things had changed. There was a new coach, the assistant who loved Beth and always advocated for her. Coach Fritz had been removed and quietly took early retirement. There was a rumor going around that these new developments were related to an incident in the locker room with a player, but no one was talking, at least for now, including the player. Beth was not sure how to feel. It was all sort of creepy, but she would not miss Coach Fritz. Beth excitedly looked at the starting line-up for tomorrow's game, starting forward, right-wing. Adrenaline flowed into her. It was time to blow off some steam, steam that had been building the last two seasons.

The three months of training had been challenging and stressful. Today was graduation from corpsman school and the new "Docs" were receiving their certificates of completion.
"After you take your oath today, I want you to stop and give yourself credit for what you have accomplished, but the hard work will continue, and you have to remember to honor your vocation on a daily basis. I challenge you to never forget, you are there to serve. I challenge you to remember why you wanted to be a corpsman and know that your patients always deserve compassion. All military personnel serve their country, but few do it like corpsmen. We define the word service. Service to our brothers and sisters but also to any civilians and yes, sometimes even the enemy. You are all they have. Ensure that you are worthy to be called a corpsman.
"Some may be asking yourselves if you want to make this a career - that will be your decision. But in the Navy, you can reach any goal you put your mind to, be anything you want to be. The only restricting factor is yourself. Never limit yourself. You can always do better than you think. Believe in yourself and put forth the maximum effort. I promise you will be pleased with the results."
After the ceremony, the two graduates were standing in the hallway looking at a mural of a corpsman treating a wounded Marine. The text under it stated, "He runs into battle zones where angels cry and Marines fear to tread."
"Wow look at that, McCreesh, amazing. Have you ever thought about making a career out of this?"
"No, Foster. I'm still leaning towards the priesthood."
"I think I found a home," Foster said. "I can see myself doing 20 years easy."

Calling the landline, Jack phoned home.
"Congratulations, Jack."
"Thanks, Mom. I'm really excited to do this job, but deep down I'm still thinking priesthood. The thought will just not go away."

"That's great, Jack. If you have a calling no one will be more thrilled than me."

"Mom, there are a lot of Protestants here. Once they find out I'm Catholic, they want to debate me. It's getting kind of annoying. What do they have against Catholics anyway? Aren't we all Christians? And all the Protestants seem to get along, but they want to argue with me. It's bizarre."

"Maybe not so much, Jack. It's quite common. For the first 1500 years after Jesus died, there was only one Christian church, the Catholic Church. That is the church Jesus passed down through the line of succession, until today, handed down to our bishops and priests, so they seem to get a little defensive when they meet a Catholic.

"The Catholic Church is the one true faith, Jack. People don't like it when you say that, and, of course, that does not mean the other Christian faiths do not have some good aspects, but it is the most authentic, meaning it has stayed true to the teachings of our Lord, and his apostles. In other words, they have kept it principally the same, the way Jesus and His apostles instituted it.

"Catholics are too timid. You have to admire Protestants because they will speak boldly about their beliefs. Most of them are all about the Bible, a Bible that was compiled by the Catholic Church. They quote St. Paul all the time, but he was one of the first Catholics, a Catholic martyr no less. And don't let them fool you, Jack. The Protestants are not all united in their beliefs, many splits and schisms, even within their own denominations. They're basically subject to their pastor's interpretation of scripture, and of course, not all Protestant pastors are going to interpret the Bible the same way.

"There may be conflict in the Catholic Church, but at least we have a basic text that outlines the faith, the catechism, a template for us. The rationale of the catechism is deeply rooted in scripture and tradition, including the church fathers. Read it sometime, Jack. It's beautifully written with impressive logic and supporting evidence. So if there's conflict in our church, it is usually because someone is going against the teaching, but the teaching is clear."

"But why do they care so much what Catholics are doing?" Jack said.

"It's a good question, Jack. Why are they so defensive and feel the need to confront Catholics? The truth is a lot of their pastors will preach against the Catholic faith and say we worship statues and other false stereotypes. Funny thing is, you'll never hear a Catholic priest criticize Protestants. Oddly, a lot of priests seem to think we should be more like them, but Protestants always want to attack us. It's perplexing, but it makes my faith even stronger. Why are they so preoccupied with us? But there are some huge problems with Protestantism. For example, when it comes to the Eucharist, they have completely blown it. They no longer believe in the real presence of Christ in the bread, most don't even celebrate Communion at their services."

"Yeah, they were talking about that," Jack said.

"Tell your Protestant friends to read John, Chapter 6, and then read what Jesus said at The Last Supper. It usually puts them back on their heels and gives them food for thought."

"What does it say, Mom?"

"Read it yourself, but it's clear. Jesus stated that He was the bread of life and you must eat this bread to have everlasting life, and then at the Last Supper, celebrated on the Jewish holy day, the Passover, He reiterated it. Interestingly enough, the Jews would sacrifice a perfect lamb in the Old Testament, then they would eat the lamb, and it was the blood of the lamb that saved the first-born males of the Jews during the original Passover. So this is all tied together and makes perfect sense for the few who will actually take the time to study the faith. The New Testament is hidden in the Old Testament."

"So for 1500 years, there was only one church. I remember studying this, The Protestant Reformation, correct?"

"Yes, it started with a Catholic monk, Martin Luther, largely objecting to the abuses of indulgences, where people donated money to have their sins forgiven. Things were getting out of hand with indulgences, but that should not have undermined all the teachings of Jesus. Martin Luther was not objecting to the basic tenants of the faith, but more about the abuse of indulgences, and he initially remained a Catholic. The drift away from orthodoxy came over time as Luther and others decided their own analyses of the faith eclipsed the church's.

"Maybe Martin Luther was a reasonably good man, but he seemed to get caught up in his own celebrity. Printing presses were now in use and his thoughts, along with his image on the front, were printed in thousands of pamphlets. Over time, he became more and more self-absorbed and eventually was relying more on his ability to interpret scripture, than the teachings of the church, which were 1500 years old, rooted in scripture and tradition.

"He later married a former nun and had children. Some think he was a decent man, albeit pugnacious and an avowed anti-smite, but when you compare him to some of the great saints of the church, men and women who endured great suffering and were martyred for the faith, he pales in comparison. Martin Luther was more about himself than God. In addition, anyone who studies the life of Luther will find he was troubled and disturbed. His church is basically the machinations of an anxious soul, a man-made religion, but few will ever look into it."

"So, this one man was responsible for The Reformation and all Protestant faiths?" Jack asked.

"Not quite. Of course, Lutheranism, but once Martin Luther started, several others evolved as well. It began a spirit of defiance and rebelliousness. It was mostly started, interestingly, by former Catholics, too many to talk about now, but I'll just mention the King of England, Henry VIII, a former Catholic himself, even a defender of the faith at one time who vehemently opposed Luther.

"That was until he became infatuated with an eighteen-year-old woman and wanted to divorce his wife. When the pope wouldn't allow it, he started his own church, The Church of England, the Anglican Church, which started another huge split, rooted in a king's lust for an eighteen-year-old woman, Anne Boleyn, who he later beheaded. His actions resulted in the persecution and murder of many faithful Catholics, including priests, especially priests, and the obliteration of many beautiful and charitable monasteries that served the poor, not to mention all the wonderful churches."

"Wow, Mom. It's very interesting, the history."

"It is. The Catholic Church is in bad shape these days, Jack, but the teachings are still rock solid. They're from our Lord, not the interpretations of one man. Even the early founders of all these Protestant religions disagreed on everything, now there are thousands of different Christian sects, all with their own man-made beliefs."

"I see. They keep wanting to lecture me on 'faith alone,'" Jack said, "whatever that means."

"It means you can live however you want and still go straight to Heaven. It's like a Protestant mantra developed by Luther and basically shattered in James, Chapter 2, but don't even try arguing,

Jack. This is straight-up Kool-Aid. It's called 'justification' and it's the main thing they always come at us with. I completely disagree with it, and it makes no sense, but who wouldn't want to believe you can sin all you want and go directly to Heaven simply because you believe, sure makes it easier, sets the bar quite low."

Foster came into the room just as Jack was getting off the phone.

"Hey, Foster, do you know anything about The Protestant Reformation? It's so interesting."

"No, McCreesh, you're the only one I know who thinks about stuff like that. What I was really thinking about is doing a little celebrating, celebrating our graduation. How about going into town and getting a couple of beers?"

"Okay, pal, but maybe we should change out of our uniforms first. Remember what they told us. Sometimes things happen in clubs and uniforms draw attention, not everyone loves the military."

"I don't feel like changing. Let's just go, McCreesh. Two or three beers and that's it. We will be gone before it gets crowded. I'll call an Uber."

Later that evening, the men were leaving the club. They had stayed a little longer than planned, drank a little more too, but it was only 10:00 p.m. and an Uber had been ordered.

Exiting the club, Foster said, "I gotta' hit the head, meet you outside, brother."

When Jack walked out, he noticed a little ruckus. It was breaking up. As the small group disbursed, one man was left lying on the ground. Jack could see it was serious and yelled to some onlookers to call 911.

He went over to the man who was bleeding and started to render first aid, direct pressure, using his handkerchief. Despicably, a couple of men were hostile and started cursing at him. He thought he heard a click. He turned and rolled away just as a man was lunging at him. A scuffle ensued; the knife hit the pavement. Jack was on his back with the man on top of him. He started screaming, "Foster, Foster!"

Just then, Foster came out, heard his name being shouted, and sized up the scene, a man on top of another uniformed man, punching him. It was Jack! Running towards the scuffle, he saw the man on top pick something up off the ground. As he sprinted, Foster visualized himself wearing football shoulder pads and a helmet. He crushed the perpetrator with a perfect linebacker tackle taking him to the asphalt and leaving him stunned. He knelt on his shoulders and restrained him. It appeared more nefarious bystanders were going to jump into the fray, but decided against it, as military personnel were pouring out and encircling, most dressed as civilians but some in uniform, including a few burly Marines. Jack immediately went back to providing first aid. Just then the police and ambulance arrived. The man lived.

Jack, who was rendering first aid a few moments ago, was now receiving it for a stab wound on his forearm.

Doc Richard Foster

Chapter 11

The two corpsmen were holding their Meritorious Mast awards.

"Wow," Foster said. "I can't believe I got an award for something I did the day I graduated corpsman school."

"Yeah, I thought it would take you a little longer than that," Jack said smiling.

"Very funny, McCreesh, but listen up, this is my favorite part. 'Your bravery in the face of a clear threat and imminent danger, and your bold and decisive action reflect the highest standards and traditions of the United States Navy. Your professionalism and courage are a credit to yourself and your command.' I can't believe it, McCreesh. This is like a dream, an award from the Navy."

"You deserve it, Foster. That man was a wanted fugitive, a violent felon. Plus, he sure was attempting to do harm to me, not sure what he'll be charged with, but thanks for disrupting him with a linebacker lambasting."

Foster laughed. "You saved an unconscious guy, and I saved you. We make a good team, McCreesh. Too bad we couldn't work together."

"Well since we're both going to a Marine unit, and both going to Camp Lejeune, we'll be near each other and we'll probably be training together when we get to Lejeune. Training to indoctrinate us into Marine life, that might be rough."

"I can't believe how much training we're getting, McCreesh. Two months of boot camp, three months of corpsman school, and now two more months with the Marines."

"Yeah, I'm getting a little burned out. I'm going to sleep a lot this weekend."

"I love it McCreesh. I'm going to take advantage of everything the Navy has to offer. I want to keep going and keep learning, maybe even take college courses, and that bonus, twenty thousand dollars in my savings account. It's just awesome! I never dreamed of having that much money. I just sent my mom $200.00. I would have sent her more, but I don't want it to go for drugs if she gets out."

"That's nice, Foster, nice that you could do that for your mom."

"Yeah, McCreesh. I'm going to live right. I'm not going to live a selfish life like my parents. If I have kids, I'm going to take care of them, be there for them, not put some evil drug ahead of them and let them suffer and be all alone in the world, confused and abandoned, and only cause them heartache and misery and never do a damn thing for them."

Foster grabbed a tissue and wiped his eye. Jack put his arm around his shoulder.

"It's okay, buddy. Your mom loves you, Foster. The drugs are just too powerful. You're right, Foster. The drugs are evil, pure evil and that's what makes them so powerful. I'll pray for your mom."

"Thanks, McCreesh. I appreciate you."

Beth McCreesh was at the high school field hockey dinner receiving the MVP award. Tearing it up from the moment she got her starting job, she had been the leader in scoring and assists and had taken her team to the state semi-finals where they had lost to perennial power, Western Seminary. It had been a great experience with many hard-fought victories and team bonding. Everyone admired Beth for her energy and enthusiasm. Even the freshman who lost her spot to Beth had come to love and admire her. Beth had become her mentor, teaching the freshman so much, not only about sports but about life.

Mollie and Patrick were beaming with pride as Beth picked up her award. The coach got up to speak, and it was all so positive. There was a feeling of optimism for the next season as if Beth had left her impact on the whole team. Now it was off to play college field hockey and major in education, be a teacher. The colleges were lining up, including some Division 1 schools. There was going to be scholarship money. The question was how much, and how to figure out the next best move. It was an exciting time for all. Too bad Jack couldn't be here.

Marine Base Camp Lejeune, North Carolina was another intensive training, combat first aid, simulating real battle conditions, including gruesome body parts and blood. It was meant to be stressful and it was. The men were fascinated with the Marine culture and the intensity of the USMC. After their graduation, they were assigned to a battalion.

Reviewing the orders they were ecstatic.

"I can't believe it," said Foster. "2nd Marine Division, 1st Battalion, 8th Marines. We're in the same company. Maybe we will be in the same platoon. Anyway, we'll be near each other. I think they're about a dozen corpsman in a company, so we will be seeing each other on base. This is great, McCreesh."

"Wow, Foster. I'll be happy to have a friend around. I don't mind telling you this has been a bit of a culture shock for me. Even though my dad was a Marine, I really didn't think they were this crazy. These inspections are over the top. Now I know why they call them 'Kill Hats.'"

The men were assigned to different platoons and each had two, twelve-men squads under their care. They would now be called "Doc" by all the Marines. Currently, the company was getting ready for deployment, doing a work-up, and they would be training at Camp Lejeune for the next few months. The corpsmen were expected to do everything the Marines did, with no exceptions, including long hikes with a full pack. They would be going into the field and living in fox holes and tents, and it was wintertime. Jack had one rough night where his water carrier, the Camelbak, leaked all over him while he was sleeping. There was no way to dry off. He just had to endure the cold and dampness, not much sleep that night.

After a two-week stint, the men got back from the field. The hot showers and steaming fresh food were heavenly. Jack was at the chow hall walking with his tray when one of his new Marine buddies yelled over.

"Hey, Doc, we saved you a seat, over here."

"Thanks, Crossin."

"You survived your first trip to the field, Doc, congratulations."

"Thanks, I'm glad to be back on base. It was rough. I guess I'll get used to it. That nighttime training was brutal. I think I need help with my night vision goggles, couldn't get them to work right."

"Oh, that's not you, Doc," said Crossin. "They're old and beat-up, hardly any good. We get all the Army's old stuff. I heard the Army's new ones are awesome, but their old ones are pretty much worthless."

"You get the Army's old stuff? Really?" said McCreesh. "I thought the Marines would get the best. I mean, the Marines are the elite, at least that's how I look at it. First to fight, you should get the best, or I mean we should get the best."

"I wish you were running the Pentagon, Doc. But the Marines are like an afterthought, the smallest branch. We aren't even really a branch but under the Department of the Navy. I think there are only about 200,000 Marines. Everything we have is second-hand. We're like the Army's red-headed stepchild, even our bases are run down. Right now, there are eight washers and six dryers for a whole company, and half of them are broken and no one cares. No one bothers to get them fixed. You'd think with all the people on this base, someone would know how to fix a washer. It's probably a $10.00 part, but no one cares about Marines, especially the infantry, the grunts. It's part of the culture of the corps I guess, be tough and not be concerned with comfort."

"Well I can understand wanting Marines to be tough," Jack said, "but you could at least give them the courtesy of having clean clothes when they come back from the field, decent laundry facilities."

"Let me tell you something, Doc," Crossin said. "We are the unwanted, using the outdated, being trained by the unqualified, for the ungrateful. That pretty much sums up our lives as grunts. We are promoted more slowly, treated more harshly, and no one cares about us, including the higher-ups, even though they would never admit it, but in a way, all this mistreatment is what makes us brothers. We're all in it together. The average infantry unit is a bunch of crazy bastards, a lot of dysfunctional backgrounds. Sometimes it might look like an angry, twisted group, but these are just the kind of guys I'd want to go into combat with, but not the kind I want to go up against."

"Wow, you're really opening my eyes to some things," Jack said. "It's all the more reason to want to give the grunts good medical care. You guys deserve it. It's going to take some getting used to, but I'm glad I'm here."

"Glad to have you, Doc," Crossin said. "There's something else you should know if you're going to be living with us."

"And what's that?"

"Did anyone tell you what Marine stands for? It's actually an acronym."

"No, I don't know how I missed that with all my training."

"Marine, it stands for 'muscles are required, intelligence not expected.'"

The next morning, Jack couldn't believe what he saw, Foster standing in the doorway with his hefty sea bag.

"McCreesh, guess who your new roommate is?"

"You got to be kidding me, Foster. This is awesome, unbelievable! I haven't seen you around the base for a few weeks. I was wondering what happened to you. It's fantastic to see you, Foster. You look great. It'll be like old times. I think it's pretty cool how they put us corpsman together, but I never dreamed we'd be hitched up again. Wow, I can't get over it. We have so much to talk about. How are you liking this?"

"I love it, everything, McCreesh. I love my job and my Marines. I love when they call me Doc, Doc Foster. I mean how many people get to be called doc? It's so cool, and last week we went to the rifle range. I was blasting that M-16 like a devil doc, McCreesh, even made sharpshooter. It was so much fun, reminded me of back home. And I love our uniforms, almost the same as the Marines. I could've been a Marine, McCreesh, but then I wouldn't get to do corpsman work. One guy even told me on the hike that I inspired him to continue. Watching me, a Navy sailor, carrying more weight than him, encouraged him. He was thinking about falling out, but when he looked at me it motivated him. I motivate Marines, McCreesh."

"Nice, Foster, and we have that hike tomorrow, O-dark thirty, so maybe you can start motivating me, or at least help me tape up this giant blister."

The next day Jack and Foster paired up on the twelve-mile hike. In addition to the full pack, the docs had to carry all of their medical gear. Their packs were among the heaviest.

"Man, it's cold Foster. Aren't you cold?"

"Yeah, Jack. You just have to ignore it."

"Ignore it? How do you do that?"

"Just don't think about it. When it pops into your mind, think of something else."

"You are amazing, Foster. You're turning into a beast."

"You're the one that taught me, McCreesh. Remember, it's 98 % mental, you were right."

"It's not feeling that way now with this blister on my foot."

"Keep going McCreesh, I got you. I can give you my gloves if you want."

Beth was touring Villanova University's campus with her parents and the coach.

"This is our locker room and workout facilities. You can see it's all state of the art, complete with a trainer and whirlpool."

They walked outside and the coach turned to the parents. "We're so impressed with Beth. Obviously, she comes from a great family. Players of good character, that's what we're looking for. That's how you build a successful program and represent the traditions of a Catholic university like Villanova."

They continued to tour the campus, a beautiful layout located on the western suburbs of Philadelphia, an exclusive neighborhood, the Main Line. It was obviously safe and secure away from the vice and temptation of the inner city, unlike some of the other schools they had toured. Villanova was offering an 80 percent scholarship. Exiting one of the campus buildings, Mollie grabbed an alumni magazine.

Driving home to New Jersey, Beth was excited.

"I think that's it, Dad. The coach seems so nice. That's where I want to go. What do you think?"

"It's great, Beth," Patrick said, "but it's your decision."

"What do you think, Mom?"

"It's a beautiful campus, Beth. I agree with your dad. It's your decision."

"Okay, great, I think I'm going to sign with them."

A half-hour later Beth had fallen asleep in the car.

"So, what do you really think, Mollie?"

"What do I really think? I think all these Catholic colleges are pathetic. Just look at this alumni magazine. There's nothing faith-based anywhere in it. It's basically a self-aggrandizing piece about how successful, rich, and talented all the alumni are, and how much money they're raising, all the expensive new buildings, all the rich donors. I find it revolting. It's like a promotional piece that screams, 'Hey, look at us, look at how great we are.' It's the opposite of Christian values and filled with ego and materialism. There's nothing about God or faith anywhere in this magazine, but all these Catholic colleges are like this."

Patrick slowed down for the toll booth and grinned. "I know, Mollie. I know you're not a fan of the modern Catholic university, but putting that aside, and realizing almost all colleges are liberal, are you okay with her going to Villanova?"

"Yes, if that's what she wants, but I'm going to make sure she is strong in the faith before she goes. I am going to prepare her. I don't want her indoctrinated into some Catholic social justice warrior with a wishy-washy faith."

The platoon was preparing for ten days of training at sea and the Marines were waiting for a plane. Jack and Foster were chatting. When the plane finally came, it filled up quickly. The Sergeant asked for a corpsman.
"I'll go," said Jack.
"No, I will, McCreesh," said Foster.
The Sergeant interrupted. "I'm only going to need one corpsman on this mission. It's only half the platoon. Someone needs to get on there now, the other stays."
"It's me, McCreesh. They're mostly my guys."
"Okay, Doc Foster, don't say I didn't offer."
"Got it, Jack. Love you brother, semper fi."
A V-22 Osprey landed, it was a most impressive plane, an engineering marvel, a plane that could land like a helicopter but reach speeds over 300 mph in the air, flying like a plane when necessary, quite a versatile weapon against the enemy. And it did not need an aircraft carrier runway to land, just a large flat surface. As the Osprey departed, Jack waved to the plane, not knowing if Foster could see him. Five minutes later, Jack thought he heard Foster yell his name. He even turned around to look, but there was no one there.

The plane would never make it to the ship. It crashed into a ball of flames before getting to the ocean, engine failure, a software problem. Everyone aboard perished - eleven Marines and one corpsman - Hospital Corpsman First Class, Richard Foster.

Chapter 12

Monsignor Sabatini called down to the kitchen. "The bishop would like to know if the fruit salad you sent up yesterday was made with fresh or frozen?"

"I'm not going to lie. It was frozen. Sorry, we were short-staffed, and I was trying to get ready for the dinner party."

"Okay, I will tell Bishop Cesare it will not happen again, are we clear?"

"Yes, absolutely."

The chef glanced red-faced at his helper, grabbed a ladle, and threw it across the room.

"I told you he would notice."

"Don't stress, you had no choice," the helper said. "You're doing the best you can."

Meanwhile, next door in the chancery office, the bishop was stretching out on a leather couch, looking at vivid pictures on his cell phone. Ah, Alex and I in Italy, the Mediterranean, just grand, seafood, sand, and sunsets, spaghetti and clams at the beach, white wine, and Alex looking great with a tan and designer sunglasses. Just then the desk phone rang.

"Your Excellency, Monsignor is here."

"Send him in." He turned off his cell and put it in the drawer.

"Good Morning, Monsignor. I hope we can make this brief. I have a tee time at 10:30."

"Of course, Your Excellency."

"We have two items to discuss. First, we're getting complaints from Holy Trinity again."

"Oh, Father 'Dudley Do-Right Donahue.' What is it this time?"

"We're getting reports he's saying the Saint Michael prayer after every mass," Monsignor Sabatini said. "They're dismayed with the unpleasant nature of it, references to Hell and the Devil."

The bishop slapped his hand on the desk. "Why would anyone still be saying that archaic prayer like it's the 1940s? And that story of some pope getting it in a supernatural trance, incredible. What was that pope's name again?"

"It was Pope Leo XIII, in 1884, a trance at the foot of the altar, after mass," Monsignor Sabatini said, "witnessed by a few Vatican staff members."

"Whatever. I will be drafting a letter tomorrow to Father Donahue. I will put a stop to this."

"There is something else, Your Excellency. The ladies who make the perogies at the church every summer for the festival customarily take a few dozen home, perhaps freezing them. Father Donahue put a stop to it and said they were stealing from the church."

"He did what? Outrageous," the bishop said. "Get him on the phone before I leave for the club. What else is there this morning?"

"Father Kenneth is outside in the waiting area. You said you wanted to see him before he leaves for rehab."

"Okay, very good. Send him in. I won't be long. Set up a phone call thirty minutes hence with Father Donahue, and tell my driver to be standing by. I wish to go directly to the club after my meeting. Make arrangements for my private golf cart."

"Good morning, Your Excellency."

"Sit down, Father Kenneth. This should come as no surprise, but we will be sending you to rehab again. You have caused me a great deal of aggravation with this latest incident, not to mention the lawyers' fees and settlement money. The family of that boy was quite aggressive, and we had to pay them $75,000 to send them away quietly. After you complete your treatment, I'll be transferring you to a diocese in Pennsylvania. Bishop Rahmney has been kind enough to accept you. Plus, he needs priests. I trust this meets with your approval."

"Actually, I was hoping to stay in New Jersey."

The bishop raised his eyebrows. "You were hoping? You're lucky we're not sending you out of the country, which is where you'll be going next if there are any more 'incidents.' Our broom is only so big. It can only do so many sweeps!"

The bishop sat up and took off his glasses.

"Hoping to stay? The nerve of you. You should be kissing my ring and thanking me for getting Bishop Rahmney, who is a dear friend of mine, to agree. Your track record is pathetic, abysmal. You're damaging our image."

"Maybe people who live in glass houses shouldn't throw stones, Your Excellency."

"What? What did you say? How dare you!"

The bishop gently picked up his phone and glared. His eyes suddenly went dark like a vampire's. "How about I call the police right now and have you face real justice? I have not broken any laws, Father, but you have. From what I have been told, jail is not pleasant for child molesters."

"Forgive me, Your Excellency. How rude and clumsy of me. I beg your mercy."

He stood, approached the bishop's desk, and kissed his ring.

They gathered the troops for an important announcement. Jack knew, he just knew.

"The plane crashed. There were no survivors. We have twelve dead brothers."

Jack fell to his knees and started sobbing, his hands covering his face. He didn't want to open his eyes. God, how could you allow this? How could you take a man who had suffered so much, and just when he finds his calling and is filled with joy, he burns up in a horrific accident before he even has a chance to do his job, a job he trained so hard for. He was going to help so many people in his future 20-year career. He was a rare breed. *Find yourself some other jackass to join your priesthood. Your church is lame anyway.*

An hour later, Jack was sitting in his room looking at all of Foster's gear. It was too much. He called his mom.

"Mom, Foster is gone. He's dead. There was a plane crash. He died, Mom, along with eleven Marines." Jack wiped his eyes with his sleeve.

Mollie shook her head as she tried to absorb the news. "Oh, no! Oh, Jack, I'm so sorry."

"Mom, how can this even happen?" Jack asked, his voice cracking. "How can God allow this?"

"Oh, Jack. I know this must be so hard for you. My heart is breaking for you. I don't think this is a good time to talk about this, the whole question of suffering in the world. Now is a time for grieving. It's okay to cry, okay to grieve. The best advice I can give you is to pray for all your deceased brothers."

"I don't feel like praying, Mom. You don't understand, that could have been me. Foster went in place of me! I offered to go, but he insisted. Now I feel guilty."

"Yes, Jack. Of course, you do. It makes sense. And if you got on that plane and died, would you want Foster to feel guilty?"

"No, absolutely not."

"Do you think he wants you to beat yourself up?"

"No. I see what you're saying. Thanks, Mom." Jack wiped away another tear.

"Listen, Jack. I feel awful about this but feeling sorry for you is not going to help you. After you take a few days to feel sad, maybe even a little self-pity, I want you to get back in the game. That's what Foster would have wanted. Once you're feeling better, we can talk more. In the meantime, try and help someone else. There are Marines all around you who are distressed. Remember, you are their corpsman, their doc. They need their doc. Corpsmen all throughout history have had to deal with dying brothers. You are not alone. And there's someone not on the base who is suffering, Foster's mom. I want you to write her a letter. Tell her about her son."

"Okay, Mom."

"Your Excellency, Father Donahue is on line two."

"Okay, I got it."

The bishop took a deep breath and picked up the call. "Father, we've had more complaints from your parishioners. Your parish generates more grievances than all the others combined, so let's try this again. I want you to tone it down."

"Tone it down, Your Excellency?"

"Yes, we've had this conversation before," the bishop said. "Yet now you're praying the outdated St. Michael's prayer after mass. This is just the kind of thing I warned you about. People don't want to hear about being saved from the fires of Hell or casting Satan into the abyss."

"Maybe they need to hear about it, even if they don't want to," the priest said. "It's essential Catholic teaching."

"Father, I don't have time to debate this. I have a commitment at 10:30. I'll be sending you a directive regarding this matter that must be printed in the bulletin, and what is this about accusing these poor women of stealing from the church?"

"It is not their property, Your Excellency. It was an opportunity to remind people to live nobly, and not make excuses and rationalize bad behavior, regardless of how trivial it might seem."

"Poppycock, Father. I want you to apologize to those women, volunteers no less, and next year you can just turn a blind eye."

"Yes, Your Excellency."

The next day, choking up the whole time, Jack wrote the letter and addressed it to Inmate Dixie Mae Foster at the Beckley County Correctional Facility.

Dear Foster's mom,

I trained with Richie and we became close friends. It's hard to explain to someone who was never in the military, but Richie and I were inseparable through Navy Boot Camp, the Corpsman School, then Marine training, (a total of about 7 months). We were so happy to be assigned to the same base, and amazingly, right before the accident, we were reunited as roommates, which thrilled us both. He was like the brother I never had. Actually, the last words he ever said to me were, "love you brother, semper fi."

Once he got through boot camp he was like a ball of fire, and as you know he received an award for valor. I was the one he rescued. That was me. He saved me from serious harm, perhaps worse. You should be so proud of Richie. He was a great Doc. He had such a bright future and was so happy and proud to be a Navy corpsman. Honestly, I am having trouble accepting this and it has me questioning my faith.

I can tell you that Richie talked about you. He loved you and was hoping the best for you. It's never too late to get it right. Your son, A/K/A Doc Foster, will be watching over you. His spirit lives.

Sincerely,

HN, Jack McCreesh

Three days later, there was a massive service with hundreds of Marines assembled to pay their respects before a reverent display of the deceased men's photos. A line formed in front of each. Foster's line was a bit shorter since he had only been on the base a brief time, but many Marines, who had never even met him, took the time to pay their respects to Doc Foster. Finally, Jack made it to the front and kneeled down. He started talking to Foster, and thanked him for his friendship, told him he loved him and would miss him. He tried to pray but couldn't. He could feel himself being overcome with emotion and started to leave, just then he heard Foster's voice, "Love you, brother, semper fi." It was clear as day, felt like a jolt. Jack could barely walk and made his way to a bench.

An hour later, he tried calling his mother but got the voicemail. "Mom, I heard from Foster. I want to tell you about it, call me back. You're the only one I can talk to about this."

Father Kenneth walked out of the chancery and began texting Fabio.
I have an Amazon gift card for you.
Meet me at the rectory at 5:00.
Ok Uncle.

Fabio rang the bell. Father Kenneth combed his hair and checked himself in the mirror. He felt butterflies in his stomach as he briskly walked to the door.

"Hi, Fabio, come in."

He handed him the gift card. "Wow, $100? That's awesome. I can just buy whatever I want?"

"Yep, it's your decision, whatever you want."

"I want to take my time and think, Uncle Kenny, but thank you."

"Take all the time you need. Plus, I wanted to talk to you. I won't be here much longer. I'm going to be taking a sabbatical for a while, and then they're sending me to Pennsylvania where there's a priest shortage. Perhaps I'll be able to see you in the future but that remains to be seen."

Father Kenneth motioned for him to sit down on the couch. He sat close to him and looked him squarely in the eyes. "Fabio, have you told anyone about our secret?"

"No, Uncle Kenny."

"Good, that's great. I knew I could trust you, Fabio. It shows good character. Most people can't keep a secret. I'm afraid there are those who wouldn't understand. I think, for example, the bishop, who is my boss, wouldn't understand, so we can't let that happen. Okay, Fabio?"

"Okay."

"And of course the bishop is not only my boss but is the boss of a lot of people. The bishop is the boss of everyone who works for the diocese, all the schools, church-owned facilities, and other agencies. Your aunt works at Holy Name School, doesn't she?"

"Yes, she's a teacher."

"And you wouldn't want to see her lose her job, would you? Because that could happen if our secret gets out."

"No, I won't tell."

"Okay great, Fabio. I am so impressed with you. I knew I could rely on you. Do you want something to eat?"

"Yeah, I'm starving."

"We can take care of that. Get something out of the freezer. We'll microwave it for your dinner. Then you can have all the sodas and snacks you want. How does that sound?"

"Awesome, Uncle Kenny."

"And later I have something new for you. Have you ever tried brandy? I have some vanilla brandy I want you to try. I think you'll like it, but just a small glass since it's your first time."

"Vanilla is my favorite ice cream."

"Mom, thank God I got you. I really need to talk to you."

"Sure, Jack. I'm here for you, always."

"I heard Foster's voice, like a powerful blast in my mind. I can't explain it."

"You don't have to explain it. It was real, Jack, believe it. He lives on."

"I know, Mom, but I'm still struggling with this. It was such a horrific accident and heart wrenching to see the families come, so much heartache. More than half of the planes the Marines have aren't even airworthy due to a shortage of parts. That's what a crew chief told me, and those that are operational are not in the best shape either. How can these politicians waste so much money but not give the Marines good parts for their airplanes? And how can God let a horrible accident like this happen?"

"Suffering is part of life," Mollie said. "This is Earth, not Heaven. Things will never be perfect, and I told you when you signed up to be a corpsman that you had to steel yourself, that you might see a lot of death and carnage on a battlefield"

Jack said, "I think I could've if this happened in battle, but it was a pointless accident, and Foster was my best friend."

"You think bad things shouldn't happen to people you love," Mollie said. "That's just not realistic. You need to toughen up, son. It could be said that everything is God's will because God either wills it or allows it. We have to take what God gives us and persevere.

"Everyone wants to go to Heaven, but no one wants to die. There is such a thing as an afterlife. Study what the church says about life after death. Now you can believe, like me, that Foster is in a better place. I don't know about the other men on that plane, but Foster had such a gentle soul and had suffered so much on this Earth, my guess is he made it to Purgatory."

"Why not Heaven?"

"We don't really know, Jack. Very few go directly to Heaven, but if you make it to Purgatory you're guaranteed to get to Heaven. Purgatory is for a period of purification. It seems that when we're in Purgatory, we don't even want to enter Heaven until we are purified. It would be like if you played a football game in the mud, and were dropped off at the prom right after, you wouldn't want to go in until you were cleaned up."

Jack stepped outside to get more privacy.

"Are there fires in Purgatory, Mom?"

"It's not really clear, Jack. Some describe it more as spiritual suffering, but perhaps it is hard for us to fathom. Apparently, there are different levels, so some are suffering more than others, but all are edified knowing they will ultimately be going to Heaven.

"Most of us are going to come up short in the eyes of God, but we have to make the best effort possible. Hell is real and it's for eternity. Think about the afterlife often, Jack, and remember the sacraments help so much, especially Confession. People really shouldn't fear death so much if they're living right, but if they're not, well, they probably should, but many who've had near-death experiences come back with less fear of dying.

"Bottom line, Jack, we can't really be sure of anything. That's why they call it faith, but I believe in a final judgment. Foster is either just a burned-up body or his soul lives on, as the church teaches."

"It's funny, Mom, I had a couple of dreams about him. He was shrouded in smoke and seemed sad."

"I'd say it's a sign he's in Purgatory, and no one is praying for him. The souls in Purgatory can't do anything to help themselves. Once our time on Earth ends, we no longer can help ourselves, but while we're here our good deeds can help our salvation."

Mollie got up from the kitchen table and lowered the oven temperature. She paced as the aroma of chicken and baked potatoes filled the air.

"Remember what I taught you, Jack. The Holy Souls can pray for us and we can pray for them, but once they're there, they are totally dependent on our prayers. Sadly, so many are forgotten. Few are thinking about the Holy Souls, even though a few simple prayers, or having a mass said, could relieve their sufferings. We're too busy with the clamor of life and we forget our loved ones. Honestly, Jack, I pray for my parents every morning, and offer up minor sufferings all day long."

"Offer up?"

"It's another powerful concept the church has neglected. It's a way of offering discomfort for the Holy Souls. Say you have to cut the grass on a really hot day, beforehand you tell God you're going to offer it for a Holy Soul."

"Do you think it works, Mom?"

"It's all very mysterious, Jack, but I've had many signs and coincidences over the years. I'm convinced there's a power to it, a power most will never employ, even though it's so easy. People don't want to talk about this stuff, Jack, including, sadly, our priests. People just want to keep the thought of Hell out of their minds. Our Blessed Mother, when she appeared at Fatima, showed the children visions of Hell.

"Fatima was authentic, Jack, and the miracle of the sun was witnessed by over 70,000 people. Newspapers all over the world reported on it at the time, but you'll rarely hear it mentioned in church. The whole point is to get to Heaven and avoid Hell, and the church has put this issue to the side, buried it really. Plus, once you stop thinking of the afterlife, things can seem so much easier. You don't have to put any more effort into your faith life, stay home on Sunday and watch football and stuff your face, the life of many modern Catholics who have forgotten or never been taught the faith.

"When you become a priest, Jack, you need to 'preach it.' The Catholic Church represents truth, a truth based on the life and teachings of Christ. 'Preach it,' Jack. Preach the truth.

"Pray for Foster, Jack, and have masses said. When you are on a long hike, or out in the field in a fox hole, offer it up."

"I will, Mom, and I'll start praying for Foster and talk to the chaplain."

"And once a soul gets to Heaven, Jack, they will appreciate your efforts. When they're with God, they are in a position to help us. Just remember, Jack, when I die, don't go around telling everyone, 'Mom is in Heaven now,' because I won't be. When I was in college, I wasn't living right, years when I never went to mass. I need you and Beth to pray for me and have masses said, not go around talking about me as if I was some saint. I am telling you now, you had better not forget me and the state of my soul."

"I won't, Mom. I promise."

Jack put down his cell phone. *Everyone wants to go to Heaven, but no one wants to die. Fascinating.*

Riding home from the golf course, the bishop was feeling chipper after several after-dinner cocktails. Classical music played softly in the background. He had good news for Father Paul. "Father, you have served me well and demonstrated your loyalty to the chancery, and now I'm pleased to offer you a pastorate at St. Dominic's parish in Short Hills. I know you wanted your own parish, Paul, and as you know, St. Dom's is one of the most sought-after, such sophisticated parishioners. I think it would be a great match if you're interested."

"Oh, yes, absolutely, Louie. Thank you so much. I love the idea. The property is magnificent."

"Wonderful, let's have some drinks in the hot tub to celebrate."

Father Daniel Donahue clicked on the e-mail from the bishop.

Father Donahue,

The following statement is to be placed in the bulletin:

Although the Saint Michael's prayer has a place in one's faith life, it has been decided the appropriate circumstance is not as part of The Holy Mass. The historic Roman rite is carefully theocentric and does not underscore angels and saints. The emphasis is on our Lord and Savior. In the Holy Eucharist, under the appearances of bread and wine, Christ is contained, offered, and received, this will be our emphasis, our focus. The faithful are at liberty, indeed encouraged, to utilize the many prayers and devotions our beautiful and rich faith offers, outside the sacrifice of The Holy Mass. We draw strength from Word and Sacrament, especially in the celebration of the Eucharist. Modeling Christ's work, we embrace our commitment to Christ's call. In summary, the Saint Michael prayer is not to be recited at the end of mass.

Chapter 13

Seated on the upholstered bench with another priest, Father Kenneth glanced out the window of the airport shuttle as it made its way to Saint Dymphna's Rehabilitation Center. He loathed the name. Saint Dymphna, patron saint for the nervous and mentally ill. The thought of it made him uncomfortable. He was thinking of Fabio. He hoped he would see him again. Maybe Fabio could take a bus. A bus ride from New Jersey to Northeast Pennsylvania (where he expected to be assigned subsequent to treatment) would not take that long.

As the shuttle turned the corner and the rehab was in sight, Father Kenneth cringed thinking about what some of these confrontational counselors would say. After all, he was a repeat offender, a relapser. It was his third time at this treatment center.

The rehab center was impressive, with an imposing red brick structure, the administration building, standing at the center surrounded by out-buildings and beautifully manicured lawns and rolling hills. The facility had previously been a seminary but had been converted due to a lack of vocations and the need to address the many "behavioral issues" present in the modern-day clergy. The rehab was equipped to treat a variety of disorders, including inappropriate sexual activity and impulses, drug and alcohol addiction, mental health issues (bipolar, anxiety, clinical depression) and various other compulsions and maladies including OCD and PTSD. Most of the priests were there due to a combination of improper sexual activity and substance abuse, quite a challenge for the staff.

Father Kenneth made his way to his room and began to unpack. Dinner would be in an hour. He knew the schedule and was going to try and make the best of things, an anticipated three weeks.

Mollie had just been called into the section chief's office at the Social Security Administration where the chief was seated with his assistant.

"Mollie, we're so pleased with your performance. You do the work of two people, and we think if you could manage a whole section, others could learn from your methods. We're under a lot of pressure from the management to increase our productivity. What would you think about taking a supervisory position?"

"I think I could do that if there's a need, but I'm telling you right now, if you put me in this spot, I'm going to do my job. If people are slacking or not helping our clients, all these elderly people, I'm not going to tolerate it."

"That is what we want, Mollie, strong managers. You have an intensity about you. There's only one thing we're concerned about. Please don't take this personally, but we don't want you to push your religious views on people."

"My religious views?" Mollie chuckled. "What are you talking about?"

"It's kind of a touchy subject, the whole religion thing, but it seems you are overly sensitive to profanity and people just being human, and we don't want it to be an uncomfortable work environment."

"So you think it's good for people to be able to just scream out the F-bomb whenever they feel like it? You think that's appropriate and a good stress reliever."

"Well, I guess you could put it that way. It's the way people are, so we're asking you to put your religious views aside."

"I really don't think this has anything to do with religious views. This kind of behavior used to be considered inappropriate everywhere in our culture. Actually, let me tell you what I think about 'religious views' as you put it. Anyone who curses and uses profanity all day is representing their own form of religion, or a particular system of faith, a world view if you will. A view that is dark and filled with defiance and victimhood. Dare I say the word profane means 'to go against the sacred' so that in itself is like an anti-religion, even a form of religion, but you are saying that's okay."

"Some cursing is okay, yes."

Mollie took a deep breath. "Okay, so you are an advocate for vulgarity, a word which comes from the Latin 'vulgaris,' meaning the language of the uneducated. It's defined as morally crude, lacking in cultivation. So this is what you want in your workforce?"

"Mollie, why don't you just lighten up? We are offering you a promotion. We really need you as a section chief."

"If you're looking for someone who is going to tolerate crude, offensive behavior you need to find someone else. I might be able to employ a measure of patience, but I'm not going to accept indecent conduct. It's disruptive and disrespectful to others. I don't think I'm the person you're looking for."

She got up and walked out.

The assistant said, "What's her problem?"

"I don't know, but if I had three more like her we would crush our quota every month."

"Monsignor, I want the workers to put up wooden barriers. There was a reporter from the newspaper snooping around here yesterday with questions about my remodeling plans. Before the real work begins, I need barriers up, and we need to hire a couple of security guards - big brawny ones to keep out the meddling media."

"Yes, Your Excellency."

"And how are things coming along with the new security system?"

"The cameras will be in next week."

"Remember, I want some with audio capability, and make sure we have audio down near the garage where our maintenance guy is always blabbing with vendors. There's something about him that does not sit right with me. I'm going to find out what's on his mind. People will see the cameras, Monsignor, but no one is to know about the audio. Is that clear?"

"I don't think that kind of listening is legal, Your Excellency."

"That will only be an issue if its existence is known," said the bishop. "The vendor has already assured me of his discretion. It came at a price, but it was worth it. It will help me to manage this massive diocese more efficiently. We will be the only ones who know about the audio, so there shouldn't be a problem. Don't you agree, Monsignor?"

"Of course, Your Excellency."

Father Kenneth grabbed a coffee and sat with another priest, Father Hank, "Happy Hands," Haney. Group was in thirty minutes.

"You were here a few years ago with me, weren't you, Hank?"

"Yes, I'm doing the relapse program"

"Me too, three weeks," said Father Kenneth. "Then they're transferring me out of state to Pennsylvania. I'll have a new assignment by the time I get out. My bishop said next time he would be sending me out of the country. That really has me shaken."

"Oh, I don't know. I've thought about that. I have a priest friend who had some issues and even completed treatment here a few years ago. They sent him to Samoa where there's no extradition treaty. He loves it. He gives out candy to the children after mass. They swarm right up to him. I was emailing him. He says he doesn't feel tempted and no one there knows his history, so he is able to move on. But the children in a lot of these poorer countries love American priests. I mean, not that I'd do anything, but I prefer to be around young people."

"Interesting. I never thought of it that way. Maybe it wouldn't be so bad. I'm hoping the group this morning won't be so bad either, but that's wishful thinking."

Fifteen minutes later, the group started. There was one counselor, Walter, who had spent years counseling victims and was less sympathetic than his colleagues to the plight of the clients, all of whom were priests or brothers. There were twelve men sitting in a circle. He started the group.

"Good morning. We have two new priests here today, both prior patients, which should tell you something about the insidious nature of your compulsions. Let me start with Father Kenneth. So from what I understand, you had sex with a teenage boy in the band room at the school. Is that correct?"

"Yeah, sort of."

"Sort of? There obviously was an encounter of some kind. Witnesses saw you leaving together. Was it of a sexual nature, yes or no?"

The other patients were glaring at him. He knew they would not accept anything but the truth.

"Yes, it was of a sexual nature, but the boy could have left at any time. He was old enough to walk out. It's not like I was holding him there. I guess it was a mistake, but I was attracted to him. I didn't force him to do anything he didn't want to. I was depressed and lonely and drinking a lot at the time."

"So you decided having sex with a fifteen-year-old in the band room was a good way to deal with your loneliness and depression? And we might as well throw in alcoholism."

"I didn't decide ahead of time. I was attracted to him and it just happened."

"It's not your fault," Walter said. "You were attracted to him, so that makes it okay."

"Well, I wouldn't say it that way."

"Then how would you say it?"

"I'm not sure," said Kenneth.

"Do you regret it?"

"I'm not sure."

"That means no," Walter said, "and it also means the next time you're attracted to a minor, and the opportunity presents itself, you'll do it again."

"I don't know about that."

"I do, trust me you will," Walter said. "Unless there's a fundamental change in your thinking and some kind of psychic shift, but I'm not seeing it, not at all, but I guess we still have three weeks, not feeling optimistic though, not yet."

Walter looked at his clipboard and continued. "Next we have 'Happy Hands' Haney who likes to play 'find the keys in the cassock' with eight graders, twelve-year-old boys. How did you end up back here Hank?"

"Well, first off, I think it's unprofessional for you to call me Happy Hands."

"Please forgive me, but maybe you're not in a position to lecture someone about unprofessional conduct," Walter said. "You have a history of groping young men, altar boys, but you're going to preach to me about professionalism, which is obviously not something you practice. But okay, no more Happy Hands, I promise. So, I ask you again, why are you here, Hank?"

"I had a friendship with a thirteen-year-old boy."

"A friendship? How nice. Why would that get you here? It sounds so innocent."

"It started out innocent. I was helping him to deal with his confusion over same-sex attraction. I noticed he seemed different. I offered to counsel him."

"Offered to counsel him, so kind of you, volunteering your time. So he was confused, and instead of counseling him, you decided to help him by performing sex acts on him, in order to clear up the young man's confusion."

"I wanted to help him explore his sexuality."

"Oh, really? Or maybe you didn't care about him and you wanted to explore your own sexuality. And why is it necessary for a thirteen-year-old to explore his sexuality? Perhaps you could have taught him about abstinence, self-discipline, celibacy or any number of spiritual practices the church offers to deal with harmful forms of self-indulgence."

"He was mature for his age," said Hank. "I don't think it's harmful, not really. Sexuality is natural, not harmful."

"Mature for his age? That's ridiculous. And you don't think it's harmful because you got what you wanted. You are a selfish, self-absorbed predator, but you think you're harmless. It doesn't matter if this is a same-sex attraction. It would be the same if this was a thirteen-year-old girl. You're a forty-year-old man. You have no right to have sex with any young person who is confused and vulnerable. You're hurting them in so many ways and they'll carry these scars for life. They will always feel betrayed by the church, a church that should represent goodness and purity. A good and holy priest could have made a difference in this young man's life, but obviously, you're not a holy priest, not even close. Statistics show that these victims have a much higher rate of substance abuse and suicide, but you don't care."

"I care, at least I came here."

"Well, you didn't have much choice, but okay fine, what are you going to do differently when you leave?"

"I don't know yet. Ask me in three weeks."

Later that night, Hank was holding court in the kitchen. He didn't see Walter walk in to grab a coffee. "Yeah, you should have seen this kid. He was magnificent. We would have sleepovers and watch movies."

Walter was stunned. He pounded his half-filled coffee mug on the table and walked over to Hank with fire in his eyes. "Hey, Hank, are you actually sitting in this rehab bragging about having sex with a minor?"

Hank forced a smile. "Oh, uh, Walter. No, not at all. We were just talking about movies."

"I heard what you said, Happy. Just pathetic, you're still elevating and romancing your deviant behavior. Keep it up, Hank. When you land in state prison, you'll have all the time you want to fantasize about your conquests. I want to see you in my office first thing in the morning."

"Why, what did I do?"

"We will discuss it tomorrow."

In the meantime, upstairs in the library, Kenneth, who had just received the details regarding his pending transfer to Pennsylvania, was writing to Fabio as cell phones had been confiscated.

Dear Fabio,

I just wanted to let you know I will be living in Pennsylvania in a couple of weeks. I just learned my parish will be in Pike County, so you will not be far. I can still help you with your schoolwork. Pike County is on the border of New Jersey, so that's great.
You could take a bus, and I would pay for your ticket.
I will text you the address in a couple of weeks. In the meantime, I am on a spiritual retreat and have set aside my phone in order to have more peace and serenity.
And remember, I have a lot of confidence in you.

Best regards,

Uncle Kenny

Two days later Walter grabbed Father Kenneth after group. "I need to see you right now, in my office."
"Why, what's wrong?"
"We will discuss it."
They walked in, and Walter firmly closed the door.
"Who is Fabio Alou?"
"He is a friend," Kenneth said.
"You mean a friend who happens to be a fifteen-year-old boy from your old parish."
"Yes, he was a member of my parish."
"Why are you writing to him?"
"Just to say hello. I used to help him with his homework."
"Really, you were helping a fifteen-year-old boy with his homework?" Walter said. "How interesting, I wonder what's inside that letter?"
"You have no right to screen my mail. It is illegal to read my personal mail!"

"We did not screen or read anything. The address is on the outside of the envelope. Now, I'm giving you a choice. You rip that letter up in front of me right now or your letter to that boy and its mysterious contents are going to be the topic of the group this afternoon. I'm going to ask your peers what they think might be in that letter, and if they think it's a good idea for that letter to go out."

Kenneth turned white as a piece of chalk. "Okay, I'll rip it up."

Walter handed him the letter. "Shred it right now."

"Alright, take it easy. There's nothing bad in it anyway."

"Really, then how about letting me read it first?"

"Never mind," Kenneth said, as he tore it into small pieces.

"In addition, we want you to sign a release authorizing us to notify Fabio's family that you have been treated here," Walter said.

"What? That's a violation of HIPAA laws!"

"Not if you sign a release."

"I'm not signing it."

"Okay fine," Walter said. "Your relapse program was just changed to long-term treatment, six months minimum."

"You can't do that."

"Try me, and if you refuse to authorize the letter, I will also recommend that this relationship with your 'homework buddy' be investigated to determine if there was inappropriate activity."

The blood ran out of his face again. "Give it to me."

A few days later a letter was received by Maria Alou, who while going through the mail in a drunken stupor and seeing a letter from Saint Dymphna's, deemed it junk mail and trashed it. She was more focused on the past due bills.

Bishop Cesare was enjoying his new toy. He could pull up fifteen different cameras, some with panning capability, six with audio, including the garage, the kitchen, and the living room. He planned on being tolerant of a certain degree of negativity. It would be impossible to keep people if he overly scrutinized everyone. It was more of a test of loyalty. An obvious lack of loyalty would be dealt with swiftly and harshly.

It was five games into the college field hockey season, and Beth was still trying to get settled. It was an exciting time, but she was feeling some anxiety and was on the phone with her mom.

"Mom, I thought my scholarship was a great deal, but now I'm not so sure."

"How so, Beth?"

"I thought when I graduated, I'd owe about $40,000, but I think it's going to be a lot more, even with the scholarship. There are all these extra fees that no one mentioned. It started with an orientation fee of $250, then a student union fee of $1,000. I don't even know what that's for, and a campus fee of $100, an athletic fee of $400, and then a lab fee of $ 300.00, and I'm an education major. I don't even have a lab, yet no one can explain to me why I have a lab fee, but they're all certain I have to pay it.

"And then there are the books! That's going to cost me another $1,500. I asked my English professor if I could use one from last year and she insisted I needed the new one. Tell me, Mom, how does English change from year to year, or algebra, science, and history? This is a rip-off."

"You're a smart girl, Beth, and don't be surprised if some of your professors authored those books, and college professors often have very cozy relationships with book publishers, if you know what I mean."

"You mean they get money."

"Well, let's just say there are incentives, but of course, the students aren't going to know about it. They just need you to buy the $ 95.00 e-book. But don't worry, Beth. Dad and I are prepared to pay at least half of everything in cash."

"Thanks so much, Mom. But really, I'm stressing more about field hockey. The coach doesn't care at all about schoolwork. We have two pre-med majors on the team, and she couldn't care less about their studies, or any of the players really. I never imagined a sport like women's field hockey would take precedence over education. I mean, why get so worked up about field hockey, or any sport for that matter? We have to be in the gym every morning for weightlifting at 5:30 a.m. and then practice for three hours after school. It's supposed to be two and a half, but it's always three, and then we travel for games. It's exhausting."

"Let me guess," Mollie said. "The coach is not so sweet and personable like she was when she was giving us the tour. Am I right?"

"Wow, Mom. You nailed it. She is completely insane and mean as a junkyard dog. How did you know?"

Mollie chuckled, "Just a lucky guess. Listen, Beth, you don't have to stay there if this gets too crazy."

"I know, you told me that before," Beth said, "but I'm going to wait and see. The games are so much fun. I've been playing more than I expected."

Chuck Foreman from Channel 17 Action News had been hearing about the bishop's elaborate remodeling project. He was also catching rumors about other things that warranted further investigation. As he approached with his cameraman, he was surprised to see huge wooden barriers in front of the residence. After he told his camera guy to begin filming, he heard a loud voice from behind the walls, "no filming." Suddenly two burly men in bright orange vests appeared out of nowhere. He could hear a construction vehicle beeping as it was backed up.

"Get off this property."

"This sidewalk is public property," Chuck said. "We're permitted to film here."

The security men kept menacing the cameraman, standing in front of him and blocking him. Sort of bumping him and shoving but being careful not to make significant contact. Chuck could see things were escalating and decided to retreat. Maybe they couldn't get any footage of the mansion, but he had a new story in mind, a better one:

"The bishop's henchmen who guard his fortress."

Chapter 14

The Marines were on a transport plane to California. They had been anxious about getting on the plane, the memory of the recent tragedy still on their minds. Jack couldn't stop thinking of Foster and kept struggling to convert his sad thoughts into prayers for his buddy. It was much quieter than past flights. Everyone was relieved when the plane landed safely.

Today, the Marines would set up in an old hanger and prepare for field training, training in a desert resembling the terrain in Iraq. There would be buildings with actors portraying citizens and terrorists. They would live in the desert for three weeks, sleeping under the stars and eating freeze-dried MREs.

Jack was laying on his cot.

"Hey, Doc, you got anything for a sore throat?"

"Yeah, drink some water and change your socks."

"Very funny, Doc. No seriously, I think it's getting worse."

"Sure, let me take a look."

The next morning six huge, seven-ton trucks arrived to take the company to the field, twelve grunts per truck, trucks covered with canvas and open at the rear, hot and stuffy inside but preferable to hiking. The trucks were three hours late. Some said it was due to a SNAFU, an acronym believed to have originated in the Marine Corps which stands for - situation normal, all f-d up. The Marines were used to waiting in lines and standing around for hours. It was a normal situation, but one they never accepted without grumbling. Several, who were thinking about reenlisting, changed their minds after having to routinely stand in line for six hours to hand in an M-16 rifle.

It was a hot sunny day in the desert and the POGs (person other than grunt) who were driving the trucks would have the rest of the day free once they dropped off the infantry. They were anxious to be done and driving too fast while kicking up a blinding sand. Little did they know there was a senseless checkpoint at the halfway mark, a checkpoint no one was anticipating. The first truck hit the brakes, and due to the sand and poor visibility, there was a six truck pileup, seven-ton trucks crashing into each other and tossing Marines like ragdolls, throwing their gear everywhere, and resulting in serious injury and carnage.

Jack, who was in the third truck, sprang into action. He had a tourniquet secured on a Marine before anyone else even realized what happened. As he was putting a brace on another man's shoulder, he heard several Marines screaming from the lead truck "corpsman!" It sounded ominous. He jogged to the front and saw a man who had been sitting in the rear of the first truck badly disfigured. An engine was smoking, and the scent of oil and gasoline filled the air.

"He's not breathing, Doc. We can't wake him."

Jack checked for a pulse, nothing. "Radio for a helicopter!"

He immediately began chest compressions, ten chest compressions. Then he cleared the airway, rescue breaths, nothing.

"Where is the other corpsman? Get the other corpsman!"

"That is the other corpsman!"

Jack looked down in shock. It was Doc Gilroy; he hadn't recognized him. He quickly started more chest compressions, ten more.

"Come on, Doc, come on, don't leave us. We need you, Doc."

He saw his eyelids flicker. "That's it, Doc, come on, breathe, breathe."

Just as he found a pulse, he could hear chopper blades rattling in the distance.

"Come on, Gilroy, hear that? They're coming for you! They will be here in two minutes, hang on, Doc, hang on."

In no time the helicopter landed, and Doc Gilroy was secured on a stretcher with an oxygen mask and whisked away.

Jack collapsed on the side of the road and suddenly realized his shoulder was badly injured.

Beth was sitting freshly showered in the locker-room looking at her wrapped ankle and listening to the coach and team doctor. "You can't keep her out for the quarter-final on Monday! She's my number one sub."

The doctor scowled with his bushy eyebrows. "It's entirely inappropriate for you to pressure me to clear an injured player."

"An ankle sprain? That's hardly an injury."

"It most certainly is, and I believe she may have a torn meniscus. She shouldn't have been practicing today. I told you yesterday."

"But you're not sure how bad it is."

"Not until I can get an x-ray Monday. She is to sit out practice for now."

"What time Monday? The game is at three."

"I will let you know," the doctor said.

"It has to be in the morning."

"I said, I'll let you know."

The doctor let out a huge sigh and made his way to the door with a stethoscope dangling from his white jacket pocket.

"Coach, maybe I can see my family doctor on Saturday," Beth said. "He always sees me on short notice. He's a great doctor. I really trust him."

"No, absolutely not. You can sit out practice tomorrow, but I do not want you leaving the campus this weekend. Do you understand? I mean it."

"Yes, coach."

Arriving back at her dorm room, Beth called her mother.

"Hi, Mom, do you have a minute? I'm kind of having a bad day."

"Sure, honey. What's troubling you?"

"I wasn't going to say anything, but I took a bad spill a few days ago and sprained my ankle, maybe tore my meniscus."

"Injuries are part of sports, Beth. So what's upsetting you?"

"The coach. The coach is upsetting me. Today she got in an argument with the doctor because he wants to make sure I'm okay before he clears me. I'm supposed to get an x-ray on Monday."

"Really, she was arguing with him? That doesn't seem kosher."

"Yes, thank you, Mom. We have our quarter-final on Monday, and she wants me cleared."

"Take it easy, Beth. You've done nothing wrong. I'm glad you called. I'm going to call Dr. Gill's office and make an appointment for Saturday morning. I'll leave work early tomorrow and pick you up around five."

"No, Mom, I can't. The coach said I was not to leave the campus and said I couldn't see Dr. Gill."

"She what? Oh no, not on my watch. The nerve! What's wrong with her? Who does she think she is imposing a travel ban? I'll be there to get you tomorrow and if this coach has a problem with it, you let me handle her. I got you, Beth."

Mollie could hear Beth starting to cry.

"What's wrong, honey? Don't you want me to come?"

"No, that's not it," she said weeping. "I really need you, Mom. Honestly, I'm having second thoughts about field hockey. This was the last straw. The whole thing is over-the-top crazy, like field hockey is the only thing there is to life. It's like there's something sinister about it."

"That's because there is, Beth. When something like this is so out of balance, so extreme, and puts the desires and ego of one person, the coach, ahead of the well-being of all these beautiful, talented young women, it's despicable."

"I hope you aren't too disappointed in me, Mom."

"On the contrary, Beth. I could not be more proud that you are repulsed by this. These Catholic universities, which are supposed to be operating under Christian principles, are just pathetic. A lot of these colleges were founded by humble servants of God for very noble purposes, but now there's nothing humble about these schools or the people who run them.

"The Augustinians run Villanova. I doubt you'll ever hear much about Saint Augustine, one of the great fathers of the church. They are not educating you in basic Catholic doctrine. They're more interested in indoctrinating you to become a social justice warrior, an absolute deception. Most of these colleges have huge endowments but just keep jacking up their tuitions, and the priest who runs the school probably gets a salary well into the six figures. And when he retires, they will name a building after him because of his 'sacrifice and service.'"

"I'm so happy you understand, Mom. I've been thinking about this. I might want to come home and go to community college. It would be a lot cheaper and less stressful."

"Yes, I agree. It's definitely worth considering and whatever you decide you can be sure Dad and I will support you. So are you okay?"

"Yeah. Thanks, Mom."

"No worries, honey. Jack is calling in, so I'm going to grab it. Love you, Beth. Don't worry, I'll be there tomorrow, and I have a feeling Dad will be with me."

"Bye, Mom."

"Hi, Jack."

"Do you have a minute, Mom? I've had a rough week."

"Sure, honey, what's troubling you?"

"I wasn't going to say anything because I didn't want you to worry, and everything is okay, but I was involved in a bad truck accident. Another guy almost died right in my arms, Mom, another corpsman. Thank God for helicopters. I could not deal with that again."

"Oh, Jack. What happened?"

"The trucks were driving too fast through the desert and had to stop suddenly. It caused a pile-up."

"Thank God you're okay, Jack."

"Yeah, Mom, I'm fine. I'm just glad there wasn't another funeral."

"For sure, Jack. Thank God you're safe. What happened to that man? And was anyone else seriously injured?"

"He had to be life-flighted, but he's going to be okay and there were others with sprains and broken bones, but they'll be fine."

"That was a close call, Jack. Of course, we never want to go through these things, but try to develop a faith-filled attitude towards death. When I die, I don't want you to feel sorry for yourself. I want you to think about how lucky you were to have a mom like me." Mollie chuckled.

"Seriously, Jack, I've already told myself that if something happened to you in the military, I'd reject the mire of self-pity, and try and be grateful for the years we had, try and accept it as the life God intended for you.

"I was reading recently where parents in medieval Europe would have witnessed the death of half their children, and even hundreds of years later the average life expectancy in England in 1750 was only thirty-five. Deadly diseases and plagues were common all throughout history. It's always a horrible thing for a parent to lose a child, but years ago it was common. These people were remarkably tough, and I can't help but think their faith sustained them. Routine death has a way of keeping you mindful of God.

"Most who lived before us have suffered so much, yet they probably complained less. Only two of Thomas Jefferson's six children survived childhood, and another one died at twenty-five. Could you imagine burying five of your children?"

"No, that's inconceivable," Jack said.

"And years ago, there were no weather forecasters to warn people of impending tornadoes, blizzards, or hurricanes. Our ancestors dealt with a lot of tragedy and death."

Pulling up in the flower truck, Peter Matson was happy to see Gil outside the garage.

"Good morning, Gil."

"Hey, Pete. Let me give you a hand. I need to talk to you for a minute."

"Sure, thanks, Gil. What's up?"

"Do remember that guy Alex we were talking about? Remember I told you I saw him leaving the bishop's residence at the crack of dawn?"

"Yeah, I remember."

"Well, I had to stop for something over the weekend, and I saw his car again."

"Leave it alone, Gil. It's none of your business."

The next day, Mollie and Patrick picked up Beth. Dad was first with a big hug. "It might be good for you to come home for a while after this semester. Come home and rest up."

On the car ride home, Patrick wanted to support his daughter. An analysis of a Villanova Men's Basketball game he had watched recently seemed appropriate.

"You know, Beth, I was watching the men's basketball the other night. I couldn't believe the coach wouldn't put the subs in the last couple of minutes. They were up by fifteen. Why not let the subs run up and down the court a few times so the families can see them on TV? In the old days, the coaches always took care of the subs. They work so hard in the practices. I see a lot of odd things with sports nowadays, Beth."

"Thanks, Dad. Thanks for understanding. If things were different, I'd probably just stay."

"I know, Beth. If you decide to leave, it's not like you quit. You're making a wise decision to get out of an unhealthy situation."

Sunday afternoon Mollie dropped Beth in front of her dorm and pulled off. The coach, who had been tipped off, was waiting.

"Where were you?"

"I was with my Mom."

"Did you leave this campus against my directive?"

"Yes, my mom came and-."

"Meet me in the gym this afternoon at two for wind sprints."

"Coach, I'm injured!"

"We will see about that."

Just then Mollie, who was getting ready to exit the parking lot, took one last look in the rearview and noticed the coach in an aggressive stance in front of Beth. She immediately spun the car around, pounced out like a mother lioness, and slammed the door. She glared with piercing eyes as she made her way across the parking lot. She gently pushed her daughter aside and took Beth's place. "Is there a problem here, Coach?"

The coach pointed at Beth. "Yes, Beth was not to leave campus."

"Okay, but you're dealing with me now. I was her accomplice. So just exactly what is your problem?"

"She disobeyed my directive. She was insubordinate."

"How dare you! How dare you tell my daughter she cannot leave this campus to see her private physician? You're nothing but a small grain of sand on this planet. What makes you so all-powerful that you can command a player's life?"

"I'm her coach!"

"Imprisoning her in a dorm room? Field hockey is a game! You are the coach of a team that is *playing a game.* Your stupid program is not that important!"

The coach stared red-faced. "Are you done?" She rolled her eyes and with all the disdain she could muster said, "You know, I don't think there's a place for Beth on this team."

"You don't think? What makes you believe anyone cares what you think? Actually, this is something we agree on. There's no place for Beth with this team, a sick, twisted program that abuses players. A program run by a self-absorbed egotist who does not honor God, but worships at the pagan altar of Division I athletics."

"What are you talking about, pagan altar?"

"Never mind, I didn't think you'd understand."

"She'll lose her scholarship," the coach said with a scowl.

Mollie laughed out loud. "You mean she'll lose her indentured servitude. All of you private-university, plastic people may be so impressed with yourselves, and your ultra-modern campuses, but you are all like the emperor's new suit - a phony overblown illusion, but no one wants to say anything. Too many are enjoying a cozy lifestyle, including coaches and professors."

"Just because your kid couldn't hack it."

"Yeah, we don't 'hack' neurotic madness in this family. We're done. Beth was seen by her doctor, in direct opposition to her Nazi coach's directive. He said she shouldn't play for the postseason."

"Nazi? How dare you call me a Nazi?"

"You're right. I apologize. It's an insult to Nazis everywhere. Let's go, Beth."

Sheepishly walking into the chancery office of the Scranton Diocese, Father Kenneth braced himself for his meeting with Bishop Mitchell "Mittens" Rahmney in his new diocese. He felt queasy as he sat waiting. He reached for some Tums. He took a cup of water from the dispenser. The gurgling water tank seemed to mock his stomachache.

"You can go in now, Father," said the receptionist. As he entered, CNN was playing on a suspended flat screen.

"Good afternoon, Father. Come in and sit down." He turned off the television.

"Are you settled in yet at your new rectory?"

"Yes, thank you, Your Excellency. It's fine."

"I wanted to meet with you sooner, but things have been busy. I hope you understand I did you a huge favor by allowing you to transfer here," the bishop said. "That comes with a price."

"A price?"

"The price is loyalty. I expect you will be faithful to me in gratitude for what I've done."

"Of course, Your Excellency."

"However, the report your counselor sent me does not inspire confidence."

Father Kenneth sat stone faced, gazing, his eyes glossed over. He chose not to respond.

"But you seem to be doing well and I trust you are managing your problem."

"Yes, Your Excellency. Treatment was most helpful."

"I'm delighted to hear that, Father, because the local high school, Central Catholic, is requesting a priest. You are in close proximity. Do not disappoint me, Father."

"Of course not, Your Excellency."

After exiting, Father Kenneth wiped his forehead with a handkerchief.

Having said the 8:00 a.m. mass, the bishop returned to his residence and had breakfast. Afterward, he walked to the chancery office where he met with Monsignor Sabatini.

"Good morning, Monsignor, help yourself to a Danish. They're fresh from the bakery."

"Thank you, Your Excellency."

"We have some personnel issues to discuss. First, I want you to take a look at this post someone forwarded to me. It's from Evelyn's Facebook account." The bishop swiveled his computer screen. "Read this post."

From the Catechism of the Catholic Church:

Political authorities, may for the sake of the common good for which they are responsible, make the exercise of the right to immigrate subject to various juridical conditions, especially with regard to immigrants' duties toward their country of adoption. Immigrants are obliged to respect with gratitude the material and spiritual heritage of the country that receives them, to obey its laws and to assist in carrying civic burdens (2241).

I am pro-immigration. Legal immigration as The Catechism suggests. Laws should be obeyed.

Build the wall!

"What do you think, Monsignor?"

"It's interesting."

"Interesting? It's outrageous!"

"Interesting that it is from the catechism. I don't recall that clause," the Monsignor said, "but if it's authentic, and I believe it is, she is simply posting it."

"She is taking it out of context and misusing it for a political agenda," the bishop said. "I will not tolerate someone on our staff politicizing the catechism. There was always something about her that didn't sit right with me. She's an alt-right nutjob. We need to start looking for a new communications director. My public relations message is critical. Keep her on until we find someone else."

"Perhaps her post demonstrates poor judgment, Your Excellency, but do you really think it warrants dismissal?"

"Yes, she is clearly insensitive to the plight of the immigrant. In the same way, the Israelites had to escape Egypt, these people have a right to migrate to sustain their lives and the lives of their families. I cannot and will not tolerate someone who is insensitive to the sufferings and difficulties of the migrant. The good of the earth belongs to all people. We as Americans need to have compassion. Whatsoever you do to the least of my brothers, you do unto me."

The bishop adjusted his computer screen and looked at a notepad on his desk. "Now moving on, there is another personnel issue I want you to take care of. Just as I suspected, the maintenance man is not trustworthy. He is to be terminated."

"Yes, Your Excellency, but this man's wife is getting chemo treatments and he has a handicapped son. I didn't know if you were aware."

"No, I was not aware, but it doesn't change anything. We all have our crosses to bear."

"I see, Your Excellency. What reason should I give?"

"Do we really need to have a reason? Just come up with something, perhaps budgetary cuts. I shouldn't have to think of everything. Simply have the security man escort him off the grounds, Monsignor."

Father Paul was sitting in the den at his new rectory. "I have my own parish, Dad, and the bishop is great. He's given me full autonomy. No one looking over my shoulder."

"How is the place, Paul?"

"Magnificent, everything has been updated. Beautiful Corian countertops, hardwood floors, new stainless-steel oversized appliances, and all the latest tech gadgets including a state-of-the-art security system. There are five bedrooms and three and a half baths, beautiful baths, so you and Mom can visit anytime, Dad."

"Great, Paul. It sounds like a good assignment."

"Oh, yes. Trust me, there are some envious priests out there. This is a highly desirable parish and a great steppingstone, many influential types at this parish, heavy hitters if you know what I mean. It was a gift from Bishop Cesare.

"Driving the bishop was a great chance to ingratiate myself. He's well-connected, rumored to be first in line when the archbishop of Newark retires next year, probably leading to Cardinal. Imagine that, Dad. I'll be on a first-name basis with a Cardinal. I'm in with the inner circle."

"It never hurts to be in good graces with the bosses, Paul. Mom and I are happy for you."

"Thanks, Dad. And I saw some more of those KKK protestors on the news. Was that your people?"

"Yes, Paul. We have put together a team of KKK posers who are available to make a showing anywhere a conservative republican speaks, or any right-wing rally. It's working great. Even a lot of republicans are being fooled and being cowed into denouncing 'the white supremacists.'"

Hermann chuckled. "It wasn't easy. We had to have the outfits and hoods custom made. You can't even find them on the internet, which should tell you something about their membership numbers. We also bought some hats and t-shirts with racist messages that our people can wear depending on the event. The media just eats it up. You'll be seeing more of our people with the fake gear."

"I'd say it's dishonest, Dad, but you and I both know that's how these conservatives really are, deep down."

"Exactly, Paul. We're just using a practical means to expose them. It's funny. In reality, the KKK has *maybe* a membership of 3,000 in the whole country. The Southern Poverty Law Center can't even quantify it. It's a bunch of losers, white high school dropouts. A scrawny group that barely exists and does virtually nothing, but they have given us a great tool with their getups."

Just then there was a knock on the door. "I have to go. Someone's at the door. Nice talking to you, Dad."

Father Paul put on the hip-hop channel, took a large gulp of champagne, and pranced to the door. He took one last look in the mirror before greeting Leon.

"Leon, you look great. I love your sweater." He gave him a hug.

"Come in and sit down. Let me get you a glass of champagne. Were you able to get the nose candy?"

"They fired me, Alice. They said it was budget cuts, but he must be spending a million dollars on remodeling. It doesn't make any sense. Plus, I went to file for unemployment and it was denied! They said the diocese is opposing it. I have no income."

"That's despicable, Gil, I'm going to talk to my cousin. He's a lawyer specializing in wrongful discharge. Maybe you could sue for discrimination. You were the only African American on staff."

"Maybe, but it's just not my nature to sue."

"I don't think it's wrong, Gil. Sometimes you have to fight with whatever means you have. I suspect a lawsuit that would generate any kind of scrutiny would be something the bishop would want to settle quietly. You may have more leverage than you think. In the meantime, you have a standing offer to move in with me until you can get on your feet."

Gazing at the gorgeous fall foliage in the Pocono Mountains of Pennsylvania did not do much to lift Father Kenneth's spirits. He couldn't escape the melancholy. It had been three months since he left treatment. By avoiding alcohol completely, as recommended by his counselors, he had been able to stay on the straight and narrow for ninety days, but now he was driving across Route 6 after leaving the liquor store on his day off.

He lit a cigar and sat on his deck soaking in the afternoon sun. He started to feel a warm glow from the alcohol. The thought of texting Fabio popped into his head. Why not? I'll just send a text message to say hello. It's not like it's a crime just to text someone. Plus, he's in another state.

Hey Fabio. What's up? I have a great place in the mountains in PA.
Hi Uncle.
How is school going?
Bad.

Father Kenneth grinned, leaned back on his lounge chair, and gulped his brandy.

Chapter 15

Three years later.

Bishop Cesare was now the Archbishop of Newark. Father Paul George, was now Monsignor George and was the rector at a seminary (in the same diocese), attached to a large university. It was preferable to running a diocese, fewer minor details and more staff. Plus, the bishop needed someone he could trust and rely upon to ensure the seminarians were given the proper formation, and the right kind of men were being recruited.

Monsignor Paul George phoned the bishop. "Good morning, Louie."

"Good morning, Paul. How do the new candidates look?"

"We've got a good selection of delightful men, just a few that might be problematic."

"Tell me more, Monsignor."

"First off is a John McCreesh, former military, a Navy corpsman, promoted several times. I think he might be a bit much, a regular GI Joe, even got two awards. One for saving a stabbing victim and another for reviving a man after a truck accident, and it looks like he's studied martial arts. He's straight as a Republican's tie."

"Oh, he sounds like a real gem, but we need the bodies, Paul."

"Of course, but listen to what he wrote in his packet under three main reasons for wanting to be a priest. First, to fight the forces of darkness, second, rescue the unborn, and lastly, save souls from Hell."

"Save souls from Hell? He actually wrote that in his packet? And fight the forces of darkness?" The bishop chuckled. "We have a real trooper here, fresh out of the armed forces. But he does have medical training, maybe we can stick him at Saint Mark's as the hospital chaplain. Either way, we have sufficient time to indoctrinate him. Trust me, in five years our little sailor boy will have a more modern theology."

"And here is another. Seth Abrams, former Marine."

"A former Marine?" The bishop let out a big sigh. "Oh well, we can't be too picky, Paul. I don't know what's attracting these men to the priesthood. We'll just have to try and form them into something sensible."

Jack arrived home to a grand welcome. A party was scheduled for the following day. He had left the Navy with an honorable discharge and had been accepted into the seminary in his home diocese.

After taking an Uber from the airport, Jack entered the home to a round of hugs. Beth spoke first. "I really missed you, Jack, and so did a lot of other people. Everyone is so excited about your party tomorrow. And I'm just warning you, I saw your old girlfriend, Nora, at the mall yesterday and I invited her. She really wanted to come."

Jack laughed. "Don't worry. We've been keeping in touch. Nora knows my plans."

"We're all excited about your plans, Jack," Mollie said. "It will be such a blessing to have a priest in the family."

"And a doctor too," Patrick said. "Is it alright if I call you Doc McCreesh?"

"Sure, Dad, and if you're sick, I'll tell you to drink some water and change your socks." Patrick loved the grunt humor; it took him right back to his Marine days.

Jack had spent his last two years in the Navy working at a hospital. He missed his Marine buddies but was grateful for the break from rigorous training and exhaustive hikes. His shoulder had never been quite right since the truck accident, and it was a constant nuisance while assigned to the USMC. Once he got a hospital assignment, he was able to rest it and even went to a chiropractor. It seemed like it was healing up but would still give him trouble from time to time, especially on cold damp days.

Working at a hospital had given Jack the chance to take college courses, most of them online. He even received almost two semesters of credits for his training and experience. He was close to getting a degree. With all this education, he judged he could be ordained as a priest in about five years.

"I have to check on dinner," Mollie said. Patrick made his way out to cut the grass.

Jack said, "I want to talk to you, Beth. Let's go into the living room. I have something for you. I'm going to grab some iced tea. Do you want anything?"

"No, thanks, Jack."

He came back in and handed her a card. Opening the card, Beth was stunned by what she saw, a check for $10,000. "Jack! What are you crazy? It's too much, Jack."

"It's only half of my enlistment bonus. It's easy to save money in the military if you avoid partying and gambling." Jack thought of many of his buddies and chuckled, "but most don't. I have more than I need, and the GI Bill will be paying for my seminary. I just wanted to wipe out your college debt, Beth. I thought it was great when you escaped the insanity of college athletics, and now you're almost done with court reporting school. You're one of the tough ones, Beth."

"That's how a corpsman's sister rolls," Beth said.

Jack laughed. "Yeah, but Mom was telling me there's an eighty percent dropout rate."

"I think it's actually more like ninety," Beth said. "At least for my class. Most could probably do it, but they get discouraged."

"The demon of discouragement," Jack said.

"You sound like Mom, but Dad kept telling me not to look at where I needed to get to but how far I came. We started at 40 words per minute, and now I am closing in on 225. I passed the 225 once, Jack, but I got to pass it two more times, and I'm stuck. I keep coming close, but if I don't pass it next week, I'll need to enroll for the fall semester. I have a good job waiting for me at a freelance firm in Scranton. It's so frustrating. After I passed it once, I thought I'd nail the next two right away."

"Everything in God's time."

"You sound like Mom again."

Jack smiled and hugged his sister. "It's so good to be home, Beth. Relax, you will pass those tests. No one gets to this level and doesn't cross the finish line. You are at the 98 percent mark. Look how far you've come."

"Now you sound like Dad." They both laughed.

For a considerable time, Father Kenneth had been staying out of trouble. Years ago, Fabio had come to visit him twice for help with his homework. Both times he plied him with alcohol and molested him. But once Walter, the counselor from the rehab, called Fabio's mother to ensure she received the letter, the visits ceased.

After speaking with Fabio, who would not reveal the whole story, Walter arranged for a tutor. Then the counselor called Father Kenneth. After an irritating back and forth, he decided to end the call. "I have notified the bishop's office. Keep it up. Keep sucking down the booze and messing with juveniles. You are headed for state prison. In the end, it will be the best thing for you, and everyone else." Click.

It had left Kenneth shaken. He decided to try 12-Step meetings. At rehab, he had learned that all the addictive behavior was related. After thinking about it, it occurred to him that drinking often led him to sexual impropriety. A few drinks were enough to flip the switch. He decided he didn't want to go to state prison as a "pedophile priest," even though it was not technically pedophilia; his targets were not children. They had passed through puberty. Regardless, it made sense to try and address the alcohol issue.

Kenneth was surprised he enjoyed the AA meetings. He went almost every day for eighteen months. It really helped with the loneliness and he learned many meaningful spiritual techniques, a new way of thinking, acceptance, and gratitude. The AA people had an authentic, down in the trenches style faith. It was inspiring. The influence was even making its way into his homilies. People were getting practical spiritual guidance they could apply to their daily lives, instead of lukewarm Catholic platitudes. The parishioners were starting to appreciate this pastor. He started to read the Bible and pray at his bedside, actually kneeling down. It was working. He was even doing fine at the high school. Urges of all kinds would come at him but he had found the strength to defeat them.

But then one day, after an uninspiring AA meeting, he kicked it all to the curb - the same people saying the same things. Is this going to be my life, going to these stupid meetings? He decided to take a break. That was six months ago, and he had not returned. He had not planned on stopping entirely, but he did.

And today had been a particularly lonely day. Unspeakable loneliness. He opted to get a bottle. After all, he had not had a drink in almost two years. *Just this one time.* After returning to the residence, he poured a half glass of brandy and reveled in the warmth. It was filling the void.

Jack was in the backyard greeting his guests while wearing a blue Navy polo shirt. His mom wanted him to wear his uniform, but Jack had tired of military regalia. Jack was talking to his Uncle Jim.

"When do you leave, Jack?"

"In two weeks."

"Are you sure about this?"

"Yes, I'm sure I want to go to the seminary, but that's the beauty of it. I can change my mind at any time. It's a process of discernment, so every year as I move forward, I can reassess."

The party had been catered and the food was pleasing and plentiful. Mollie had hired one of Jack's friends to bartend. Beth deejayed the party with her I-phone, Apple music, starting with patriotic tunes, then oldies, eventually transitioning to more modern pop, while throwing in an occasional classic rock number. The weather cooperated and the big tent fit perfectly in the back yard next to the shed. It was a festive, relaxed atmosphere with many friends and relatives. Although Jack had not wanted a party, he felt edified and honored with the graciousness expressed by many, especially relatives he had not seen in years.

Halfway through the party, Patrick got up on the deck with a megaphone.

"Attention K-mart shoppers." Everyone laughed.

"I just wanted to take a minute and thank you all for coming and to say how proud we are of Jack. As a former grunt myself, that is Marine infantry for you civilians, I can tell you that corpsman and medics are among the most revered in all the military. And although, thank God, Jack did not see live combat, he still managed to receive two awards. Jack might be too humble to say anything about them, but I'm not. Humility was never my strong suit." There was a smattering of laughter.

Meanwhile, Beth had switched the tunes back to patriotic music. Patrick continued as *Stars and Stripes Forever* played in the background.

"When Jack was training with the Marines in the California desert, there was a bad truck accident. He was in the third truck and immediately started to administer first aid. Then he heard Marines calling. Turns out there was an unconscious man in the first truck, a fellow corpsman. Jack immediately called for a helicopter and began CPR. I was in combat and I know how stressful these things can be. Jack maintained his composure and kept this man alive until a chopper arrived. He was the only corpsman available and if he'd hesitated this man would have been lost.

"But that's not all. As a brand-new corpsman, Jack witnessed a stabbing, a street fight, nefarious characters. His training kicked in, and in spite of the obvious perilous circumstances, he leaped into action, putting his own life at risk and stopping the bleeding of a badly injured man. Actually, another man, who also got an award, Doc Foster, ended up saving Jack, who found himself in the middle of some kind of gang conflict. Foster later died in a plane crash."

Mollie went over and put her arm around Jack. "We're so happy and thankful that God brought Jack home safely but we all should be grateful to those in our military who sacrifice their lives, whatever the circumstances." Patrick paused and took a sip of beer. "Well, I guess that's enough out of me. Do you have anything you want to say, Jack?"

Jack had not been planning to speak, but the mention of Foster had stirred something in him. He grabbed a napkin and wiped his eye.

"Yeah, Dad, I do have something."

He walked through the crowd, climbed up onto the white vinyl deck, and hugged his father who handed him the megaphone.

"Thanks, Dad. I appreciate my dad's remarks, but today I want to tell you a little bit about the best friend I ever had, Doc Richie Foster. Foster used to joke he got his name because of all the foster homes he was shuffled through.

"The kid had it rough. He used to talk about it. I can't imagine what it's like to grow up without a family, with no support or guidance, and although there are some good foster families, that was not Doc Foster's experience, very bad homes. His meth-addicted mother could've come and rescued him at any time, which was always his hope, but she never did. She loved her drugs more than her son. It left emotional wounds that wouldn't heal. And his father, well he never was around and never did a damn thing for him either."

Jack took a deep breath. "At the beginning of boot camp I was helping Foster, but as time went on, he was helping me. He transitioned from boy to man, grew stronger physically and mentally. It was amazing to watch. He was so happy to be a corpsman, a doc to his Marines. We were like brothers. He saved my life. He literally saved my life. Then God took him in a senseless plane crash. It was hard for me to process and still is sometimes. One of the last things Foster did before he died was send money to his mother in jail. The mother who had never done one damn thing for him. He had a giver's heart and his memory still inspires me. Although his career was short, he was a great corpsman. I wanted you to know a little about him."

Jack paused his eyes moistening.

"At this time I'd like to make a toast." He raised his glass. "To my friend and fellow corpsman, Doc Richie Foster, who died doing what he loved, serving his Marines. Love you, brother, semper fi."

The next morning Jack was having a coffee with his mom.

"I had another dream about Foster last night. He seemed a little less troubled, almost like he was trying to smile. The mist surrounding him was thinner. It was so vivid."

"I think it's because we all prayed for him last night," Mollie said. "He's thanking you for the prayers and masses. Keep it up, Jack. You're helping him."

"Don't worry, Mom. I'll never forget him."

Gil Rodgers' plumbing business was up and running. After mulling things over, he had decided to sue for wrongful discharge. Alice had judged it correctly – the bishop knew a jury trial might bring out some embarrassing testimony. Gil had been quite pleased with the quick $125,000 settlement (after attorney's fees) and had used it to start his own business. He and his family had resided with Alice for four months until he was able to get his unemployment compensation. The bishop, who heard on his audio surveillance that Gil was living with Alice, had subsequently fired her too. She later filed an age discrimination suit and received a similar settlement. Since she had been planning on retiring anyway, she took it all in stride.

Gil had all the plumbing business he could handle. There was a shortage of reliable plumbers in New Jersey. He decided to operate as a sole-proprietor and do mostly simple jobs. It was a winning strategy. The money flowed in and the workdays were pleasant. Gil enjoyed helping people and always made it a point to be prompt, something that separated him from his competition. His wife Dusty had gone back to work as a drug and alcohol counselor. Things were looking up.

Tomorrow morning Jack would be leaving for the seminary. "I'm so proud of you, Jack. First, a decorated corpsman and now a seminarian."

"Thanks, Mom, but I didn't really do that much. Many have done so much more."

"I know, Jack. I'm just happy you're living right. I want to talk to you about the seminary Jack. There are some things I need to warn you about."

"Warn me?"

"Yes. We live in strange times. Don't get me wrong, God needs men like you to enter the pastorate, but I've been hearing things about a sort of gay mafia in the diocese. You're likely to encounter it."

"You mean effeminate priests."

"That's not really it, Jack. I don't have a problem with an effeminate priest who is faithful. It's more like a radical in-your-face gay type who is living in direct opposition to the church, a subversive. I'm afraid they are in our seminaries. You need to be alert. Forewarned is forearmed."

"Okay, Mom. I think I understand. I knew there were issues but maybe it's worse than I thought."

"It is, Jack. I had a long talk with the plumber today. He's a member of our parish and worked for the bishop. You wouldn't believe some of the things he told me. You know how I feel about gossip, but we need to know what's happening in our church. Be careful, Jack. Keep your mouth shut and your head down until you know who you can trust. And you can't trust Archbishop Cesare or any of his minions."

"Really, the archbishop?"

"Consider him the head of the local lavender mafia, the gay godfather. We're all sinners and, of course, we have some gay relatives we truly love. But if you have same-sex tendencies and want to actively promote that lifestyle, it's fraudulent to join the priesthood with the intention of undermining the church. And although homosexuality is sinful, it's not really the main issue. It's the subversive nature of it. If a bunch of straight priests were regularly having sex with women, and forming a covert alliance to undermine the faith, it would be just as bad."

"Maybe I should look for a new seminary or go out of this diocese."

"You can't escape it, son. You might as well start the battle here. Remember, Jesus said, 'Blessed are you when people scorn and hate you.' Be prepared for adversity."

"I'm not looking for a soft life. I plan on being a militant priest."

"That's it, Jack. The militant church needs militant priests. Pray to the Holy Spirit. He will guide you. Face everything with courage and be willing to suffer. And, of course, know that I am praying for you, always. I'm so proud of you, Jack."

Chapter 16

Riding to the seminary Jack's heart was singing. He had always dreamed about this day. He could not believe his whole life for the next five years would be entirely about seeking God's will and studying scripture, all while being surrounded by like-minded men, his fellow seminarians. Finally, to be around people who had a similar world view, a view where there was a living God active in their lives. Plus, he would not have to worry about worldly things like paying bills and preparing meals. It was all focused on seeking God, an ideal situation.

Jack unpacked his things and settled into his room, a plain, spartan space with only the bare essentials, designed to limit distractions. They called it a cell. He loved the simplicity of it. The dormitory also included a recreation room with a pool table and various table games, including chess, and another room, a lounge with a television and a shared computer for email. A 9:00 p.m. curfew was also in force. Seminarians were encouraged to study scripture prior to retiring for the evening.

Hearing someone across the hall, Jack wandered out into the hallway. He spied a short, broad-shouldered man in the room across from his. He couldn't believe it, the haircut. It was a "low fade." It had to be a Marine! Jack always thought it was interesting, humorous even, how the grunts, some of the toughest men you would ever meet, would pay so much attention to their hair. If you were new out of boot camp, a "boot" they called it, you did not dare wear a low fade, until you completed your first deployment. Haircuts in the Marines were a symbol of rank and status and it was ill-advised to go against the norms; there would be disagreeable consequences.

Jack knocked on the open door. "Good morning, I'm Jack McCreesh. Pardon me, but you look like a grunt." Just then Jack noticed a USMC tattoo, some of the letters represented by bullets, on the man's forearm, and he knew.

"Yeah, 0331, first battalion, first Marines. I was a machine gunner. I just completed a four-year hitch." He put his hand out. "My name is Seth Abrams."

Jack's eyes glowed. Thank you, God. A Marine - God, country, corps! During his enlistment, Jack had found some of the Marines a little hard to take, especially the complaining profane types. But there was something so noble about a number of them. Their peers would refer to them as "a good Marine." A Marine who was principled and faith-filled was a splendid soul, tough spiritually and physically.

"Great to meet you, Seth. I just finished up as a Navy Corpsman. I spent two years with the infantry."

"Wow, a doc here at the seminary. That's great. A pleasure to meet you, Doc."

The next day, after morning prayers and a quick breakfast, the seminarians gathered in the auditorium for introductory remarks by Rector Paul George.

"Good morning, my brothers in Christ. Allow me to welcome you to Good Shepard Seminary. The Seminary is, in itself, an original experience of the church's life. Thank you for answering God's call, a call to discernment and holiness. A commitment to holiness means continually putting into practice the teachings of Christ. Here you will have an opportunity to build the foundation that will promote holiness. The priesthood is a vocation of joy and ministry.

"Evidently, you've experienced a stirring of some sort. Our goal is to help you to identify the nature of that stirring and realize God's will. For most of you that will mean a vocation to the priesthood. For others, it may be something else. Either result is fine as long as you are aligning yourself with God. As all are redeemed, so all are called. Our goal is to make you servants of Christ in whatever capacity that might be. Unless we train seminarians capable of warming people's hearts, accompanying them through the darkness, dialoguing with their hopes and despairs, and mending the wounds and brokenness, what hope can we have for the future?

"Here, you can encounter Christ. You can enter into silence, reflect and pray. Through scripture study and deep personal prayer, we will hear His message. The challenges of ministry are more demanding than ever. Our dedicated and diverse staff is determined to meet all your ministry needs to prepare you for a priesthood in the contemporary world. We will form you into well-rounded, mature men, ready to embrace your vocation.

"Although this program will provide you with spiritual formation in the theological disciplines, we will do even more to equip you with utmost integrity and nobleness, qualities the Catholic Church requires of its ministerial priests.

"There is one thing I wish to caution you about, and that is closed-mindedness. Our modern church requires one to be less rigid, open to new forms of evangelization. The way of the world is rigidity and narrow-mindedness, intolerance even. The way of the spirit is broad and wide. Open your minds to new systems of comprehending and perceiving. Let go of prejudice and narrow-mindedness. Broadening your frame of reference, that is what a seminary education is all about."

Father Kenneth returned to the rectory after celebrating the Sunday noon mass. Feeling hungry, and a bit hungover, he went to the refrigerator and grabbed the dinner plate his housekeeper had left. He wanted to eat something substantial before he started hitting the bottle. Sunday was his favorite day to drink. No one bothered a priest on Sunday, and Monday was his day off. On Monday, he only needed to say a noon mass at the parish. Most times he didn't even bother giving a homily, although the laity could really use some edification in the modern culture; they would not get it at Father Kenneth's daily noon mass; Father had lost his zeal.

Later that evening, after several strong brandies, Father Kenneth was online planning a ski trip. He had been cautiously befriending several of the sophomore boys, careful to be discreet and not do any form of obvious grooming. He felt like the bishop was watching him, but in reality, no one was paying much attention. There were several ski resorts in the Poconos, but none of them had overnight lodging. Overnight was just so much more fun for the kids. He thought about finding some funds, maybe even the parish youth group account, so they could stay at the Holiday Inn. He knew some of the boys loved to ski.

Once he was satisfied with his ski trip plan, he went on Facebook. *I wonder if I can get any of the boys to "friend" me.*

Monsignor George's parents were visiting. "This is a beautiful layout," his mother said. "I love the small lake."

"Yes, it's so scenic. I like to just stroll around. As rector, I can do whatever I want. My title is also president, which I prefer." The Monsignor giggled and continued. "It's my own little fiefdom."

Hermann said, "Good for you. You have a nice setup here, Paul and an opportunity to influence these seminarians, impacting the church for years well into the future. I trust you'll teach them how to fight for economic justice and human rights, and how important equality is for the welfare of society, the greater good."

"Don't worry, Dad. We're going to make sure our men are on the right side of things when it comes to the vital social issues of our age. Diversity is not something we will tolerate with certain things."

"Glad to hear it, our movement needs men in the pulpit," Hermann said. "It's a great way to reinforce our message, a captive audience every Sunday. If you have a few moments, there's something else I wanted to talk to you about, Paul."

"Of course, what is it?"

"Even though the presidential election is not until next year, we want to be proactive. My donors are interested in setting up a Catholic group to promote a more progressive agenda. We're going to call it 'Catholics For a Better Way,' or 'Catholics For Social Justice,' something like that. It will be a front group. Well, I shouldn't say front group, but we won't have a real membership base, just a few token members and we'll take bold progressive positions on contemporary issues and send out news releases to our allies in the media."

"I think that's a great idea, Dad. If there's anything I can do-"

"Yes, perhaps. I wonder if any of your professors could assist us, act like a think-tank and provide us with well-reasoned propaganda. We need intelligent analysis and tactful news releases giving us maximum impact. We're targeting the lukewarm, uninformed Catholic who's easily swayed."

Monsignor George chuckled. "Lukewarm and uninformed are the bulk of the church. It's a good target, brilliant, Dad. I can think of a number of professors who would be eager to help."

After a few days of an orientation schedule, school started.

Seth and Jack sat down for their first course of the day, "Foundations in Scripture." The professor, a stout Catholic nun with

THE LAVENDER MAFIA

a doctorate's degree began. She didn't wear a habit. Her gray hair was cut short. She had piercing brown eyes and granny glasses. A plate of cookies sat on her desk.

"Welcome to Good Shepard. I'm Dr. Marion Semple and I'm honored to have this opportunity to help with your formation. I must warn you, I'm somewhat unconventional and will not hesitate to offer new, non-traditional ways of viewing the scriptures. The church has been stuck in something of a time warp for many years. It's only in the past few decades that the inelasticity of the church has been challenged. I'm not here to tell you what to think. However, I will not hesitate to give you alternative views that may appear controversial. Perhaps they're my views, perhaps they are not. Perhaps they will become your views, perhaps they will not. That is the beauty of education, to expose the student to bold new ideas and widen your horizons. So I implore you to enter into your seminary training with an open mind. A stubborn padlocked brain, rusted shut, will not fully realize the seminary experience.

"I'd like to start today with a story from sacred scripture, the Book of Matthew, Chapter 14. Can I have a volunteer to read?" A man in the front row raised his hand. "Thank you, please read verses 13 through 21."

After the reading, the professor took a sip of coffee and began to pace. "Now what you have here is the well-known story of Jesus, the miracle worker, chronicling how He took just five loaves and two fishes and fed five thousand. The people had been listening to Jesus preach. They were tired and were going to be sent away, but then Jesus told the disciples to feed them. When they told Him what little they had, He said, 'bring it to me.' Then He apparently blessed the meager rations and passed them, allegedly multiplying them in a way that was sufficient to feed five thousand people. Everyone was satisfied, and there were even leftovers. Quite a miracle, wouldn't you say?"

No one answered. The question appeared to be hypothetical. Nobody was sure where she was going. While she waited, the professor went over and began to munch on a large cookie. Many found the behavior odd. Still chewing, she continued while spraying random cookie crumbs. Some in the front could pick up the scent of oatmeal.

"Yes, indeed it was a miracle, miraculous no doubt. But perhaps not in the way you think. Modern theologians, who presently have more resources, have determined that, yes, undeniably, there was a miracle that day. I call it the 'miracle of love.' You see, in those days people walked everywhere, often traveling very far, and they didn't know where their next meal would come from. There were no fast-food restaurants, so they would carry food in their garments, especially loaves and sometimes small fish. Food was often scarce, and people of that age were stingy with their provisions. But as Jesus passed the baskets the food began to multiply. People who were carrying food hidden in their robes began to share and place it in the baskets. Jesus knew they would do this as he was a highly advanced rabbi, a genius of human nature. Jesus was able to free the selfish, fearful people of these blockages and release them into the realm of giving and sharing where they could experience Christian joy, bliss if you will."

Later, walking from class, Jack said, "What did you think of the professor's Jesus story, Seth?"

"I'm not sure, Doc. I thought it was kind of cool, but it's a lot different than what I was taught."

"Yes, but be careful. Although it might sound good, these stories are intended to undermine the divinity of Christ. In other words, miracles aren't miracles, they're just nice stories."

"Oh, I see what you mean, Doc. Like a diluted faith."

"Yes exactly, Seth. Keep your antennae up. Jesus was God. I believe Jesus was God or I wouldn't be here. I suspect we're going to have to disregard some things we're taught. I'm already disregarding that last lecture."

The boys headed off to lunch. Food was served cafeteria-style. Jack and Seth were the only ex-military seminarians out of a class of twenty. Having both lived the life of an infantry grunt, they shared a similar world view and often knew what the other was thinking. It was just a perspective you gained in the USMC.

They were sitting alone when another man came up. "Hello, my name is Jakob Kowalski. Do you mind if I join you?"

Jack noticed a Polish accent. "No, not at all," Jack said. The man was sturdy and lean with deep blue eyes and short blonde hair, a crew cut. He had a serious demeanor yet was polite and seemed agreeable. He was also blunt.

"I did not like in the least bit that ridiculous lecture this morning about the miracle of love. So sweet and syrupy, yet more like sour cream. I was going to tell her to stuff herself with hay."

"Stuff herself with hay?" Seth asked.

"I think he means, she is full of it," Jack said.

"Yes, you are right my friend," Jakob said. "Sometimes I forget I am not in Poland."

"Say it any way you want, Jakob. I'm so happy to hear there's someone else who feels strongly about this. My mother told me to expect this sort of thing all throughout the training, pockets of modernism. I suspect it will be predominant, but I'm determined to endure it so I can speak the truth once this is over."

"Yes, I am the same kind of man," Jakob said. "I am going to teach the true faith and fight the good fight."

After just a few days, the men had already formed into like-minded small groups. Jack, Seth, and Jakob were close friends and there were two more regulars that usually sat with them. There was another table that stood out. A group of eight who were noticeably louder than the others. Laughter and squealing could be routinely heard from their table, and so could profanity. Although forbidden, you could often hear cursing in their private conversations since they never seemed to consider lowering the volume. Jakob nicknamed the table "the mean girls." There was also another group that seemed more sensible who just followed the protocol and did not seek attention.

After lunch, the men had some free time until their afternoon course. They wandered around familiarizing themselves with the grounds,

The midafternoon class was "Fundamentals of Theology," with Father Ahmed Keita, a priest who had been educated in West Africa. After introductory remarks and passing out his syllabus, Father sat down at his desk. He paused for a moment like he was praying. He had a sense of peace and calmness about him and spoke softly. Then he began.

"Original sin started in the garden, in the book of Genesis, the very first book of the Bible. In this book, we are introduced to Satan, who through man's weakness altered the course of all mankind. So our nemesis the Devil appears very early in the scriptures and is present all throughout, and is prominently featured in the last book, Revelation. And our Savior repeatedly talked about the Devil, emphasized his existence. Yet, somewhere along the way, in our modern church, Lucifer has disappeared. Can anyone tell me where he went? It seems he's no longer spoken of. Was he defeated? Did I miss something?"

Jakob raised his hand and the professor acknowledged him.

"Yes, I'm happy to answer your question, Father. The Devil is alive and well, and if you look you will find him in this monastery."

"Good answer, bold, confident, and brash. That is the spirit we need in the modern church, yet it is sorely lacking. What's your name?"

"Jakob."

"Ah, Jacob, yes, one of the patriarchs. You are most welcome in this classroom young man. It ranks as one of the best responses ever to that question and you have helped me to make a point, a very strong point I wanted to make."

He got up from his desk and raised his voice. "The Devil is everywhere. The church has forgotten about him, but I have not. Throughout our studies, we will be discussing the enemy. The word 'Satan' comes from a Hebrew word meaning 'adversary.' The Jews knew they had an adversary, but today we have forgotten. If the church had maintained the full armor of God, instead of putting down the shield, the church would not be in such a sorry state, steeped in sin. We put our guard down and forgot about the adversary, and now the adversary is thrashing forward like a German blitzkrieg, virtually unopposed.

"We have this horrible sex scandal in the church and the bishops keep expressing regret and talking about hurt and disappointment. They categorize the evil as 'uncomfortable and unsettling issues.' It's pathetic how they keep apologizing while deflecting responsibility. But they never identify the real culprit – Satan. His name is unspoken, but he is the demon behind the curtain. Weak priests and cowardly leaders falling prey to Satan's wiles and trickeries, yet how odd that the church seems reluctant to name him, but I digress.

"Can anyone here tell me something about the Church of England?"

Jack answered. "Yes, the Church of England was founded by King Henry VIII in the early 1500s when the pope would not allow him to get a divorce and marry an eighteen-year-old woman, so he basically started his own church and persecuted Catholics who remained faithful."

"Yes, very good. The Church of England, also known as the Anglican Church, although a heresy in my opinion, did initially maintain many of the teachings of the Catholic Church. However, two years ago, in a feckless attempt to broaden its appeal the Anglican Church removed any mention of Satan from its baptismal ritual because it was uncomfortable for parents and godparents to be asked to reject the Devil. The church had deemed itself sufficiently progressive and declared it no longer needed to renounce Satan in order to live in freedom or some such blather, indicative of a larger trend throughout all Christendom.

"Every day more and more Catholics are rejecting the idea of Satan as a cunning adversary. Polls show that less than twenty percent of Catholics believe in the Devil as a living being, most see him simply as a symbol. A symbol. A symbol of what? Evil, of course, but calling him a symbol does not lessen his power. On the contrary, it strengthens it. By not clearly identifying and regularly acknowledging the existence of the Prince of Darkness, the church facilitated Satan's ascent.

"*The Catechism of the Catholic Church* makes it clear there are demons, led by Lucifer, angels who irrevocably rejected God and who are now in direct opposition to Him. Around each man lurks a seductive voice, the voice of temptation. It is the voice of a liar, the father of lies. Jesus said he was 'a murderer from the beginning.' But the Devil is simply a creature, a powerful spiritual being, but his power pales in comparison to divine power.

"Align yourself with the Almighty. Put on the full armor of God. Lucifer's favorite targets are Catholic priests. Many have been effortlessly crushed, and it's caused irreparable harm to the church. There was no fight in these clerics. They fell into worldly ways and became complacent. Many were annihilated, at least spiritually if not physically. To be a priest, in the order of Melchizedek, you must be willing to pick up your cross. If you are looking for a soft life you are in the wrong place. The church needs warriors. To be a priest you must be a teacher of truth, not tepid drivel. Why would any servant of God be hesitant to preach the truth? The truth about the enemy, an enemy who hates all mankind and wants to separate as many as possible from God, forever.

"Which brings me to another topic that has been set aside by the modern church. The topic of the afterlife, Heaven, Hell, and Purgatory. We will be discussing these places in detail, especially Hell. Hell is eternal. Once you're there, you cannot leave. It's final. It may make you uncomfortable to hear this, and mystery is part of it, but Hell is real. Choosing not to believe, like some lame, modernist clerics, does not make it disappear. Jesus confirmed its existence. How can a man be a priest if he neglects the teachings of our Lord? It's reckless, but regrettably, it's quite common. A good shepherd is going to be mindful of the afterlife and warn his sheep, whether they want to hear it or not. Saint Ignatius described Hell as 'a horrible cavern of black flames.' Or as Dante said, 'Abandon hope, all ye who enter here.'"

Chapter 17

Sister Marion Semple concluded her lecture, "That, you see, is why modern-day archeologists and scientists tell us there was no 'parting of the Red Sea.' After years of intensive study, and forensic archeology, combined with clues provided by ancient writings, the evidence strongly suggests the Israelites were able to cross the Red Sea due to low tide, and they simply walked across in several inches of water."

Jack was squirming in his chair; this was the third lecture that removed the divine nature of a long-standing miracle chronicled in scripture. He raised his hand.

"So you're saying it was low tide? After thousands of years, now you are changing the story to low tide?"

"I am not *changing* anything," Sister said. "This is what our modern methods have been able to uncover. I am simply giving you the most updated information."

"Does your updated information also tell us how the Pharaoh's soldiers, with their horses and chariots, all drown in a few inches of water?"

"Well not exactly, but the more sophisticated Bible scholars, who have considered this new information, believe the author of the book of Exodus, who some believe was Moses, if there really was a Moses, but regardless, the modern scholars believe the account of the Egyptian soldiers all being abruptly drowned by the waters of the Red Sea was simply an embellishment, to titillate the readers of the age and endear future generations to the Hebrew faith, perhaps allowing the leaders to better control and manipulate the populous."

Jack sighed and shook his head.

Another student, Luther, raised his hand. A tall, wiry man with bright red hair who had been a star basketball player in high school, he was also the de facto leader of the "mean girls."

"Doctor, I appreciate your analysis and find it fascinating. There will always be those who are stuck in the past, programmed by children's Bible stories. We were advised by our rector when we arrived to be open to new ways of perceiving things, but apparently, some were not listening. I know I speak for others when I commend your scholarly methodology. I say, 'Bravo, Doctor.'" After speaking he looked over at Jack and sneered.

Sister Semple dismissed the class. "And remember, the afternoon classes have been canceled. You are all required to attend Father Karpman's talk. I've been so looking forward to it all week."

Later that day, Monsignor George took to the microphone. "Today as a guest speaker we have renowned writer, journalist, and hottest Catholic author in the country, who brings his own unique brand of spirituality, Father Jonathan Karpman. Father Karpman will be discussing social issues confronting today's church."

"Thank you, Monsignor. It is a great pleasure to be here today to help form the hearts and minds of our future clergy. My message today is the message of the gospel. A message of charity, love, and understanding, the example set by our Lord. I have been asked to speak about the more delicate issues facing the church, issues many pastors try to avoid.

"First, I would like to discuss climate change. My book *The Climate Conscious Catholic* will give you more insight, but I'd like to make a few brief points. When it comes to climate change, we all have a part to play. Every action you take, no matter how small, impacts our lives and promotes a more sustainable environment. Our governments need to get involved. People will not do what needs to be done on their own. Some think it's just a power grab, a way for the government to take more money and have absolute control over our lives. And that any so-called solutions the politicians put forth will not have any real impact anyway - that they will funnel the money to cronies and sham companies. Just because one solar power company went out of business after a 500-million-dollar grant, doesn't mean similar projects are not worth pursuing. There's always a learning curve with new technologies, and the day will come when our investment will pay off in the form of cleaner air and water for our children.

"Our opponents say the climate is always changing anyway, and the Earth is too massive for human beings to have a major impact and only a tiny fraction of carbons are the result of human activity. Then there are those who say carbon, some even scientists, is good for the environment and promotes plant growth. They are pro-carbon. It's absurd!

"There're even those who are asking for more leniency with coal-burning power plants. They state new cleaner processing methods, one they always mention is the Allam Cycle, emits no carbon, none. Do not believe any of this evil propaganda. These fossil fuel companies have lots of money to fund studies and buy whatever outcome they want.

"This is a crisis, and America needs to lead. We need to pay more and have less in order to lead the world in addressing climate change. And yes, countries like China and India pollute much more, but they'll never get on board unless we lead and are willing to sacrifice. I'm convinced everyone has the ability to contribute to the defeat of climate change and select sustainable lifestyles. Let's begin here. Teach your flock to live simply, respect mother Earth, and be willing to pay higher taxes and utility fees in order to save our children. Every individual action which contributes to fundamental human improvement and worldwide solidarity helps to fashion a more sustainable environment and, hence, a better planet. If you want to know more, get a copy of my book. They will be available afterward.

"The next thing I want to discuss is immigration. Please be mindful my thoughts on immigration are rooted in the gospel. Jesus said, 'take courage, be not afraid.' I believe what is behind the anti-immigration sentiment is fear. Our fears cause intolerance and racism. Racism creeps in and people don't even realize it. There are countless subconscious racists. These irrational, baseless fears have the ability to control people and dominate them in ways they don't even realize. These prejudices keep us captive and hold us in bondage as intolerant racist Catholics, preventing us from encountering Christ in these people.

"Our country, the most powerful nation on Earth, a country which has the ability to protect and feed its residents, has a responsibility to assist migrants. Often, they are subject to punitive laws and harsh treatment by enforcement officers from both receiving and transit countries. This is not consistent with Christ's message. More powerful economic nations have an obligation to accommodate migration flows. All persons are worthy of human dignity."

He continued along the same lines, emphasizing racism then concluded his remarks about immigration. "The United States Catholic Bishops have stated the following, and I quote, 'The

Catholic community is rapidly re-encountering itself as an immigrant Church, a witness at once to the diversity of people who make up our world and our unity in one humanity, destined to enjoy the fullness of God's blessing in Jesus Christ.' We are a nation of immigrants and need to welcome the concept of the immigrant church.

"Lastly, I want to talk about building a bridge for our LGBTQ brothers and sisters. Much of what I discuss can be found in more detail in my book, *The Lost Sheep. An LGBTQ Catholic Homecoming*.

"There's still a lot of bigotry in our church against this community, even among our clergy. I know of a priest who recently asked a gay man, who was living with another man, not to approach for communion. At least he did it quietly, and off to the side, but I wonder if this same priest would say that to a heterosexual man who was living with his girlfriend, or a straight couple using contraceptives. Apply it equally. If it's against church teaching, let's be consistent.

"The woman at the well taught Jesus to be more tolerant of those on the margins, even those who have engaged in improper sexual activity. Remember, this woman had five husbands and the man she was with now was not even her husband. Many gays and lesbians have already experienced a lot of hardship in their lives and don't need to feel the heavy hammer of the church when they are simply seeking an encounter with God.

"My Catholic friend recently married his boyfriend. Why weren't they able to marry in the church? They are a beautiful union of friendship and love, a love perhaps beyond your understanding, but a love, nonetheless. Maybe someday these men will be able to marry in the church and freely share the 'kiss of peace' at mass. Instead, they feel disconnected and don't trust their fellow parishioners. Some have been fired from teaching jobs and other positions at Catholic-run institutions once their LGBTQ lifestyle became apparent.

"At my church, every month we have an LGBTQ mass and we have a rainbow runner leading up the center aisle. I wear a rainbow cross on my vestments, and we have coffee and donuts afterward. It's a beautiful community. I believe gays are more compassionate than most Catholics. Since they have endured considerable suffering, they're more attuned to suffering in others. And the Catholic church is responsible for ninety percent of that suffering. It's the last organization having trouble letting go of its stiffness.

"I envy today's seminarians. I predict you'll see major changes in the church in your lifetime and I know you'll feel the spirit of Christ guiding it. What a beautiful thing. You can read more about it in my book. All my books are available after this talk or on Amazon. Of course, if you buy today, I can autograph it. I am open for questions now."

After several softball questions, Jack saw this was turning into a love fest. As it continued, Jack could feel the heat on the back of his neck. With a few minutes left, he raised his hand.

"First, I have a statement, then a question," Jack said. "Jesus did not condone the lifestyle of the woman at the well, not even close, and since He was God, I don't see how this sinful woman was in a position to teach Him anything, but regardless. You talk all about how the church has alienated LGBTQ, but you do not mention anything about a Catholic group already ministering to same-sex attraction parishioners, a beautiful, aptly named group called 'Courage.' What about Courage?"

"Courage is all about celibacy," the priest said. "Gays shouldn't have to live a chaste life. Heterosexuals don't have to live a chaste life."

Jack said, "They do if they're not married."

"But there's no avenue for gays to marry in the church, so that's the problem. It's not fair."

"Life is not fair," Jack said. "It's sinful for anyone to have sex outside of marriage, even though all can maintain church membership, just shouldn't be receiving communion, but are you saying we should change the definition of this as sin, a definition that has stood for two thousand years?"

"Not necessarily. That's not for me to decide. That's for the magisterium of the church. For now, I'm just asking for more acceptance of the LGBTQ community by the church, LGBTQ themed liturgies, gatherings, and the like, so our LGBTQ brothers and sisters feel ministered to."

"I still think Courage is already doing that," Jack said, "but of course Courage requires one to sacrifice and suffer for the faith. No one wants to pick up their cross. But what you are suggesting is that the church celebrates sin. Spin it any way you want - it's still sin.

Shouldn't people struggle with their sins quietly and privately, and not broadcast them? I feel like you are elevating sin."

"I am not elevating anything," Father Karpman said. "Just asking people to stop being so mean and intolerant. We are all sinners."

"I agree," Jack said. "We're all sinners. The church is capable of addressing the state of anyone's soul. It doesn't exclude anyone. But why have a sin-based group that basically endorses sin? Are there any other groups like that? Should we have a heterosexual fornicators group too? Or a contraceptives support group? And a monthly mass for them? As you said, if it's against church teaching, let's be consistent."

"Okay, now you are getting ridiculous," Father Karpman said. "Plus, we're almost out of time."

Jack said, "I have one more question? Do you, or do you not, accept the church's teaching that homosexuality is intrinsically disordered and under no circumstances can these acts be approved. Do you agree with that teaching?"

"I'm sorry, we are out of time. If you read my book, you'll get a clearer picture of where I stand. All of my books are for sale during the reception. Just see Leon at the back table."

Jack sat down with Seth and Jakob.

"Good job, Jack," Jakob said. "I was going to say something, but I felt like I was going off the rails. I was praying 'the shut-up prayer.'"

"I understand, Jakob. It seems pointless arguing with these people anyway. Let's get something to eat."

After getting their food, they sat down. As Jakob and Seth were talking, Jack's mind drifted. He remembered his mother's skepticism about climate change. She told him all about the dire predictions she had heard in the 1970s. Back then, it was global cooling. She said in her lifetime she had survived the population explosion, holes in the ozone layer, the Ebola virus, acid rain, and an invasion of killer bees. She would laugh when a commercial came on showing a polar bear floating on an iceberg as if it was stranded. Like it was a victim of ice caps melting and now the poor, lonely bear was aimlessly floating in the Arctic and clearly doomed. Few stopped to think that a polar bear could simply jump in the water and swim away. They were excellent swimmers and could swim in frigid water for hours.

Jack looked over at the table where Father Karpman was sitting with the local bishop, Rector George, and Archbishop Louis Cesare. Men were lining up to talk to the author priest and get their books signed, a real celebrity. And the higher-ups at the table were all smiles. Something was clearly amiss in the church.

Just then Jakob interrupted. "Why are you so quiet, my friend?"

"Just thinking, Jakob. Priests like Father Karpman are dispiriting."

"Agreed," Jakob said. "I was turned off from the beginning when he was introduced with his 'unique brand of spirituality.' There is only one brand, and it's not his. And 'hottest selling author?' It sounded so worldly. What is this, Ooprah' or a Catholic seminary?"

Jack and Seth burst into laughter. It was just so funny the way he pronounced Oprah's name, with a double O.

Later, after dinner, Jack was in the rec room reading the newspaper. Luther was there with his full posse and noticed Jack's buddies were absent. He decided it was time for some fun.

He alerted his minions and then walked over and dumped a cup of water on Jack.

"Hey sailor boy, look out for that wave." There was loud laughter. "I thought you could use a little cooling off. There was steam coming out of your ears when you were giving that homophobic rant at the lecture."

Jack, who was a few inches shorter, stood up and looked him in the eyes. I am not homophobic. I am not afraid of homosexuality or homosexuals, not in the least."

Luther's posse gathered behind him. Luther grinned, "maybe you should be."

"I have a question," Jack said. "What's a clown like you doing in Catholic seminary? What would a crass, vulgar man-child like you be looking for here?

"How dare you -"

"You should've just stayed home and listened to Cindy Lauper songs. You know, *Girls Just Want to Have Fun.*"

Luther turned red and balled up his fists. Just then Seth and Jacob walked in. Luther's friends had the wisdom to restrain him.

"You'd better watch your back, sailor boy."

"Thanks for the warning. I will Cindy."

Getting back to the dorms, Seth said. "What was that all about?"

"Apparently, Luther didn't like my remarks at the lecture. He dumped a cup of water on me."

"What did you do?" Seth asked.

"Not much, it's only water. I just asked him why he was here. I mean they don't seem to take this seriously. I'm not sure what's up with that group, but I have my suspicions."

"Let me tell you something," Jakob said. "I wasn't going to say anything, but on my third day here Luther came into my room and introduced himself. When he shook my hand, he took his forefinger and stroked my palm. I grabbed him by the throat and put him up against the wall. I told him if he touched me again, I would kill him. He seemed terrified and has stayed away from me ever since. I decided to keep it to myself."

It was 1:00 a.m. and Jack couldn't sleep. He decided to try a hot shower. Not wanting to disturb his peers, he chose to creep over to the shower in the gym adjacent to the dorm and accessible via an enclosed walkway. As he quietly walked in, he heard voices behind the curtain of a shower stall. He quickly hid in an adjacent shower and waited. Shortly after, he heard the water shut off. He peeked out and saw two nude men walk out of the shower room giggling. They each grabbed a towel. It was Luther and Monsignor George. He was stunned. As they exited into the locker room snickering, he thought he heard someone say, "Next time we can have a threesome."

He waited until he was sure they left and then took a quick shower. After what he witnessed, it would still be a fitful night's sleep.

The following day, after lunch, Jack was summoned to the rector's office. His mind was racing. *Did they see me?* There's no way they saw me. I'm sure of it. Pretty sure. Maybe they saw me. What do I say?

"The Monsignor will see you now."

Jack walked in.

"Thank you for reporting Mr. McCreesh. Take a seat. I'll get right to the point." Jack's heart sank. "I am quite disturbed by your conduct. You were out of place."

Jack's eyes darted around the room. *How did they see me? I wasn't out of place. You were the one out of place.*

"I'm sorry," he stammered. It was all he could muster.

"You should be sorry. When we have a guest speaker here to provide us helpful insight into current, difficult issues, hostile questioning is inappropriate and uncalled for."

Jack breathed a huge sigh of relief. Thank God it wasn't about the spying, not that he was spying. He simply stumbled upon the scene. He took another deep breath and gained his composure.

"I was just trying to clarify church teaching."

"You are a seminarian, basically clueless, and you decide to question one of our most prominent clerics, a top-selling author no less, in a disrespectful way like -"

"I don't think I was disrespectful, I -"

"I'm not interested in what you think. Shut up and listen. The Archbishop was aghast at your impudence. We have our eye on you, Mr. McCreesh. If you expect to graduate this seminary, you'd better learn to modify your rigid orthodoxy. That is not where the church is headed."

"Yes, Monsignor, I will try and be more broadminded. Is that all Monsignor?"

"Yes, you're excused. Remember what I said."

As he exited, he could not stop thinking about the shower scene. It was all so bizarre.

A few minutes later, Jack was talking to his two buddies.

"Jakob, you were right about Luther. I saw him coming out of the shower last night with the rector, Monsignor George."

"You what? The rector?" Seth said.

"It does not surprise me in the least," said Jakob. "Luther is one of them and obviously so is the rector."

"I went to take a shower in the gym late at night and I saw them walking out of the shower stall together, but they didn't see me."

Seth said, "So what can we do? This is outrageous!"

"We need to be careful, Seth. There may be something we can do but we have to proceed cautiously. There's a gay network in the priesthood, and if we report it to the wrong person it will have no effect, except to get us crushed. We need to be clever about this and do what we have to do to get Holy Orders. Then we can fight as ordained priests."

"Wow, Jack. I knew there was a problem," Seth said, "but I didn't think it was a network."

"The church needs a new breed of priests," Jack said. "Warriors who are willing to put it all out there and fight, fight and die if necessary. Are you guys with me?"

"One hundred percent," Jakob said. "That's why I'm here."

"Excellent. What about you, Seth? Are you onboard?"

"Aye, aye. Count me in, Doc."

Seth Abrams was barely five feet seven. After arriving at the seminary, he was disappointed there was no weight room, but he stayed strong with strength training exercises - push-ups and pull-ups. In high school, Seth had been an all-scholastic wrestler, wrestling at 132 pounds. He had gained another 20 since then and studied martial arts in the Marines, attaining brown belt ranking. Since he was laid-back and reserved, some underestimated his abilities.

It was a Tuesday evening; Seth heard a knock on the door and answered. Luther came in with two underlings who stood behind him grinning.

"We have a proposition for you soldier boy, like an offer you can't refuse. And if you resist, we will report you, and say you made advances towards us. Three against one."

Seth hated when someone called him a soldier, especially a "soldier boy." Marines were not soldiers. Soldiers were Army. Luther was despicable.

"You got the wrong boy. I think you'd better get the 'F' out of here."

"No, we're not leaving. It's not going to be that easy."

Seth took a second to ponder. Three against one, he knew he would have to be proactive to have a chance. Be aggressive. Use the element of surprise. He warned him again. "Get out of my room. If you take one step forward, I'll consider it an act of aggression."

Luther stepped forward.

Seth dropped him with a right cross squarely on the jaw. Another man stepped forward and he was flipped to the floor with a judo move. Seth used the attacker's momentum, pulling him forward and tripping him, causing him to hit his head on the desk. The third man ran off. Judging Luther as the biggest threat remaining, he pounced on him while he was getting up and punched him two more times in the face. Seeing the fighting skills of the Marine, the tripped man got up and ran out too. Seth then dragged Luther out into the hallway and before shutting and locking the door said, "Don't come back. Next time it will be worse."

Chapter 18

It was Friday morning and Luther was on the phone with Monsignor George. "You need to do something. That flipping Marine gave me a black eye!"

"He did? That's outrageous. What happened?"

"I went to his room to see if he was up for some adult fun, but then he cold-cocked me for no reason. I think he's a homophobe."

"So it was unprovoked?"

"Yeah, I was trying to confirm he was straight. I was hoping he wasn't, but he didn't have to slam me just for flirting with him."

"I have a busy day scheduled," the Monsignor said. "I'll talk to him on Monday, but I can tell you now, his days at this seminary are numbered. I will not tolerate this kind of behavior."

Father Ahmed Keita was on a roll. Three times a week, Jack looked forward to his afternoon lecture. He was like a beacon of light in a modern liberal seminary.

"Your goal as a priest is to lead your flock to Heaven. If you leave the seminary, your goal as a father is to lead your family to Heaven, perhaps via Purgatory. Take time to ponder the afterlife, then never stop pondering it. During your priesthood, keep it in the forefront of your minds. The catechism defines Heaven as 'the state of supreme and definitive happiness.' Isn't that worth thinking about?

"Conversely, examine what Jesus and the saints said about Hell. Read what the children at Fatima experienced. There is so much information. Investigate for yourselves. As priests, we are required to accept the teachings of the church, teachings that represent truth, although now it is more in vogue for clerics to modify and splice the faith, a slippery slope, a slope that can slide you into the depths of darkness, forever. Your souls know the truth. Your hearts just need to be open. Ask the Holy Spirit for guidance.

"Sometimes I hear people say, 'I don't believe in Hell,' even priests. It's weak, so weak, distressing. But have they investigated it? Have they spent hours pondering it? It's the most important question we face - the question of our eternity. Most spend very little time thinking about it, and if they do, they quickly dismiss it. They find it unpleasant, so they dispose of it by saying they don't believe. But now is the time to think and face reality, the reality of Hell for eternity, and take appropriate steps to save your soul and the souls of those in your care.

"Hell is bewildering, but it's clearly a place of horror. I cringe when I contemplate the visions that have been reported. Unspeakable terror. How could God do this to anyone? But then you see the way God is arrogantly abused and trampled upon, even by the church, and it becomes more plausible.

"The church does not take a position on who is in Hell. The church confirms souls in Heaven, after extensive research and two bona fide miracles, the church will proclaim someone as being in Heaven with God, a saint, but the church does not proclaim souls as damned. Much about Hell is unknown. There is even conflicting information.

"On one hand, Sister Faustina, who wrote a famous diary about her visions and conversations with Jesus, seemed to indicate after our death we will have one final chance to turn to God, and that only those who choose not to are damned. Of course, her diary is considered 'private revelation' and not a doctrine of faith, but it does provide a degree optimism, and it could still mean a long time in Purgatory for some, perhaps extremely long.

"On the other hand, when I was a child growing up in Africa, I was taught if you died with mortal sin on your soul you'd go straight to Hell, and that missing mass on Sunday was a mortal sin. Applying that standard most Catholics are damned. The catechism characterizes missing mass as a grave sin. So do I think if someone misses one mass and dies, they go to Hell? It doesn't matter what I think. God's justice will be perfect. I would simply tell you this - instruct your people to go to mass. Teach them it's a grave sin not to fulfill their Sunday obligation - telling them anything less is a travesty and a mortal sin for a priest.

"Then there are others who have spoken of different layers of Purgatory, the very lowest level only slightly better than Hell, except there's one huge difference - those in Purgatory eventually get out.

"There are many books about what suffering souls have allegedly communicated from the netherworld. There is a museum in Rome which has remarkable items that were provided as a result of visits by souls in Purgatory, like palm prints burned on furniture and clothing. It's a small museum but a most interesting place. I strongly suggest you visit if you're ever in Rome. And teach your flock to pray and have masses said for these souls. We are the only ones who can help them. So many have been forgotten, and yet the church is silent.

"Ultimately, we are all sinners, but we need to put up the best fight possible. Go to Mass, go to Confession, avoid serious sin, and strive to do better every day. Fight against abortion and do it forcefully! The idea of Hell is terrifying, but our good deeds will be factored in as well. So while you are trying to avoid sin, remember to help others. It will elevate the quality of your life.

"In the end, many will refuse to believe. I direct you to the story of the beggar Lazarus and the rich man in the Book of Luke, Chapter 16. The rich man, who was on the wrong side of the chasm in the afterlife, in a place of torment, wanted Lazarus sent to warn his brothers on Earth. He was told it would not do any good because they still would not believe. How true it is today. Evidence is all around us, yet many, if not most, still refuse to believe."

Jack approached after the lecture and asked for a private meeting. He needed to talk to someone he trusted. Perhaps this devoted priest could help him. He was given an appointment for the following Tuesday.

It was Friday night and there was an event scheduled, "Pizza with the Priests." Three diocesan priests were booked to have pizza with the seminarians and offer guidance and support. Jack and his buddies were looking forward to some real pizza and a change from the cafeteria fare. It was to be an informal event and a quarter keg of beer had been ordered.

The men were all seated in their typical cliques when three priests came bounding in. One of them, who had spiked, floppy blonde hair, was carrying a fifth of peppermint schnapps. After putting the bottle down, he said, "I'm father Axel, you can just call me Axel." The three priests were all dressed in jeans and tight t-shirts. The mean girls' group seemed to warm right up to them, Jack and his friends not so much. They were loud and already seemed drunk.

Axel put a game box on the table. "Anybody up for playing *Dirt and Punishment*? It's the hottest new adult board game. There are even hands-on activities." Luther picked up the box and started smiling at his crew. "This looks interesting, very interesting."

"Not until later," Axel said. "First let's eat, drink, and be merry. The pizza guy is outside. After we eat, we can play beer pong and do shots to loosen up. You need to be buzzed to play *Dirt and Punishment*. We don't want any dull boys." One of the other priests said, "Yeah, we like naughty boys." Half the group roared.

Jack and his friends were not amused. They decided they would have some pizza and go upstairs to the lounge and watch a game. Just as they were finishing up the pizza, Axel, who kept pouring shots for himself and his buddies, said, "What we really need for this pizza is sausage, some Polish sausage." He glared over at Jakob and laughed, so did several others. The sexual innuendo and crude talk were really getting to Jakob, but he simply sat stone-faced.

Everyone was almost done eating. Luther got up to make an announcement. "Father Axel has given me a DVD to play. As the priests are here to offer guidance and direction, they have decided to give us some insight into human sexuality." He was grinning ear to ear as he loaded the DVD attached to the 60-inch flat-screen. A moment later, a hard-core, gay-porn movie was playing.

Jakob immediately stood up, went over to the player, and ejected the DVD. He held it up in front of everyone with a look of contempt and snapped it in half. Father Axel's face turned crimson. He faced off with Jakob. "How dare you destroy my property!"

Jakob stood motionless. He was an intimidating figure, not so much because of his size. His physique was considerable but not exceptional. It was the glare in his clear dark blue eyes. They were flashing fire. Jakob held the broken DVD up to Axel's face.

"This diabolical DVD is not your property. It is the property of Lucifer. It is my duty as a Catholic seminarian to destroy it. It was my pleasure to crush the head of the snake. Maybe I should take a look at that juvenile board game. Perhaps it is also the property of Satan."

Luther grabbed the game, "Screw you. If you don't want to play, you don't have to. Just get out and let us have our fun."

Jakob looked like he was in a trance. Jack thought he might explode into a rage. He went over and said, "Come on, pal. They aren't worth it."

Seth was also calming him down. He didn't want another altercation. Luther had been walking around with a black eye, and Seth expected to be questioned. He put his arm around Jakob. "Come on, Jack is right. Let's go."

Jakob seemed to snap out of it. "Yes, you are right. We do not belong here."

After they left, Axel said, "If anyone wants to powder their nose meet me in the lavatory."

Five minutes later, one priest and two seminarians came out with white residue around their nostrils. *Dirt and Punishment* was placed on the table and the fun began. The drinks would flow and there would be two more trips to the bathroom for nose powdering.

The group of traditional seminarians went to the lounge and looked for a game to watch. Jack said, "I think you broke Father Axel's heart when you smashed his DVD, Jakob." They all laughed. It was maddening, but they were going to stick together. Jack got a text from his Mom asking if she could call. He agreed and stepped out into the hallway.

"Hi, Jack, I just wanted to check-in."

"I'm glad you did, Mom. You were right about everything as usual, but we're okay. A small group of us is sticking together. We're going to stand strong and provide opposition."

"Yes, exactly, Jack. God needs brave seminarians. I am so proud of you, son."

"Thanks, Mom. It's a network like you described. I'm almost paranoid to talk about it over the phone. It's like an indoctrination. I'm trying to lay low, but I did argue some. I'm learning to be more discreet." Jack laughed and continued. "I'm not going to tell my professors I'm skeptical of climate change. They might throw me out for that, although it has nothing to do with the seminary. Groupthink is in full force here.

"And I was looking at that book you told me about, *The Population Bomb*. I can't believe that guy floated the idea of sterilizing the populous through the water supply. That is straight-up evil. And he was wrong about everything. We were supposed to have run out of everything by now, mass starvation, societal upheaval. And there are still people writing favorable reviews on Amazon, even though it was written in the 1960s. Talk about Kool-Aid! I can't believe the book was a top seller."

"Yes, Jack. Truth never matters to these people. You can't let facts get in the way of your twisted agenda. This guy is still considered an expert, and a tenured college professor at Stanford even though everything he wrote turned out to be nonsense."

"And who is the other guy who made the movie saying the ice caps would be melted by now and that our country would not be using fossil fuels by 2015?"

"That was Al Gore and the movie was *An Inconvenient Truth*," Mollie said. "All the predictions he made were phony, but the tens of millions of dollars he made, and the three houses he owns, are real. You see, Jack, fear sells. People love the terror of it. 'The sky is falling' is a great story, and the media is 100 percent behind it. Anyone who steps out of line, God forbid they should work on a college campus, will be crushed, and few would dare come to their aid. But there have been so many books with erroneous predictions over the years it's astounding, yet they get away with it, even prosper, but most don't look back or remember. It's all about today's headlines. And the media owns the narrative.

"There are a fair number of articulate scientists who will counter climate change, but they won't get much media attention. It's interesting how the climate alarmists changed the name from 'global warming' when it became clear the Earth was not warming. Changing it to 'climate change' was rather brilliant, this way they're always right because it's been changing since day one." Mollie chuckled. "I'm going to tell you something, Jack, but maybe you shouldn't repeat this. It's controversial, to say the least. There are some brilliant scientists, like Dr. Patrick Moore, who wrote *Confessions of a Greenpeace Dropout*, who say carbon is good for the environment, and that we need more. He said, 'carbon is the basis of all life on Earth.' Very interesting, but not alarming, so few will buy his book. Putting people in a panic is what sells. But even the climate change chicken littles admit spending trillions might only reduce carbon emissions one percent. And that's good because we actually need more." Mollie laughed again. "Don't worry, Jack. God is in charge."

God is in charge. I gotta' remember that. He would have a good night's sleep.

Father Axel was feeling high as the heavens when he got behind the wheel. His passengers, the two other priests, were also feeling no pain. It was 1:30 a.m., late but nothing crazy. They were blasting AC/DC's *Highway to Hell*, when Axel failed to negotiate the curve on the winding two-lane highway, crashing into a garage attached to an occupied residence. It all happened so fast. The car was totaled.

All would survive, but one of the passengers would be hospitalized. Police would later find two empty plastic packets with white residue in the center consul.

Monday morning Seth was called to the rector's office.

"Sit down, Mr. Abrams. We have a serious situation to discuss. It has come to my attention you assaulted a fellow seminarian. You are being suspended from the seminary pending further investigation."

"You are suspending me before you even ask for my side of the story?"

"I saw the black eye on the seminarian, and he has provided a written statement."

"And you are not interested in my version," Seth said.

"Not really."

"I see, but you don't need to suspend me."

"Yes, I do, and I am," said Monsignor George.

"No, what I mean is don't bother. As of this moment, I'm officially resigning. I'm disgusted with what I've seen here. I can't serve under this kind of leadership. It's revolting. You are a disgrace to the priesthood, a wretched human being."

The Monsignor stiffened in his deluxe desk chair and turned red as Seth continued. "But you should be more careful about getting on a Marine's bad side. We don't surrender without a fight."

"How dare you speak to me like that! Is that a threat? What's that supposed to mean?"

"It can mean whatever you want it to mean."

"You are in no position to threaten me, Mr. Abrams, and you can forget about appealing to the bishop," the Monsignor said. "I can assure you it won't do you any good."

Seth grinned, "Ahh, that's not really what I had in mind. As you know, Monsignor, I have been trained in the art of warfare. I anticipated this and have prepared countermeasures, but unlike some foolish politicians, I know better than to reveal my tactics. Imagine it as an artillery bombardment. However, there will be no fox hole for you to crawl into."

"How dare you! Get out of my office and be off this property within one hour! I'll have security ensure your prompt departure."

"Maybe we can meet in the gym shower for a threesome first."

"What? What are you talking about? Get out! Get out now!"

Monsignor George called his secretary. "See if Archbishop Cesare is available for a phone call. It's urgent I speak with him."

Jack and Jakob walked in while Seth was packing. "I'm leaving boys. The Monsignor was getting ready to expel me, so I saved him the trouble. I have no regrets and the highlight of my seminary experience was smashing Luther." Seth smiled and continued. "Do not despair men. I will continue to fight. I'm going to look for a more orthodox religious order, maybe as a missionary priest, overseas in a third world country. I always felt that's where God was calling me."

"That is the right attitude," Jakob said. "We must go wherever God leads us. I am going to try and make it through this seminary, but perhaps God has other plans. Either way, I'll never yield or moderate. This fight will only end when I am dead and buried, but I am going to miss having you as a brother."

"Me too," said Jack. "We're both going to miss you, Seth, but I understand."

"Thanks, guys. I'm not worried," Seth chuckled. "It's the good Monsignor that should be worried."

"Hello, Paul. What is it now?"

"Thank goodness I got you, Louie. We had a couple of incidents here recently. I had to dismiss a seminarian. There may be problems."

"Why would there be problems?"

"He's a former Marine, kind of intimidating."

"What's he going to do, storm the seminary? Don't worry, Paul. These guys are all filled with bravado when they're being dismissed, but inevitably they fade into the sunset."

"I hope you're right, but there's something else. A priest who visited here over the weekend totaled his car, hit a house, and was apparently very drunk. The police also found drug paraphernalia. You'll probably be hearing more about it."

"His bishop already contacted me. I called the chief of police and took care of it. You have to move quickly on these matters before the paperwork starts to advance through the system. The chief owes me since I got his nephew into Seton Hall. He never would have been accepted. I even made sure he got extra scholarship money. Not only that but last year I got his son a job as a janitor at

St. Pete's. The kid is a drunk. I told him to make sure the kid at least shows up and no one will bother him."

The archbishop put his feet up on the desk. "Father Axel has been a problem. This is the second drunk driving incident I got him out of. I told him next time he's going to have to do rehab, and I might even let the police prosecute."

"I'm glad you're the archbishop, Louie. You do a great job smoothing things."

"You got to have your priorities straight if you want to do this job. I make it a point to have influence with all the major police departments in the areas under my purview, but you don't want to go to the till too many times or you end up indebted to them and no longer have the upper hand."

Chapter 19

Riding to the ski resort on the school bus, Father Kenneth was feeling quite pleased with his ski trip. The bus was full and all his favorite male students, mostly sophomores, had signed up. By using the parish youth group fund and additional monies from the high school's activities account, he had been able to provide a ski package, including a hotel, at a very attractive rate. He had also negotiated effectively with the ski resort and the hotel chain as it was still early in the season. For many students, the deal was just too good to pass up.

Father Kenneth, who was a good skier, had promoted his trip on Facebook and had already promised one boy, Freddie, private lessons. Freddie, who loved to watch YouTube videos of UFOs and extra-terrestrials, was a bit shy and awkward and had only been coaxed into going after Father offered to pay for his trip and help him with beginner lessons.

Arriving at the hotel late on Friday afternoon, Father unpacked a bottle of brandy and put it on the dresser. Another bottle was left in his luggage. He had plans to take Freddie and three of his friends to the Friendly's Restaurant adjacent to the hotel. In twenty minutes, he would be meeting them in the lobby. A double shot of brandy was poured into a hotel water glass. He drank it right down. His anxiety began to lift. He had another and felt emboldened. Taking a moment, he straightened up the room and hid the bottle in a dresser drawer.

Walking to meet the boys, who would be dining as his guest, Father Kenneth was feeling buzzed and enjoying the added bounce in his step as he strutted off the elevator. Young men were delightful company and he would keep the conversation light and friendly. There would be no risqué or lewd suggestions, no matter how tempting. It was too risky in a group situation. Father saw them standing in the lobby. "Are you guys hungry? Ready for some Friendly's hamburgers? Maybe a little ice cream for dessert?" They were all smiles as they walked with him through the parking lot. They could already smell the meat sizzling.

At dinner, Father asked each of the boys if they had a girlfriend. He was especially interested in Freddie's response and was happy to learn he didn't, and that he felt awkward around girls.

After the waitress brought the check, Father invited the boys back to his room for a movie, a pay-per-view. They could pick any movie they wanted. There were no takers. Arriving back to his room feeling frustrated, he poured another drink and stared at the ceiling. He was really hoping to have company tonight. That's how he'd envisioned the trip, hanging out with the students. The rejection hurt, especially after the great trip he had arranged. He lit a cigar and stepped out onto the patio. It was cold but not bitter and the chilly wind felt good. He looked towards Friendly's and blew a lonely cloud of smoke, then watched as the breeze took it away. The plan was to drink until he passed out.

After falling and knocking over the lamp, the priest decided it was time for bed, but just one more thing. He went to Freddie's Facebook page and was enthralled by the photos. He couldn't resist messaging him. *Love you, Freddie.*

Seth was staying with his parents in Northern New Jersey. He started surfing the internet. He found a story on Channel 17's news site. It was about a bishop's extravagant remodeling plans and his henchmen guards. This reporter obviously had good instincts. Chuck Foreman. What a great name for a reporter, sounds like a fighter. I have a feeling Chuck has more interest in church affairs than the average newsman. I think I'll give old Chuckie a call and tell him what's up. Winning the people's hearts and minds, that's what I learned in the USMC.

Father Kenneth woke up feeling groggy and thirsty, cottonmouth. He was supposed to meet Freddie at 10:00 a.m. on the slopes to give him a few tips. When he looked at the alarm clock, he realized he had overslept but would make it on time if he hurried. He took a quick look at the pay-per-view selection and found a movie Freddie would like. A speedy shower, a stop at the hotel's continental breakfast, and then off to the slopes to meet Freddie. He was excited when he saw him outside the rental shop. As light snow fell, they went in and got their gear.

As Father was helping Freddie, he took the opportunity to touch him in any innocent way he could, like when he was helping him put on his skis. He even brushed some snow off of Freddie's hair. Freddie was totally unaware of Father's true thoughts and feelings. Knowing about Freddie's love of UFOs and all things extraterrestrial, Father proposed they watch *Men in Black* later that evening. Freddie agreed.

They went down the beginners' slope together a few times, and Freddie did better each time, really getting the hang of it, but when the other boys came Father was feeling like he needed to eat and maybe have a beer to take the edge off. He told Freddie he would check on him later and went in to eat lunch. The beer with lunch worked so well he decided to take another back to the room. The combination of the fresh air from the slopes and alcohol had made him drowsy; he nodded off for two hours.

Upon awakening, he decided to go out to the slopes and look for the boys. After making several runs, first on the beginners' slope and then the intermediate, the priest was frustrated he saw no signs of anyone. It was almost 4:00 p.m. and he was getting tired, enough skiing for the day. He went back to the room and had more brandy. He texted Freddie. After thirty minutes there was no response. He decided to go out and look around, ultimately finding the gang at the pool. He thought about getting his bathing suit, but the group was breaking up.

"Hey, Freddie, why didn't you answer my text?"

"I was swimming, Father. I left my phone in the room, but I really want to watch the movie later. What time should I come by?"

"Come at six. I'll grab some snacks, and you can order whatever you want from room service."

"Okay, thanks. I always wanted to see that movie. I've read about the men in black. It's so cool."

It was 6:15. After taking a shower, Father was relaxing with a drink while waiting for a knock on the door. He got a text instead.

I'm not coming. We went roller skating. Took an Uber. Thanks anyway.

Father Kenneth was crushed. Stood up. Another night alone on his awesome ski trip. He was going to text something back, something nasty, but he knew it was a bad idea, so he just texted, *Okay. Maybe next time.*

He reached for the bottle and was glad he had brought an extra one. He really didn't think he was going to need it, but it was turning out he needed it more than ever. Opening the fifth, he poured a full glass and was on a mission to anesthetize himself. He looked for a movie to watch but nothing interested him. He noticed *Stand by Me* in the Red Box machine earlier. He loved the movie but had watched it incessantly over the years. He was tiring of it.

A few hours later, Father was flipping through the channels, completely hammered. It felt good to be in a semiconscious state. Yet, the loneliness was still taunting him. It was 10:00 p.m. Maybe the boys are back from roller skating. He texted Freddie.

Want to get pizza?

He waited. There was no response. He banged his glass on the table. Then, excitedly, he remembered he had the list of names and room numbers. He has to be in his room. He picked up the folder. Ah yes, there it is, room 404. He decided to pay a visit.

When Father banged on the door, Freddie was in the room with three of his friends watching a movie. As one of the boys opened the door, his eyes widened. Father Kenneth was hunching over and looked bloated. There were snack food crumbs all over his wrinkled maroon sweater.

Father was slurring his words, "Where's Freddie?"

"He's right here."

Freddie paused the movie and got up. "What do you want, Father?" He took a moment and sized him up. "I think you're drunk. I'd say plastered." The other boys laughed.

Father said. "Why didn't you answer my text? We could get a pizza."

"I was watching the movie," Freddie said, "and we ate at the roller rink. Maybe you should go back to your room and lay down, Father."

"What movie are you guys watching?"

"Stop shouting, we can hear you, Father," Freddie said. "We're watching *Men in Black*. It's really good. Maybe you should call it a night, Father."

"But you were supposed to watch that *with me*, Freddie," Father said whimpering.

"Maybe another time," Freddie said. It was becoming more obvious the priest was not only drunk - he was incoherent. The boys were still finding it amusing but it was getting weird, creepy even. "Please leave now, Father."

"I want a hug first."

Another boy said, "Father, leave now or we're calling security."

The priest went over to a small table and sat down. He began babbling as an aroma of stale booze filled the room. "I want to watch a movie. It was my idea. Let's get a pizza. Freddie, I want a hug. Do you guys want a pizza? Can I watch the movie? It was my idea."

A call was placed to security. Within a few moments, two husky security guards arrived.

"Come on, Father. We want to get you safely to bed, time for bed."

"I'm not leaving until Freddie gives me a hug."

"This is your last chance. Either you get up or we'll drag you out."

The priest folded his arms, "All I want is one hug."

The guards instantly scooped him up and removed him. Father was dragged to his room and placed on the king-size bed. He immediately passed out fully clothed, sneakers and all. The boys simply shrugged it off and went back to the movie.

The next day, Father woke up on the bed, still clothed, with a hangover and blurry images of being escorted out of Freddie's room by security - he knew it was bad. The shame and anxiety were overwhelming, but he barely remembered. He tried not to think about it. When he saw the boys on the bus, he simply nodded and took a seat down front. Thankfully, it was a short ride home where he would take Tylenol and rest up. He was scheduled to do the 5:00 p.m. Sunday mass. It would be a quick one tonight.

Monday afternoon the cameramen gave the signal and Chuck Foreman started.

"We have an exclusive story tonight you will only hear on Action News 17. A man who resigned from Good Shepard Seminary is telling us he was propositioned by another seminarian who he ended up assaulting. He claims he punched the man because he would not leave his room after he rejected an unsavory offer. He alleges the rector of the seminary is sympathetic to the men with same-sex attraction and that the rector was seen coming out of a shower late at night with a seminarian. We have not been able to speak directly with the witness, and we have no hard evidence of what happened in that shower, but it certainly gives the appearance of impropriety. In addition, he has been telling us about a 'Pizza with the Priests' event at the rectory where a gay porn DVD was presented as sex education and a vulgar X-rated board game was promoted by the priests. We will have the exclusive interview with the seminarian, Seth Abrams, in one hour on Action News at 6."

The next day Jack was walking across the campus and looking forward to meeting with Father Keita. So much around him appeared wicked. He hoped by speaking to him he could gain insight, or maybe survival skills. He knocked and walked into the small office. It was tidy with and simple with a modest wooden bookshelf.

"Good morning, Father. Thank you for meeting with me."

"Of course, young man. What can I do for you?"

"Your lectures have been helping me to keep my sanity, Father, but you're the only one. The other professors seem like they're trying to undermine the faith. It makes no sense."

"Yes, my son. I understand. Do not be afraid. You're doing better than you think. Regretfully, I am something of an outlier at this seminary. My days here are numbered. Since the day I got here, I've been in conflict with the rector. He does not like my orthodoxy. When they get rid of me, there won't be anyone left who is preaching the truth. They are preaching lies. You need to maintain your orthodoxy in spite of their attempts at indoctrination. It will take toughness and tactfulness, but remember, you are not alone. Ask the Holy Spirit to guide you and always remember, God sees your struggles."

"Thank you, Father, but the watered-down faith is only part of the problem. There seems to be a gay network in the seminary like it's the preferred lifestyle. We already lost one faithful seminarian to it. How can this be?"

"I could talk to you about this at length, Mr. McCreesh, but the quick answer is the smoke of Satan has entered the church. Remember, Jesus called the Devil the prince of this world, so don't get discouraged. As long as we are on the Earth we're going to struggle.

"As far as the gay undercurrent, yes it exists. Honestly, as a young man, growing up in Africa, I went through a period where I struggled with same-sex attraction. Fortunately, I met a good and holy priest who taught me about spiritual warfare. I was able to defeat it. Please understand, Mr. McCreesh, I am sympathetic to anyone who struggles with sin, it's our nature, but I'm not going to condone or endorse it.

"A priest stands in the place of Christ. If a man wants to promote a same-sex lifestyle, organizations exist where they can sponsor their ideas, but they do not belong in the

Catholic Church operating as subversives. It's dishonest. If a man can't accept the teaching authority of Christ, then why would they come here? Why would they give their lives to something they don't believe in? Is their entire mission to undermine Jesus Christ and His teaching? If that is the case, there needs to be opposition – relentless, determined opposition. But be judicious, sometimes it will best to remain silent until you get the permanent mark of a priest on your soul. Have courage, Mr. McCreesh. When God is for you, who can be against you?"

"Agreed," Jack said. "Speaking to you has been most helpful. Thank you, Father."

"You are welcome, young man. Always remember, we have our Lord's assurance, the gates of Hell shall not prevail."

In the meantime, across campus, Archbishop Cesare was arriving on the property in a chauffeured limousine. He was meeting with Monsignor George to discuss recent events, especially this pesky reporter from Channel 17.

"Good afternoon, Paul."

"Thank you for coming, Louie. Please, have a seat. Can I get you anything?"

"No thank you, Paul. Let's just get right to it. What do you need?"

"I need your help," the rector said. "This is a nightmare all because of that infernal Marine. This story is spiraling out of control. Did you see him on the news last night? It was shameful. Maybe your public relations people can help squash this."

"We're already on it," the Archbishop said. "When there's a sex scandal it affects all of us. I've been getting tons of angry emails, even had to take my Facebook page down. That Marine really dropped a bomb on us. I can't believe he called Chuck Foreman, of all people, but don't worry, Paul. It will pass. These scandals hit the news and then they're gone in a few days. Just tighten things up around here. Try and work with the straight men. It's better if you can operate more covertly. Discretion makes us more effective."

"I think I can do that, but I'm afraid this story may have long legs. Now Chuck Foreman is calling like a pit-bull nipping at me. He's a dreadful reporter. I wish I never let that jarhead into the seminary. The stress is unbearable, to see our seminary on the news like that. I have two voicemail messages from Chuck. I don't know how to respond."

"Our PR firm suggested we need to control the narrative," Archbishop Cesare said. "Instead of trying to dodge him, it's recommended you invite him here for dinner and present him with the other side of the story. Let him interview seminarians who are more in line with our views. Let him see the facility for himself and see we are devout, dedicated men."

"I think that's a great idea. We have some impressive seminarians. This could work."

"I think it will. These newsmen can be quite gullible."

"What if it doesn't work?"

"Don't worry, Paul. I'll make sure you land on your feet. You have nothing to fear."

"Thanks, Louie, that helps, but I think I'm going to call the doctor and ask him to increase my medication."

"Stop worrying. You'll be fine. Now, I want to meet the seminarians so I can prepare my invitations for the beach house clambake. I will be picking six. I blocked out those dates you asked for. I think you will find the property most pleasant in the off-season as well, less hustle and bustle."

"Thanks, Louie. And I know Leon appreciates it too."

"My pleasure, but before I get back on the road, I have one question for you, Paul."

"Yes, of course, Louie."

"Who was the man in the shower with you?"

They both giggled.

The next morning Jack woke up after having another dream of Foster. This time he thought he was trying to smile. He was determined to keep praying for him and have another mass said. Father Akita's lectures had been helpful in reminding Jack not to forget about his dear friend. Jack decided he would try fasting, maybe that would speed things up for his buddy. He thought about calling his mother to let her know he was the seminarian who had witnessed the shower scene that was being broadcasted but was undecided.

Two days later, Chuck Foreman arrived at the rector's residence for dinner. The meal was not particularly elegant so as not to appear pretentious. Three seminarians had been selected to dine. After coffee and dessert, the rector excused himself.

"Chuck, at this time I am going to leave you with the seminarians. All three were present the evening the 'Pizza with the Priests' event took place. I want them to be able to have an open and earnest conversation with you. You're free to ask them anything. If you find this satisfactory, I bid you a good night"

"Yes, of course, Monsignor George. Thank you."

The seminarians braced themselves. It would all be on camera.

Chuck began. "First, let me ask you. Was there a gay porn video at the 'Pizza with the Priests' party?"

Luther answered, "Yes, a video was played for a few moments, but it was not like it's being portrayed in the press. It was to educate the seminarians about same-sex attraction. They're going to be counseling men and women who are dealing with this. The goal was to get them to broaden their world view and not limit it to heterosexuals. By letting them experience a video like this, they will be better prepared for the priesthood."

"So, it was an educational video that was only played for a few moments?"

"Yes, that's correct. And it was optional. No one was required to watch."

"Interesting, but I must tell you, I still find it somewhat odd. Now moving on, what about the board game, *Dirt and Punishment*? I was looking at it online. It does not seem appropriate for a seminary."

Another seminarian piped in. "It's not for the seminary. We don't play it at the seminary, but we're not living in a bubble. It was brought in by the priests so we can be more in tune with the kinds of things happening in our culture and the activities and mindset of our parishioners, and again, participation was optional."

"So, the game was played by some of the men?"

"Yes, of course, but it's not like anything X-rated happened. It was simply to gain awareness."

"I see," said Chuck, "and what about the seminarian who claims he was propositioned by three men who came to his room? What can you tell me about that?"

"It was all blown out of proportion," Luther said. "The man was a Marine veteran who served in Iraq. I'm pretty sure he had PTSD, like a hair-trigger temper. A few of us stopped by his room and he flipped out on us. We were just trying to be friendly. Clearly, he had issues and was not well suited for the priesthood."

"Was there an altercation?" Just then Chuck thought he saw swollenness around Luther's eye. "Not really. He asked us to leave and that was the end of it. But he was quite rude about it and threatened us."

Chapter 20

Chuck finished his coffee at the Dunkin Donuts and motioned to his cameraman. They jumped in the Action News 17 van and drove two blocks to the seminary. He grabbed his black Action 17 microphone and began filming.

"Tonight we have more on the Holy Shepard Seminary, and 'Pizza with the Priests' story, some have nicknamed 'Porno with the Priests.' Recently I interviewed three of the seminarians who attended and here's what they had to say." He showed film clips of the seminarians rationalizing the events of that evening. Then he came back on.

"You can form your own opinion about their remarks. This is the modern church. However, since that interview more information has come to light about events that transpired that evening, events the rector and the seminarians surely knew about but failed to disclose. Due to an anonymous tip, we have more information tonight that you will only hear on Action News 17.

"We have confirmed that on the night of the pizza party, one of the visiting priests crashed his car into a house after leaving the seminary get-together where a gay porn DVD was presented as sex education and a vulgar X-rated board game was played by seminarians and priests. This reporter met with the homeowner whose house is still damaged. She stated the man had spiked blonde hair and seemed to be under the influence of something. It also appears a police affidavit was prepared, but mysteriously charges were not filed. It looks like this case may have disappeared. Action News was able to obtain a copy of the police report and it indicates the priest, Father Axel Schumer, was operating the vehicle and drug paraphernalia was found in the car. The homeowner we spoke with was appalled the driver, who she did not know was a priest, was not charged. It has also been alleged priests were reportedly acting in a vulgar, crass manner at the party. The rector, Monsignor Paul George, did not respond to phone messages asking for comment."

Jack's parents picked him up to take him to dinner. They were anxious to get the inside scoop and preferred to meet with Jack in person. There were rumors going around about surveillance by the church. They sat down at a nearby family restaurant.

"Mom, it's bad. There's definitely a Lavender Mafia."

"Keep your head down, son. I have been talking to the plumber, Gil Rodgers. He's a member of our parish. I mentioned him to you before."

"Yes, I remember," Jack said. "He used to work for Archbishop Cesare."

"You can't have faith in these people. Gil said, after he was fired, he heard rumors of surveillance at the property. He suspects it played a role in his dismissal, but regardless, he assured me you can't trust him. He heard they spy on people, literally spying with cameras and audio."

"That's crazy, Mom, but I'm not worried. There's a small group of us who are going to try and make the best of our vocations, but first, we have to get ordained."

"Good for you, Jack," Patrick said. "You're a true warrior."

"Thanks, Dad. It means a lot to have your support."

"Of course, Jack," Mollie said. "What could make a parent more proud than having a militant priest for a son, a man who fights for God? Nothing surpasses that in my eyes. Don't worry about us. We're nothing but proud. But we're a little worried about what we're seeing in the news. Are those stories true? Gay porn?"

"Yes, it's true, and my friend Jakob crushed that vile DVD. After it played for thirty seconds, he went right over and snapped it in half. It was great."

"Wow, what's going on in these seminaries?" Mollie said. "And do you believe the story about the rector with the man in the shower, Jack?"

"Yeah, I have good reason to believe it. I'm the one who witnessed it."

"You were?" Mollie said.

"You did?" Patrick said.

"I couldn't sleep, so I took a walk over to the gym showers. I saw them coming out together. Thankfully, they didn't see me. It was late at night."

"I guess we can assume the news station got it right," Mollie said. "You never know with things like this, but it's good to know the truth, however disheartening. Put on the full armor of God, son. You'll need it."

"I'm not worried, Mom. Like a good priest told me, 'If God is for you, who can be against you?' In other words, I'm happy to be on God's team, not the other guy's."

"Yes, I agree," Mollie said. "The other guy is a liar."

"Yeah, sadly, the deceiver is impacting the church on a daily basis," Jack said. "I heard another seminarian is thinking about resigning. He isn't a close friend, more the quiet type, seems like a good man. He's getting disgusted."

"Can't say I blame him," Patrick said.

"Hopefully, he'll stay. Enough about the seminary," Jack said. "How is Beth?"

"She's great, Jack. She finally passed the 225 tests. I guess we forgot to tell you. It was the day before school started, and her teacher, who had watched her trying so hard last semester, coming so close over and over again, let her test the day before school. She passed it twice in one day. She needed to pass it three times, and she passed the final two tests the day before school started. You could see the hand of God. She had been off from school and not even practicing. We were all so happy. Now she's working at the courthouse as a per diem, $250.00 per day. I think if she had graduated earlier, she would have taken that job in Scranton. We're so happy to have her nearby."

"That's great. Tell her I said congratulations. I'll have to send her something."

"That's so thoughtful, Jack," Patrick said. "She appreciated the cash you gave her."

"I left the military with a lot and thought I'd share with my sister. I was raised right."

Mollie smiled, "And I keep bumping into your old girlfriend Nora. She always asks about you."

Jack grinned. "I hope by now she understands the whole celibacy thing, Mom."

Mollie laughed. "Yes, don't worry, son. She has a boyfriend."

Chuck Foreman was a hard-working reporter.

"Tonight we have more news about the Holy Shepard Seminary scandal. Another seminarian, who declined to go on camera, and did not want his name used, confirmed much of what has already been reported and indicated he was at the pizza party where the gay porn video was shown, and a vulgar board game was played. He provided new information and stated the reason the DVD only played briefly, is that a concerned seminarian removed it and destroyed it, to the dismay of some others. Apparently, it almost caused a scuffle. Several of the more traditional seminarians left after the movie incident and before the board game was played. He gave the impression the seminarians are divided into two groups, those who you might describe as modernists, and the traditionalists who want to uphold the tenants of the faith. He also confirmed inappropriate sexual activity but declined to elaborate.

"We are still investigating the drunk driving crash by Father Axel Schumer, who attended the festivities that evening at the rectory. A police report was apparently prepared but charges have not been filed.

"In addition, a former seminarian who we interviewed previously is now telling us about a gay network all throughout the hierarchy of the church. He said they are known as the 'Lavender Mafia.' We expect to have more information from this former seminarian, Seth Abrams, in the next several days. We will continue to follow this story. Check back to Action News for updates. Chuck Foreman, Action News 17 reporting."

This time it was the rector who traveled to Archbishop Cesare's residence. As Monsignor George merged onto the New Jersey turnpike in his black late-model Lexus, he was feeling overwhelmed. There was precipitation, freezing rain. It made him even more anxious. With a sense of dread, he pulled into the mansion parking lot.

After exchanging pleasantries, the archbishop got right to it.

"This is getting a bit out of hand, Paul. The 'Lavender Mafia' remarks and the DWI story have really escalated things. I even got a call from Rome. They want me to do whatever's necessary to put an end to it."

"I don't know who ratted to that reporter about the crash," the rector said. "The insurance adjuster was on the phone with that woman the next day. I was hoping to keep it quiet."

"Someone is leaking to the media," the Archbishop said. "We need to find out who. I'm sending my security team over there tomorrow to interview the seminarians and get to the bottom of it. Trust me, they will plug those leaks better than a master plumber. They can be quite intimidating when the situation calls for it."

"Well, that's only part of the problem. We have to do something about that Marine and the meddlesome reporter, Louie. The stress is unbearable. The medications aren't working. I'm not sleeping well. I'm having nightmares about that Marine yammering on TV. My appetite isn't good. I don't know if I can continue."

"You worry too much, Paul. Don't worry about Chuck Foreman. And that Marine, he crossed the line with that 'Lavender Mafia' comment. We're not just going to sit back and cower, but you are better off letting me handle these two. Just leave it to Louie." The bishop deviously grinned.

"What are you going to do?"

"Uh – I – um – I." The archbishop arched his eyebrows, "Just trust me, they will be dealt with."

Father Paul nodded.

"But regarding the seminary," the archbishop said, "I have an immediate strategy to quiet things that I believe you'll find most satisfactory. I'll appoint a more moderate rector. Someone we can trust but who hasn't been compromised.

"And I have an auxiliary bishop spot open that would be perfect for you. Later, you'll be first in line for an appointment as a diocesan bishop. I've already discussed this scenario with Rome, and they promised to be accommodating. They wanted me to present them with an outline to smooth things, and so I did. Quite clever if I must say so myself."

"Very clever indeed, Louie. I've always dreamed of being a bishop. Wow. I'm getting goosebumps thinking about it. Wait until I tell Leon!"

"Yes, stay positive. I must bid you farewell. I have another meeting shortly, a very important one."

The communications director for the diocese issued the following statement:

After an internal church investigation, it has been determined there was inappropriate behavior at the Good Shepard Seminary when the priests and seminarians met for the annual "Pizza with the Priests" event. While there clearly was unsuitable behavior, there was no evidence of improper physical contact or sexual abuse of any sort.

However, it is critical these priests are held accountable for their actions and the diocese will be employing corrective measures, including sexual harassment training and a thorough review of the Diocesan Code of Conduct.

In addition, it has been determined, that in light of recent events, a change of leadership is appropriate at this time. Reverend John MacCayne has been named as the new rector of the facility, effective immediately.

A few days later, Bishop "Mittens" Rahmney was meeting with Fr. Kenneth.

"You have got to be kidding me. A ski trip, you organized a ski trip for the sophomore class. What were you thinking?"

"It was a good deal."

"A good deal? A good deal for who? You? This is outrageous! I have a letter here from a Mrs. Connors who is the mother of a student, Frederick Connors. I trust you know who I'm talking about."

"Yes, Freddie."

"Oh, I see, Freddie. That's your name for him."

"Yes, I call him Freddie."

The bishop let out a huge sigh. "From now on I don't want you to call students by their first names, it will be mister or miss. Do you understand me?"

"Yes, Your Excellency."

"Now is it true that you invited this boy to come to your room to watch a movie?"

"He wanted to watch *Men in Black*. He has an interest in that sort of thing."

"His interests have nothing to do with it. It is completely inappropriate for you to invite a student to be alone with you in a hotel room, or anywhere for that matter. Do you understand?"

The priest nodded agreement.

"And you're not to be alone with any students ever, and that includes at the school, or in the band room or any room. Are we clear?"

"Yes, Your Excellency."

"And is it true you went to the boy's hotel room completely intoxicated and had to be escorted out by security, and you wanted a hug?"

"I think that's true, but it's kind of foggy. I had too much to drink."

"And I guess you're going to tell me when you texted, *love you Freddie,* you had too much to drink also."

"That would be correct, Your Excellency."

"Listen to me, Father. I can be tolerant of some drinking, and even certain sexual activities if you are able to be discreet, but that does not include sex with minors. I will not tolerate it. If there is another incident get your passport ready because you will be going out of the country."

Reverend John MacCayne arrived at the seminary and made his way to the rector's office.

"Congratulations on your appointment, as auxiliary bishop, Paul."

"Yes, you as well, John. I enjoyed my years here at the seminary. I think you will too. There's a good staff in place and many dedicated professors, so you'll simply need to oversee everything. There's just one thing I wanted to speak to you about."

Just then there was a knock on the door. Monsignor George said, "Come in, Luther. I'm glad you could join us."

He motioned for him to sit down. "I asked Luther to join us, John. Luther is a role model here at the seminary, a natural leader. More than a few of the men look to him for direction and guidance. If we want to employ a certain strategy, Luther is in a position to help us carry it out. The archbishop feels we were getting a little lax around here, and I agree. We need to be more restrained. We need to appear more conventional until this media onslaught dies down. Do you understand what I'm saying, Luther?"

"Yes, absolutely. It seems like a good strategy. Nothing worse than having the media prying into our private lives here at the seminary. Private lives should be permitted to remain private."

"Exactly," said Monsignor George. "So here's where we're at. The archbishop says we are not to bother the straight men and be more reserved. Of course, seminarians may form certain relationships, but caution should be heeded. And the archbishop made one thing very clear. We are not to involve any outsiders. We're to keep it 'in-house.'"

"Okay, got it," said Luther.

"Thank you, Luther. You're excused now."

"You are very welcome, Monsignor."

"Okay, John. I'll be leaving tomorrow for my new assignment as auxiliary bishop. It's all yours starting tomorrow. If you need anything, just call."

Seth always attended the Thursday night, 7:00 p.m. mass. It was usually only a dozen and he was always the last one to leave. He liked to pray quietly for a few minutes while everyone slowly exited. As he neared his car, he saw a man approaching, a scruffy homeless man. "Excuse me, sir, do you have the time?"

As Seth looked down at his watch the bearded man shot him in the temple with a 9 mm pistol equipped with a silencer. He located Seth's leather wallet, pulled out the cash and credit cards, and then tossed it on the ground. The man slowly walked for two blocks. He quietly got in his car and removed his gray beard and tattered cap.

The following morning.

"We have breaking news, a former intern who worked a full summer almost a decade ago at Action News 17 is claiming to have been sexually assaulted at that time by a veteran reporter, Chuck Foreman. The incident allegedly occurred in the newsroom van while they were doing a story about the opening of the campground season. Mr. Foreman is denying any wrongdoing but has been put on leave by the news station. We will continue to follow this story and provide updates as more information becomes available. Joe Herbert, Eyewitness News, reporting."

Chapter 21

Four years later.

"I never thought we'd make it, Jakob, especially after all the drama the first year. Father MacCayne did a good job stabilizing the seminary. Even the "mean girls" behaved. On second thought, I'm not sure they behaved, but at least they were not too obnoxious, more or less stayed to themselves, but I couldn't help but notice some things."

"Yes, they were still up to no good," Jakob said, "but it was best to remain silent. Sometimes it is better not to call a wolf out of the woods, but I was tempted to react. It was a good opportunity for me to work on my patience."

"I think you did great, Jakob. At times, it looked like you were going to boil over and pound Luther."

"Yes, I wanted to kill him, but I prayed and asked God to help me and He did."

The men had done well. In spite of the countless liberal lectures, some of them *so boring*, the boys had supported each other and maintained their orthodoxy by vigorous self-study. They met as a group, an eight o'clock Bible study and reflection every night, except Sunday. The group grew as new like-minded seminarians would be invited. The rector did not object to this quasi-conservative group and even allotted them meeting space. It was like a support group within the seminary, a support group for traditional seminarians who wanted to carry on the tenants of the faith. Seminarians would read and reflect on the scriptures. Everyone was free to speak about any and all issues they were dealing with at the seminary, especially things they were struggling with, particularly the liberalness surrounding them. This group proved to be a powerful form of support and edification for all. Jack led the group. He stressed confidentiality was paramount, and the topics discussed were to stay in the group. He would end every meeting by saying, "What you hear here, stays here." The men would reply, "hear, hear."

Liberal seminarians were not welcome. On one occasion, a liberal seminarian attempted to infiltrate. Jakob instructed him to step outside and had a tactful discussion with him. There would be no further attempts. Jack told Jakob he was the unofficial Sergeant at Arms. He accepted the appointment and relished it.

It was getting near the end of seminary. The men had already been ordained as transitional deacons and could even give homilies. They had been assigned to local parishes and assisted the pastors during the summer. Now they were back at the seminary.

Drug and alcohol counselors are underpaid, but Dusty Rodgers enjoyed her job as a therapist at New Visions Drug and Alcohol Treatment Center. Her first appointment of the day was scheduled for 9:00 a.m. - a chronic heroin addict who was recently released from prison and was now on parole. As she perused his file, she could see he had been through every program available: inpatient rehab, drug court, daily reporting center, intensive outpatient, twelve-step meetings, methadone and suboxone programs, and even the Salvation Army Program. She let out a sigh. *I have no idea how to help this poor man.* She said a quick prayer for inspiration and picked up the phone. "You can send back my niner."

"Come in and sit down," Dusty said. "How are you feeling?"

"I'm okay. At least I didn't start using the first day I walked out of jail. I actually made it to the parole office this time."

"Good for you. That's progress. Now I see you've been to our agency several times before, but I don't believe I've ever worked with you. Is that correct, Fabio?"

"Yeah, I never met you before."

"How do you think I can best help you, Fabio?"

"Honestly, I feel like I'm going to use. That's just being real. I want to try rehab again. I feel like if I don't go inpatient, I'll be going to a different institution, the one with bars on the windows."

"Okay, sounds reasonable. I think we can manage that. We just got our funding from the state. Let me see what I can do. It will take a couple of days to arrange, Fabio, but I want to use our time together today to see if I can gain some insight. I was at a training recently. The instructor had a theory that many, if not most, addicted people have experienced trauma, and instead of focusing on what you've done, like your crimes and errant behaviors, we should be asking you 'what happened to you?' So before we go any further, I want to ask you - have you had any kind of traumatic experiences or did something bad happen to you? Is there something underlying the pain that causes you to keep relapsing despite being offered virtually every program we have available?"

"No, not really. Grew up poor with a single mom, and she drinks a lot but that's about it."

"So nothing traumatic? No physical or sexual abuse?"

Fabio paused and looked up to the right. "No, there was no abuse."

The pause made Dusty suspicious. "Are you sure, Fabio? It's very common, more common than you think. It's nothing to be ashamed of, but if something happened and you don't deal with it, you will probably never get sober."

He shrugged his shoulders. "Nothing happened."

Dusty was not convinced, but, regardless, it was probably best for him to go inpatient. Maybe she could talk to the counselor at the inpatient treatment facility about her suspicions.

"Okay, Fabio. I will arrange for your inpatient. We're having more success sending people out of state, away from their dealers. You'll be going to Delaware. They'll likely be sending a car for you in a few days. I'll let you know."

After he left, Dusty picked up the phone and called the rehab in Delaware, The Care Unit. "I have a frequent flier for you. His name is Fabio Alou, twenty-four years old. Do you have a bed available?"

"Yeah, we're good, and we can pick him up."

"Yes, that would be great. And when he gets there can you see if he will sign a release for me?"

"Jakob, tomorrow we have to go over to the university and hear a speaker. It's that celebrity priest, Harry Roberts. The talk is entitled, 'Be More Manly.'"

"It's insulting."

"What is, Jakob?"

"The title of that talk. 'Be More Manly.' Do I really need some Catholic priest telling me how to be more manly? He is making an assumption, basically questioning my masculinity, and implying my dear father did not already teach me well. It is an insult to me and to my father. I had some time to kill so I watched this celebrity priest on YouTube. If you ask me, he's too clownish and lacking in reverence, too much in love with himself and the camera."

Jack smiled, "Maybe a lack of humility?"

"I would say," Jakob said. "And if you look at his church's web site, he has posted photos on there, publicity photos, headshots like a movie star. It's ridiculous. He is in no position to tell me how to be more manly, but I have a suggestion for him – take down those smirking photos with that sissy boy grin - then maybe I will listen to you.

"He prances around and sprays and spouts like Daffy Duck on crack. They want us to listen to another celebrity priest. Celebrity and priest go together like an ox and a carriage. I am tired of listening to celebrity priests. Bring me a humble holy priest who understands that Christ is the one to be celebrated, not themselves. The whole world is crazy, Jack."

"I tend to agree with you, Jakob. I've heard of this priest. And you crack me up, I didn't know you watched cartoons in Poland, 'Daffy Duck on crack,' that's hysterical."

"After the fall of Communism we started to get more broadcasting," Jakob said, "but I never liked television. I don't worship celebrities. I don't disagree with everything this priest says, but he makes it more about himself and is very critical of Catholics in general. For some reason, these guys always think Protestants are better."

The next day, Jack and Jakob signed out a seminary vehicle, a dark blue Ford Taurus, and took a short drive to the Cardinal Spellman Conference Center, a modern facility with stadium seating for five hundred. It was half full when they arrived ten minutes ahead of time. It was an all-male audience.

Father Harry Roberts came bounding out on stage. He made a hurried sign of the cross and began. "Who brought their Bibles?" He paused and looked out. "I don't see any hands. Pathetic, no one has a Bible. If you knew anything about me, you would know to bring your Bible. If I was speaking in front of a bunch of Protestants, they would have their Bibles. Protestants know their Bible and take it everywhere. Catholics are too lazy and want a priest to spoon-feed them the scriptures. They don't want to do the work. To be a man you must know your Bible. There's an old saying, 'If you want to hide something from a Catholic, put it in the Bible.' You need to start reading your Bibles, that is if you even own one. Ignorance of scripture is ignorance of Christ, and a lot of you are ignorant, not only of scripture but of your faith in general.

"When I speak to Catholics, it's like I'm speaking to a bunch of constipated people. They have that look of discomfort like they're blocked up. When I speak to Protestants, which I do sometimes, they are smiling and filled with joy. They live their faith and are always cheerful. Catholics look depressed. If you really believed in the teachings of the church you would be happy all the time, like the Protestants. If you don't live in Christian joy, you suck as a Catholic. If you come to mass just to avoid going to Hell and don't live with cheerfulness and love, you suck as a Catholic."

Jakob was feeling a tightness in his chest. He could not believe a priest would speak in such a crass way. Growing up in Poland, he had never heard a priest use common vulgar language like this. He imagined going up on stage and punching him in the mouth but could only daydream. It was a coping mechanism.

Father Roberts continued.

"How many of you believe Christ is present in the Eucharist at Mass? How many of you believe in the real presence?" Almost everyone raised their hands.

"Okay, fine. Now, how many of you go to daily mass? And if you're a seminarian don't raise your hand because you have to go. Other than the seminarians, how many of you go to daily mass?"

About ten percent of the crowd raised their hands.

"Ok, I see about thirty hands. Those thirty men who raised their hands are authentic Catholics. The rest of you are frauds, liars! If you truly believed in the real presence you would be at mass every day. So either you don't really believe, or you're too lazy to get off your ass and get to church. Yeah, that means you may have to get up earlier and sacrifice an hour of sleep or go in the evening after working all day, and you'll probably be tired but that is no excuse. If you're not willing to sacrifice sleep or couch time to get to mass, you suck as a Catholic. A real man goes to church and prays for his family.

"Some of you might not like my frankness but somebody needs to tell you the truth. I even have parishioners who write to the bishop to complain about me. What they don't realize is the bishop and I are old friends. He gives me their names. Trust me, I'm not the kind of priest you want to cross. Plus, I've been through extensive training and formation. I'm an official teacher of the faith, a priest, a cleric. They're in no position to criticize me - to the bishop of all people. They're putting their souls in jeopardy and would do well to repent and seek forgiveness."

Father Roberts carried on, often mixing somewhat traditional teaching with jocular, flippant criticism of Catholics. "I hate hearing the Confessions of wimpy Catholics, I hate them." He smirked and used a doofus voice to mockingly imitate a man in the confessional, "I don't really got dat' much to confess Fadda." A handful laughed.

"This is no time to be a wimp. You need to man up. Look at the Muslims. They pray five times a day and are willing to sacrifice their lives. How many of you pray even once a day? And how many are willing to give their lives for the faith? Time to be a man!"

Father continued by talking at length about himself and his exhaustive schedule and boasted how he was able to maintain his prayer life in spite of his crushing itinerary. However, some thought his demeanor and lack of humility suggested a rather weak prayer life, as did his acknowledgment of "anger issues," and threats to hit people.

The priest continued unrelentingly, sometimes hitting on solid teaching but always critical and self-aggrandizing. He finished by plugging his books that "are all available on Amazon."

When it was finally over Jakob asked Jack, "So, what did you think? Was I right?"

"I'd say on balance, yes, but at least he talked about the afterlife and the sacraments."

"And a broken clock is right twice a day," Jakob said. "It is not Christlike. There is too much criticizing. It's uninspiring and out of balance. Plus, he is crass and vulgar."

"Good point," Jack said. "It's good to hear a priest talk about human sexuality, but that joke about turning a woman upside down to avoid mortal sin - that was pathetic. Vulgar as vulgar can be, but he got the laugh he was looking for."

"He is more like a court jester than a pastor," said Jakob. "What I see is a priest who may have been orthodox at one time but is now being swept away in the clamor of his own celebrity. If you watch these celebrity priests, Satan will eventually trip them up. Remember Father Caparelli? He was a great, powerful orthodox preacher who eventually morphed into a celebrity priest and began shaving his head. I thought it was odd a priest would concern himself so much with fashion."

"But some priests shave their heads as part of an order or a sign of devotion or humility," Jack said.

"He clearly wasn't shaving his head as a devout practice," Jakob said, "but to appear more fashionable, maybe even sexier, which seemed odd. Then he started to wear a goatee, a shaved head and a goatee, resembling the popular image of Satan. How interesting. He was always on television, speaking everywhere, selling tons of books and DVDs, and keeping all the proceeds for himself. He violated his vow of poverty by living the high life, including a million-dollar mansion, luxury cars, boats, and anything else you could imagine. Over time, his talks became more prideful. You could see where this was headed. Later, he was accused of using drugs and inappropriate sexual activity with multiple women. In spite of all his denials, the smoke suggested fire. An investigation led to his suspension. Initially, he was defiant and denied everything, but subsequently vanished. Even though he often spoke about spiritual warfare, he foolishly got caught up in his own stardom and became complacent. Lucifer destroyed him. I cannot believe how foolish these clerics can be."

"Yeah, I heard that priest is worth millions, but what good is it?" Jack said.

"Exactly my friend. What does it profit a man to gain the whole world and lose his soul? Every celebrity priest should learn from this example, but few will. It will be interesting to watch the career of Father Harry Roberts. If he does not regain his humility, you can expect a similar outcome. Pride comes before the fall. Satan is a powerful and cunning deceiver but is no match for a humble priest."

Archbishop Cesare was working on assigning the new seminarians who would soon be ordained and was on the phone with the pastor who had mentored Jack during the summer.

"So how did we do? Were you able to make any progress with him?"

"No, not at all," said the pastor. "He would not moderate. He's as stubborn as a mule. Usually, over a three-month period, I'm able to persuade them to temper things, but this one was completely inflexible. I let him give some homilies. He doesn't care if he upsets the parishioners. He has this thing about 'preaching truth,' like there's only one truth."

"Okay, I was afraid that might be the case. Don't worry, Father, you tried. Although it's not the outcome I was hoping for, your input is still most valuable. I will be meeting with Auxiliary Bishop George in a few minutes. We will be working on this."

"Come in Paul, how are you feeling? You look tired."

"I am, but I think the new medication is helping."

"Good, I could use your help with some of the new priest assignments. You probably remember some of these men from your days as rector."

"Yes, of course, Louie."

"I think we only have two or three that are problematic. Let's start with this John McCreesh. Father Boylan told me he is completely rigid. He's a problem, all about tradition and fidelity or some such blather."

"Yes, I remember him. That's just how he was at seminary."

"I have an idea. I'm thinking of putting him at St. Bart's in Newark. There's a vacancy there."

"You mean give him his own parish right out of the gate? Don't you think that's a bit much? And isn't St. Bart's a bad area? That's the Springfield-Belmont neighborhood, isn't it?"

"Yes, it's 'the hood.' It's been a long time since we assigned a white priest to that parish. I thought it might be interesting to see how our Lilly-white sailor boy would do there?"

"Wow, Louie, a man right out of seminary to St. Bart's? I don't know, Louie, it almost seems dangerous."

"Yes, that's the point. I think Mr. McCreesh might not last long there. If he survives the gangs, he will probably quit the priesthood within six months. I say good riddance."

Fabio left the drug and alcohol agency and walked three miles to his mother's house. She wasn't happy to see him. The management of the public housing complex did not allow convicted felons but would overlook a close family member visiting for a couple of days. She gave him permission to stay until he went to rehab, but he had to promise not to steal anything, especially her television, which was the only thing of value. In spite of the promise, his mother still hid her purse and locked the bedroom door.

Fabio found it all so depressing. After nine months in jail, his own mother rejected him. He was simply a burden to her. As he sat at the kitchen table listening to his mother, who was drinking 16-ounce cans of Budweiser and chain-smoking cigarettes, chronicling all the grief he had caused her, he could feel his desire to use intensifying. He knew his mother would not give him any money. He thought about grabbing the television but was not willing to stoop that low. No, there were other ways to get money. If a young man was willing to compromise his morals, or what was left of them, the mean streets of Newark provided ways to make quick money. *Screw it, I'm going to rehab in a couple of days anyway, might as well get high.*

"Hey, Moms, I'm thinking about going to an NA meeting. Can you give me two dollars for the subway?"

"Okay, two dollars, since it's for a meeting, but that's all."

"Thanks, Moms, and if I don't come back tonight, don't worry. It probably means I'm hanging out with people from the meeting."

As he wandered out into the murky streets, dimly lit streetlights caused sheets of gray mist to fill the air. A couple could be heard cursing and arguing through an open window. He caught the far-off wail of a siren. There was a musty dank odor of rotting garbage. It was all so depressing. He headed to the subway with his feet dragging and head bowed.

Ten men would be ordained today.

"Most reverend father and holy mother church, we ask that you ordain to the responsibility of the priesthood these ten men who have been found worthy."

The men were soon laying prostrate on the floor. Mollie was sobbing as she watched her son give his life to God. Jack felt conflicted as Archbishop Cesare rubbed his hands with oil but still found the overall service to be a profound spiritual experience. After it was over, a glorious peace covered him and knew he had made the right choice.

His family approached and he was met first by his mother. "I'm so proud of you, Jack. So proud to have a priest in the family."

Father John McCreesh

Chapter 22

Fabio arrived at the rehab higher than a Jedi Starfighter, relieved he had made it safely through his three-day binge and wasn't back in jail. He didn't expect any problems with county parole since Dusty had already cleared the treatment. After going through his intake, Fabio was allowed to sleep and spend a couple of days detoxing before he felt well enough to begin the daily schedule. Two of his old jail buddies were there and he soon settled into a comfortable routine.

It was Wednesday night, the night of the regular NA speaker meeting. A speaker from Narcotics Anonymous would be telling her story. Fabio liked the NA speakers better than AA. He related more to hard drug users. He didn't like alcohol and was repulsed by brandy.

The speaker took to the podium which faced many rows of folding chairs set up in the large gymnasium.

"Hello, family. My name is Dixie Mae, and I'm an addict."

The group responded. "Hi, Dixie Mae."

"It's a great pleasure to be here tonight. Like they say in the rooms, 'you have to give it away to keep it.' I know when I do a speaking commitment like this it's going to ensure another day sober, and it's such a blessing. I just celebrated eight years of being drug-free. For many years, I was an insane addict. I would use anything and everything, but it started and ended with meth. I was in and out of all sorts of facilities including jails, nuthouses, and rehabs, too many to count, for almost twenty years, until a tragic event caused me to take a hard look at my life, but I'll talk more about that later.

"I grew up in the hills of West Virginia. My father was a coal miner. He used to bring home moonshine on Fridays after working in the coal mines all week. Every weekend the clan would gather, and the fiddles and banjos would come out. My dad was a good provider. He was a good man but a mean drunk, and me and my younger brothers knew to stay out of his way as the night wore on. We knew ole' Dad was going to get mighty ornery once he got his fill, but when the grownups started getting drunk, me and my brothers would get ahold of some of that potent moonshine. There was always an ample supply so we would just fill a couple of fruit jars and head out into the woods. From the first drink, I loved the feeling. I did a lot of drinking throughout my teenage years, sometimes moonshine but a lot of beer too.

"I had a decent childhood, but my mother passed when I was sixteen. It devastated me. My mom was my heart. I never felt right after that. Then, a few years later, I got pregnant. My dad was so angry, and he threw me out. So, my boyfriend and me got a place. It went okay for a few years, but then we started fighting more. When my son was five, his father left. I was crushed. First my mom, and now this. I felt completely hopeless. He was the only boyfriend I ever had. I thought we would always be together. In order to deal with the loneliness, I started drinking more. Then I got a new boyfriend. He was so much fun and always had money. By the time I realized he was dealing meth, I was already in love with him and didn't care, probably because I was falling in love with meth at the same time. They both turned out to be bad romances." There was a smattering of laughter.

She went on telling war stories describing car accidents, encounters with law enforcement, job losses, everything going progressively downhill. She took a sip of bottled water and brushed back her hair.

"Eventually, I lost my son to Child Welfare Services when he was eight-years-old. For the next twelve years, I struggled. As I said, I was in and out of so many institutions and even did a long stint in state prison, which may have saved my life, but I was always thinking about my son. Even when I was using, I'd be thinking about him, but for some reason the drugs always overpowered me. I could stay sober for a short time, but then I'd relapse. I realize now I never fully committed to recovery. As it says in the literature, 'half measures availed us nothing.' So, yeah, I never really put the effort in. I would try for a few months, but once I hit a little adversity or maybe just became bored, I'd go and use.

"Then about ten years ago I caught a theft charge and the judge gave me nine to twenty-three months in the county. During this time, my son, Richie, graduated from Navy Corpsman School. I was so proud of him. No one in our family, on either side, had ever done anything like that. It really lifted me up. I had his photos on the walls of my cell. He never gave up on me and would still write. I couldn't believe it, a freaking Navy corpsman. Sometimes I'd look at his photos and just cry. I don't know if you know anything about corpsman, but they're awesome, the work they do. I had done everything wrong, yet I still had this beautiful boy. I felt like maybe God was finally doing something good in my life. It was giving me so much hope. I started to go to a program in the jail. I was absolutely determined to get clean this time.

"Then the Sargent called me to the office one morning. He told me Richie had died in a plane crash with eleven marines. I couldn't believe it. I finally had a glimmer of hope and then it was snuffed out in a heartbeat. All I could do for the next two days was lay in my cell sobbing. I was due to parole in a week and I was planning a major binge. In my mind, it was going to be a suicide mission. I just did not want to live anymore.

"Then I got a card in the mail. It was from my son. I still carry it with me." She pulled the card out of her hoodie. "I want to read it to you. Here's what he wrote. 'I will always love you no matter what, Mom. Keep fighting, don't ever give up, don't ever give up trying, Mom. You can do it. I know you can. Love, Richie.'

"That card did something to me. It was like it flipped a switch in my head. I can't really explain it, but at that moment I decided to live, to take my son's advice and fight back. He also sent me money. I was just the worst mom ever, and now my son was sending me money in jail. My first thought was to take that money and go get a batch of meth, but then I thought about it. I just couldn't do it, dishonor my son's memory. I just could not take that money and buy drugs. So instead, I used the money to get into a sober house, a women's sober house. I got a job waiting tables and then went back to school and got an associate degree. Now I work in the field. I work at a local drug and alcohol agency helping other addicts. I had an opportuning to move out of West Virginia, so I decided to leave that life behind and get a fresh start. Before I left, I even got my teeth fixed." Several in the audience chuckled.

"Life is good today. I love my job and I feel like I'm making a difference. The feeling I get, the satisfaction of helping someone else, well it's better than any drug I ever did. My son Richie saved my life. He literally saved me from complete destruction. Sometimes I feel sad thinking that I'll never see him again. I wish he could've seen me in recovery. I know he would have been so proud, but he comes to me in my dreams. It's like we're sitting in a living room.

He just sits in the chair smiling. He never says anything. Once he hugged me. It was so profound and felt real. I probably should stop talking about this or you'll all think I'm crazy, or still smoking meth." Everyone laughed.

"My life has meaning today. I have hope today, and I believe in an afterlife. That really motivates me. My greatest hope is to see my beautiful boy. I'm going to say to him, 'Thanks for the card. I took your advice. I didn't give up. I kept fighting. Look at me now, Richie. I made it.'

"I made it and so can you. If I can do this anyone can. I'm leaving this framed photo of my son on the table if anybody wants to see what a real Navy corpsman looks like. Thanks for listening."

She went and took her seat. There was loud applause. The counselor stepped up to the microphone. "Thanks, Dixie Mae, that was a great message. If any of the patients want to see Richie's photo it will be up here on the table. Now we will end with the Lord's Prayer."

Fabio loved the talk. The whole time he was thinking about his mom.

He went up to Dixie Mae. "You're talk was awesome. I'm so sorry about your son."

"Thanks, young man. What's your name?"

"Fabio, I'm an addict too, and my mom drinks. I wish she could get sober like you."

"Your mom loves you, Fabio." Dixie Mae said. "As you know, addiction is powerful. Maybe you need to show her the way. Why don't you try getting sober first? Show her how it's done. Do the program, Fabio. You can do it. Remember, your mom will be watching."

Jack was emailed his new assignment, Saint Bartholomew's. As he researched it on the internet, it became clear what kind of parish and what kind of neighborhood this would be. He took a moment and pondered the assignment. A warm glow enveloped him. It felt right. There was a lot of darkness in that area. He was determined he would bring some light. Get ready Lucifer. There's a new pastor in town and I'm bringing God with me.

Tomorrow, Jack was scheduled to say his first mass. It would be a noon mass, on a Thursday, at his home parish, the parish he grew up in. His family would be attending. After mass, he would go to his new assignment in Newark.

Preparing for his first mass, Jack felt lighter than an angel with wings as he put on his vestments. He took a moment to pray to the Holy Spirit for guidance. He was offering the mass for Foster. Jack gave a homily on truth. "There is only one truth," he said. "The truth as put forth and proclaimed by our Lord, Jesus Christ. There are many attacks on truth in our culture and even within our church." He ended his homily by saying, "My only hope for my vocation is to stay loyal to the teachings of Christ, in spite of the influences of outside forces, no matter how powerful they may be." The talk laid the foundation for his priesthood. His homily was forceful yet hopeful.

At the consecration of the bread, he held up the host. "This is My body, which has been given up for you." At that very moment, he saw and felt the spirit of Foster, the top half of his image in his dress uniform with a huge smile and shining brightly. It passed over him, hovered for a few seconds, and then waived and was gone. Jack almost lost his focus but soon composed himself.

After the service, he stayed and shook everyone's hand, a tradition for a new priest after his first mass. His parents came up, along with Beth, and congratulated him. After some friendly banter, Jack said, "Mom, I saw Foster during the mass."

"Wow, Jack. Sorry, but I have to run," Mollie said. "I have a dentist's appointment. I can't wait to hear all about it. Call me later. I'm so proud of you. Goodbye, Father Jack McCreesh." She quickly hugged him, and they were off.

Later that day, Jack arrived at his new rectory and opened the door. He was immediately impressed with the large wooden crucifix hanging in the living room. It was an older property but had a certain charm about it with its crown molding and wood beam ceilings. It was a bit shabby and drafty, but definitely a classic. It would do fine. Having served overseas in the USMC, living in tents or sometimes foxholes, Jack always found any property with a roof and some privacy most acceptable.

Jack answered the phone. It was his dad. "Jack, something bad has happened." He was sobbing uncontrollably. "Jack, Jack…"

"Dad, what's wrong?" Silence. "Dad are you there?"

Beth came on the line crying. "Jack, we were in a bad car accident on the way home. Mom is in bad shape. The doctor said she doesn't have long."

"What? What happened?"

"A drunk driver, Jack. Dad is shattered."

"A drunk driver, at one o'clock in the afternoon? That's insane."

"He was arrested on the spot, Jack. I really can't talk. Please come over. We need you. We're at the Saint Michael's Medical Center, critical care unit."

Jack started wailing, "But I never got to tell her about Foster."

Jack ran out of the rectory and made his way to the hospital. When he got there Patrick and Beth were standing in the room sobbing. They stepped out in the hall.

"Mom is not going to make it, son. She can barely speak. She said she wanted to see you before she goes. Go in and see her, Jack," he said crying. "But keep in mind she is very weak. You need to say goodbye."

Jack went in and held his mother's hand.

"Mom, it's Jack."

There was no response.

"Mom, it's Jack."

Her eyelids flickered, she tried to smile. She spoke in a whisper, "Jack, I'm so happy you made it, so happy, so proud of you. Pray for me, Jack."

"Mom, I think Foster is in Heaven." He could see she was fading. "Mom, please don't go."

"Everyone wants to go to Heaven, Jack, but no one…"

"Mom, Mom!"

Chapter 23

Jack stood in the receiving line at the funeral home with Beth and Patrick. He felt uplifted by many of the people he met and the impact his mom had on their lives. Many he had never met before, like Gil Rodgers who was one of the last ones to come.

"Hi, Jack. You don't know me. My name is Gil Rodgers."

"Oh yes, I remember. You used to work for the bishop."

"Yes, and now he's a cardinal, unbelievable." Jack smiled but didn't say anything. "Your Mom was such a wonderful woman, Jack. We used to speak briefly after mass. We were likeminded. I always felt like I wanted to have a long talk with her, especially about the problems in the church. Anyway, I was thinking it would be good if we spoke on the phone some time."

"Sure, Gil. Just call me at my parish."

As the last few people finally exited the grand funeral home, Jack was yawning as Beth came over. "I can't believe how many friends Mom had, Jack."

"Yeah, everyone loved, Mom."

"Jack, I've been thinking. You have to say the mass tomorrow."

"I'm just not up to it, Beth. I'm too shaken. Plus, I've only said one mass. It's better if the parish priest says it."

"Jack, we can't have a liberal priest say Mom's funeral mass! Man up, Jack. It's for Mom."

"I'm so disgusted, Beth. How can God do this? Another senseless death. I mean like, I just want to say F-it. What's the point? Mom was my rock. I was counting on her to help me get my footing in the priesthood. I was counting on her for another twenty years, at least. This is just so unfair."

"Since she's not here, let me tell you what I think she would say. No, what I know she would say. She would say, 'Stop feeling sorry for yourself, Jack. Pull yourself up by the bootstraps and move forward. You had the best mom ever for the first thirty years of your life. You are a man now. You shouldn't need your mommy.' Then she would say, 'We get what God gives us. You get, what you get. And what defines your character is how you respond. Are you going to respond like a small child or a grown man? A Catholic priest, no less.' That's what she would say. You're going to be doing a lot of funerals in the future. You're going to have to learn to console people and do a funeral mass. You might as well step up and start with Mom's. That's what she would have wanted, and you know it. You know it, Jack."

The church was filled the following day as Jack beautifully eulogized his mother and gave her full credit for his vocation.
"She always lived it. She made her faith real in her life," he said. "Seeing this example of someone with an authentic faith was very attractive to me. It drew me in. No matter what was going on in our family, Mom always approached it through the lens of faith. It made her strong. She was not ruled by fear.
"My mom was really something. She didn't think like others. She had a frank, honest way of seeing things. It was refreshing. I don't know if you ever noticed, but my mom did. Whenever we would be watching the local news, and there was some kind of tragic death, friends, and neighbors of the deceased would be interviewed. They would inevitably say, 'He was such a good person. He would do anything for anybody.' My mom would always laugh. She would say, 'Jack, where are all these people who will do anything for anybody? Do you think they really lived like that? Anything for anybody?' Then she would smile and say, 'When I die, don't go around saying, she would do anything for anybody, because I won't. I will do some things, for certain people, sometimes, if it's not too much trouble.'" Everyone laughed. "I know she would have wanted me to say that." More laughter.
Jack went on to tell stories of his mother beginning in his early childhood. Some brought laughter, others tears. Everyone laughed when Jack told the story about his mom confronting Beth's coach and calling her a Nazi.
He ended by saying, "Pray for my mom. Please have masses said for my mom. She is not in Heaven. It may surprise some of you to hear a priest say that about his mother, but I believe almost no one goes directly to Heaven, and my mother specifically told me not to go around saying, 'Mom is with God now, Mom is in Heaven.' She asked that she not be forgotten and that many masses and prayers be said for the repose of her soul. So that is what I'm asking for.
"Today, I thank God for the gift of my mother's life. I thank God that Beth and I had a mom like Mollie McCreesh. A mother

who was always there for us. A mother who always stood up for us and was forever on our side. She never let us down. You would always feel uplifted after talking to her. I am really going to miss her, but she prepared me for life. Beth and I are ready to stand firm as adults and face life with the strength and wisdom our mom and dad have given us. A strength rooted in our faith. A strength rooted in our faith in Christ. A faith and power we have that will always sustain us.

"Thank you, Mom. May you rest in peace knowing you were a great mother. Your life was pleasing to God. We will miss you, Mom, but I know I can speak for Beth when I say, we promise we will not let you down. Beth and I will stand strong, Mom. I promise you today, we will not disappoint you."

Jack was losing his composure and knew he had to end it. "We will never, ever forget you, Mom. We love you, Mom."

He stepped away from the podium and sat down. He took out his handkerchief and wiped his eyes. There was a pause in the service. Everyone sat still for three minutes, then Jack motioned to the lector, Mollie's brother Jim, to proceed with the petitions.

New appointments had been announced out of Rome. Auxiliary Bishop Paul George was now Bishop George and was Jack's immediate superior.

Archbishop Cesare was now Cardinal Cesare and out for dinner on a weekday evening.

"Alex, now there will be even more trips to Rome, so make sure you keep your passport handy."

Alex grinned. "Certainly, Your Eminence. Nothing like free trips to Europe courtesy of the diocesan faithful."

"Now, Alex. It's all official business. When the Pope calls, we can't refuse. And he can't expect a cardinal to travel alone."

"Yes, and I'm always prepared to assist you at the beach houses as well. You know me, anything for the church. By the way, when are we going to be hosting those seminarians? It will be lovely hosting a clam bake on the beach."

"It's next month. I have selected six. Reverend MacCayne is making the arrangements. I told him I was looking for progressive men who are like-minded and of a similar temperament. Of course, I had to meet with them and spend time with them first. I think the ones who were chosen will be happy to join our little party."

"It's great, Louie. I love the beach. The water might be a little cold but if we build a fire, we can keep the boys warm. Plus, fires on the beach are so romantic."

Jack was trying to persevere and get settled into his new assignment at Saint Bart's. It was Friday and Jack had just said the morning mass. He headed for the church office.

He walked into the sound of sharp taps on the keyboard.

"Good morning, I'm Father McCreesh."

"Hi, I'm Candace." She was a little surprised by the lack of pigment in his skin.

"Pleasure to meet you, Candace. Do you have a moment so we can talk?"

"Sure, Father."

"You are the office manager here, right, Candace?"

"Yes, Father."

"What do I need to know, Candace? What can you tell me about our parish?"

She smiled. It had been a long time since a priest asked her opinion. She was a rather large woman but carried her girth well. Her smile was big with large gleaming white teeth. Jack liked her immediately.

"First off, Father, you are looking at your entire staff. We're a poor parish. I run the parish office. A priest at this parish doesn't get a housekeeper or cook. You're on your own. A few of the women volunteer to wash and iron your vestments, so you'll always look 'fly' for mass."

A strong, vibrant woman. Just what I need. Thank you, God. "I'll be fine, thanks for that information, Candace. But I'm more interested in the church and the people. What can you tell me about the parish?"

"The people need hope, Father. There's a lot of despair in our community, a lot of drugs and crime. There are more good people than bad, Father, a lot more."

"Yes, of course. So what do you think I should do? How do you think I should begin?"

"I've been here twenty years, Father, and I'm not saying I'm the smartest person, but if you ask me, I'd say, 'Preach it, Father. Give it to them.' The last two priests we had here would put you to sleep. They never left the rectory. We need a priest that will preach the real gospel and be part of the community, even if it's a rundown hood. It doesn't matter. God is everywhere. We need a fighter. We need a pastor that will fight. We need power in our neighborhood. The power of God that only a good pastor can deliver, so 'preach it,' Father."

Jack smiled and remembered what his mom told him, *Preach it, Jack.*

Jack got up and gave her a hug. "That was some great advice, Candace. I feel like God has spoken through you. I was feeling overwhelmed, but you just nailed it. It's not complicated. Thank you, Candace."

"And there's something else, Father. The music. The music is boring as vanilla ice cream. We need to liven it up."

"Really, how interesting," Jack said. "How about I put you in charge of the music?"

"Oh yes, Father! Please let me. You will not be sorry. The organist is my best friend. Just let us have at it, Father. We will rock these walls!"

Jack chuckled. "I want that energy. You are now officially the music director. You'll have complete autonomy. I won't interfere."

Jack went to his office and sat down. He contemplated the masses he would be doing this weekend. Then, he thought he heard his mom's voice gently whisper, "Preach it, Jack."

It was Sunday morning, and while thinking about his mother, Jack wept in the sacristy as he prepared for mass. Every morning he would pray a rosary for her and also remember Foster. He really wished he could talk to her right now. He splashed some cold water on his face, paused for a quick prayer, and made his way to the rear of the church as he listened to the ancient bells chiming. *I got this Mom.*

Jack processed down the center aisle with the lector and altar boys, while the congregation delivered a raucous rendition of *Amazing Grace.* He felt chills, his spirit shinning inside, so happy to be a priest. After the scripture readings, Jack got up to deliver his sermon. Joy filled his heart.

"God bless you all for being here this morning. God bless you. I congratulate you. It might be easy for people with money and material things to have faith, but it is even more noble for people who have so little, people who have to live surrounded by darkness.

You can walk the streets of our neighborhood and wonder, 'Where is God?' It would be so easy to feel despair and get discouraged and think, 'What's the use? Why even bother?' But there are those who will not despair, those who will not give up, even in the greatest adversity. There are people like that in the world, some are in the Bible, and some are sitting right here in front of me. I want to commend you. I want to congratulate you.

"You are the greatest hope for this community and for the church as a whole, people of real faith. Everything is against you. The culture, the media, the darkness that surrounds us, and I know many of you have had great difficulty in your lives, tragedy even. More than a few of you have had to watch as the streets took the lives of your children, yet here you sit. God bless you for your faith.

"I know we hear a lot about absent fathers, but I want to congratulate all you fathers here today who are sitting with your children. I want to tell you that I admire and respect your strength and diligence, setting a good example, working hard all week but still taking time on a Sunday morning to show your children what's important. I want to recognize all the strong fathers in this parish today. There is great power in a father's presence. We need that power. We welcome that power.

"And of course, I want to welcome all the mothers and grandmothers. All the single parents, mothers and fathers. All of you who are struggling with life, all of you who have continued to persevere with faith in Christ as evidenced by your presence here today. I'm here to tell you today - God sees your struggles and is pleased with your efforts. Do not give up. Do not despair. Do not give in to the demon, the demon of discouragement.

"I want you to know God loves you just the way you are, but God wants us to fight against sin, not only in your own lives but the sin in our neighborhoods. I know all kinds of programs have been tried, and I have some ideas of things we can do, practical things, but that is not my main focus today. Today I want to talk about power. We are going to unearth power by employing spiritual principals. Do not doubt this power. If you are willing to take action, you'll begin to see a supernatural power in our parish, one that can impact the neighborhood.

"The despair in our neighborhood, the drug use, the prostitution, all the vices, and even the slothfulness, are the result of the dark side operating unopposed. I'm not saying we can fix everything, but we can start to bring in some light, some light and hope.

"We're going to start with Confession. I want all of you to come to Confession this week. Instead of just one-half hour before mass on Saturday, I will be hearing Confessions Monday through Friday morning from six to seven. I will also be hearing Confessions on Thursday evening at seven, and I'll stay as long as it takes. And Confession before mass on Saturday is now extended to ninety minutes. I expect you all to go to Confession regularly, and I am not going to stop talking about it, ever. So you might as well just go.

"We are also going to start Eucharistic Adoration for one hour from 6:00 p.m. until 7:00 p.m., Monday through Friday. I will be here to ensure that our Lord is not alone. I invite you to join me, even if it's just for a few minutes.

"And let the word go out on the streets - everyone is welcome in this church. I want all the drug dealers and streetwalkers, all the gang bangers and crack heads, all of God's children, no matter where they are in their lives, to know they're welcome here. However, we ask that everyone honor the teaching of the church with respect to Communion. I have put more information about that in the bulletin.

"I'm going to be looking for some help with projects. I want to get books into the homes of young children, first and second graders. Everyone needs to be reading by third grade. I want to start a Bible study. I want to get twelve-step meetings going in our church, meetings to help support sobriety. I need your help. Please do not hesitate to step forward. I need your talents and energy.

"We're going to start to fight Lucifer right here, right now. The question is, are you willing to fight with me? Do you want to be a victim, or do you want to be a warrior? It's your choice. You pick."

There was a stillness in the air as Jack walked away from the lectern.

By attending an occasional AA meeting, Father Kenneth had been able to stay sober for two months and was staying out of trouble. The church had been promising more aggressive steps against inappropriate sexual activity, and he had been trying to be good.

Sitting in the rectory on his day off, the isolation overwhelmed him. He decided to go for a drive. Passing the liquor store, he impulsively made a U-turn and went in and got two bottles of

Fireball. He had been hearing so much about it and was curious. He went back to the rectory and started drinking. Four hours later, emboldened by the better part of a bottle, he made his way into the inner city looking for something to lift his dismal spirit. He parked his car and lit a cigar. As he wandered down a side street into the blue haze of the evening, puffs of smoke drifted over his dark San Francisco Giants ball cap worn down low. He turned down an alley. Shadowy figures with muffled voices passed as the aroma of bacon exited the back window of a greasy spoon. Within an hour he had found what he was looking for.

Three days later, Bishop "Mittens" Rahmney was getting ready for a meeting with Father Kenneth. He had just gotten off the phone with the police chief. In spite of feeling some heartburn, he poured a second cup of coffee.

Father Kenneth felt warm, his fingers nervously tapping on the chair. He thought about unbuttoning his Roman collar but wanted to look sharp. He prepared himself for the bishop's excessive cologne.

The bishop picked up his phone, "Okay, send him in."

Kenneth entered with his head bowed.

"Well, oh well, look who's back."

"Good morning, Your Excellency."

"A male prostitute, really?"

"I didn't know he was a minor."

"Well, you should've known. Again, you are bringing unwelcome attention. This is completely unacceptable."

"What was I supposed to do, ask him for I.D?"

"You are not supposed to be soliciting male prostitutes! Let's start with that. Do you disagree?"

"No, Your Excellency. I'm sorry."

The bishop arched his eyebrows. "You're sorry. Isn't that just peachy? Well, I'm not sorry to tell you to get your passport ready. I'm sending you to Honduras. There's too much scrutiny with all these sex scandals. By rights, I should be reporting you right now, but lucky for you the police chief is working with me. You have three weeks to get your passport ready, Father. You are going away for a long time."

The bishop's cologne was making him queasy.

Jack worked hard to uplift the church and make his presence felt in the community.

At first, almost no one came to Confession, but he would show up every morning and read his Bible while sitting alone in the confessional. After a few weeks, parishioners started to trickle in, some who had been away a long time. After experiencing the benefits, many became regulars and now it was trending up. Jack still wanted to see more but was happy with the progress.

Since no one volunteered to help after he made pleas from the pulpit, he started to approach people individually. Jack felt guided to ask certain people and most were willing to help when asked by the pastor. Many felt flattered. Soon children's books were being donated and distributed, a Bible study was in place, and Narcotics Anonymous was holding a Friday night meeting. The attendance was so good, they were already talking about starting a Tuesday night meeting as well.

A handful of people were turned off by Father McCreesh's "fire and brimstone" sermons and left the parish, even writing to the bishop. Jack's sermons always included references to Hell and the Devil. He was unabashedly pro-life. And though some were turned off, there were many more who felt edified. New people started to stream in to hear the white priest who "preached it." Jack reopened the large balconies that ran down each side of the church. Balconies that had been closed for years. Many people loved to sit up there. More were coming every week.

For the next several months, Jack settled into the new parish and became a force in the neighborhood. After Jack helped deliver a pregnant woman's baby, word went out that no one was to mess with Father McCreesh. The baby had been the child of a gang leader. Jack was gaining "street cred." And after seeing all the heavy drug use on the side streets, Jack had made it a habit to carry Narcan and in six months had already revived three heroin addicts who overdosed. He also applied emergency first aid to a shooting victim he found lying on the church steps in broad daylight. People appreciated his efforts and his willingness to get down in the trenches. Jack always made it a point to wear his black shirt and collar as an emblem of faith. The neighborhood needed to see it. He felt safe as everyone was accepting and friendly.

It was mid-morning and cooking smells drifted from open windows as Jack headed up to the local bodega. A homeless woman passed him with an overloaded shopping cart. He stepped around a stained mattress on the sidewalk. A man sat against a brick wall with a brown bag in his hand. As he turned the corner, a group of young men were sitting on a stoop. "Hey, Fatha,' you really need to change it up. You need to get to Old Navy, get ridda' dem' same tired threads, you need some colla.'"

Jack smiled and waved, "See you at church boys." They all laughed hysterically.

Simultaneously a reporter from the local newspaper appeared. He was doing a story on a recent drive-by. One of the young men sitting on the stoop said, "Why you always reporting bad news? Do a story on dat' priest dude right dere,' bro. Dat' dude is some good news, good news for our streets."

Jack picked up the phone in the rectory, it was Gil Rodgers.

"Hey, Jack, I hope I didn't catch you at a bad time."

"No, Mr. Rodgers. What can I do for you?"

"I just wanted to give you some information," Gil said. "I don't really know if it's important, and maybe it's nothing to worry about, but I wanted to make certain you're aware that your current bishop, Bishop George, is part of that network. He is buddies with the cardinal. Watch your back, Jack."

"Thanks, Mr. Rodgers. I kind of knew already, but they are everywhere. I don't even trust half my fellow priests. I never put my guard down. They can be quite cunning - with a sort of velvet-gloved deviousness."

"Exactly, Jack. And I wanted you to know Bishop George's father, Hermann, is a union officer, but really more of a leftist activist. He's always organizing paid protests. His group is pro-abortion, rather odd for a bishop's father."

"Nothing surprises me anymore, Mr. Rodgers. Thanks for the heads-up, but I'm not worried. I think the last thing on the bishop's mind is my poor parish in the inner city. They are all about money and there isn't much in my church."

"I just want you to be safe. Your mom was such a good woman. I miss seeing her."

"Me too."

Chapter 24

Bishop George picked up the Sunday edition of *The Star-Ledger*, then abruptly slammed it on the coffee table. Frontpage, just below the fold, "Navy Corpsman Priest," then the sub-headline, "Saving Lives in A Tough Neighborhood." There was a large picture of Jack, apparently taken from the parish website.

His brain was clamoring. He tried to put it out of his mind, but after a few moments of agony he reluctantly picked it up:

There's a former Navy corpsman who is serving as a priest in the Springfield-Belmont area and has been saving lives, some of them even being raised from the dead. No, not in the way you might think, but reviving heroin overdoses with the opioid antagonist Narcan. He has also treated shooting victims and even delivered babies.

The humble priest declined to be interviewed and would not meet with us or allow any photos, so we decided to talk to his parishioners. They say not only does he perform well on the streets, but he is even better in church with a style of preaching that has brought a lot of people back into the pews and has delivered hope to these mean streets.

The article went on outlining the new programs and services. There were also quotes from parishioners: *"This priest is relentless. He believes in us and has real faith. He's just a good priest."*

Jack thought it was all blown out of proportion and figured it would pass in a few days. At least he hoped it would. He was not the least bit interested in becoming a celebrity priest.

After reading the article, Bishop George phoned the cardinal. "Did you read *The Star-Ledger* today, Louie?"

"Yes, I just put it down."

"This is pathetic," Bishop George said. "Next thing you know, I'll have television stations calling asking me to comment or wanting to do a segment on him. We can't allow a priest like this to form a power base. It could be dangerous."

"Hmm, yes, good point," the cardinal said. "Perhaps we could move him before he becomes too much of a force with that conservative bilge he spews."

"Let's move him," Bishop George said. "I have a great idea. A spot is opening up at St. Agnes's. I think it would be most fitting to send him to a parish with a very active LGBTQ ministry."

"Oh, Paul, how could you? I love it. Let's do it."

"Consider it done, Louie. And I think I'll send that Polack priest to St. Bart's. Let's see how they like his accent."

Fabio completed treatment. The counselor at the rehab recommended he go to a half-way house in Delaware, away from his drug connections, but he decided to go back to New Jersey. Staying in Delaware was the recommendation, but everyone knew an experienced heroin user could walk into any major city and find "dope" within a couple of hours. Heroin addicts who were complete strangers could somehow identify each other. Most had that look - scruffy and undernourished. It was a subculture in every city hidden from the average person. All you needed to do was offer to buy a couple of free bags of dope and someone would hook you up.

The bus arrived in Newark just after lunch. Fabio decided to check into the parole office and then stop to see his mother. He was going to try and do right this time.

The parole officer met him in a small, windowless interview room.

The officer started banging the keyboard and pulled up his screen. "We need to get an updated photo. We can do that next time. I see you completed your treatment successfully, so that's good."

"Yeah, I'm trying."

"Are you having cravings or thoughts of using?"

"No, I'm good. Maybe just a little."

"I want you to go to meetings. Here is a meeting log, at least three a week. Are you on board with that?"

"Yeah, I'll go."

"You don't sound too motivated. Trust me, Fabio, you will not make it without some support. You really should go every day, but I want you to find a job too, so where you at with that?"

"I haven't really thought about it. I just got out. Plus, I got felonies."

"Companies will hire felons if they see you living right. When you leave, check the bulletin board. Now, what about your residence? Where are you going to live?"

"With my moms."

"We've been over this before, Fabio. Your name needs to be on the lease, and you know that's not happening. I can overlook it for a few days, but I need a valid address by next week. Didn't the rehab set you up with a halfway house?"

"Yeah, but I've tried those places before. Half the people are getting high."

"Maybe, but that means half the people aren't. You should've gone there. That was a dumb move. You need to find a sober house locally or somewhere to live."

"But I don't have any money."

"You are a grown man. Figure it out, Fabio. If you have to live in a shelter, I would accept that until you find something more permanent."

"A freaking shelter? F-that."

"It's better than jail. That's where you're headed if you don't get your act together."

"No thanks. I'll find something, a friend or something."

"Okay fine, but no one with a criminal record."

"But I don't know anyone like that."

"You should have gone to the halfway house. So just to review - you need to find a place to live, get a job, go to the NA meetings, and make a payment of $100.00 per month. Remember, check the bulletin board on your way out. There are also some sober houses on there."

As Fabio walked out of the interview room his head was throbbing. He was going to look at the bulletin board, but there were two people blocking his view. He decided he would do it later. For now, his goal was to take some Tylenol and lie down. He got on the bus and headed to see his mother. It was getting cold and he wished he had a jacket. The weather had shifted since he went to rehab. As he walked the streets, he purposely avoided the blocks where he knew the dealers would be out. He passed a sausage vendor. He felt hunger pangs but didn't have money. The headache was worsening. He took a shortcut down a side lane past some dented garbage cans, his sneakers crunching on the gravel. He gave a quick knock and opened the door.

"Hi, Moms."

"What are you doing here?"

"I just got out of rehab and I went to the parole office. I just want to lie down on the couch."

"No, you can't stay here. I told you before. They're getting very strict. I can't lose my housing. You need to leave."

"But, Moms, I just want to take a nap. I'm hungry and I have a headache."

"I don't have any food. I'm leaving for the store. Go to the soup kitchen. I don't trust you here alone. I love you, son, and I wish you the best. I'm sorry, but you have to leave now."

"Do you have an extra jacket I can use?"

"No, Fabio, stop at the shelter. They have them."

Fabio exited the apartment with his shoulders slumped and his still throbbing head held down. It was late afternoon. Darkness would be settling in and the streets would be coming to life. He had tried to do the right thing, but no one was helping. He began to pity himself. *What's the use? I can't do this. I'll never get sober. F-it.* He decided to do what he needed to do to get some quick money. He headed down into the subway and jumped the turnstile.

A few hours later, he had enough for five bags of dope. He felt shame and disgust, but now he could get rid of the headache. Prior to going to jail, he had been using twenty bags a day, but since he had been sober for a month his "levels" were down, and he wouldn't need as much. Five bags seemed just right. He had heard people were overdosing on some heroin branded as "Trump's Russian Roulette." He sought it out. Overdoses were like free advertising in the drug world - they broadcasted potency. *That's the stuff I want.*

The night was black and cold as Fabio sat shivering in a t-shirt on a park bench, all alone. He shot the first two bags and felt a balminess come over him. He loaded another hit. It was sheer ecstasy. *This is some good dope.* He started to nod off and then went unconscious. Soon he stopped breathing. He floated out of his body. He was horrified as he gazed down on his corpse with a needle in his arm and realized he must be dead. Such a miserable way to die! Suddenly, small blotches of purple haze flashed in his eyes and he found himself traveling through a tunnel, a whirling vortex of gray smog. As he emerged into a dank, murkiness, he heard a voice. It sounded otherworldly. "My wretched servant failed you."

Jack was headed to the local community center to hear a speaker who had been highly recommended by his office manager, Candace. "You gotta' hear her speak, Father. Although her style is different, she reminds me of you. I feel like you both are saying the same thing. It's the same spirit."

Jack watched a YouTube video of the speaker and was intrigued. He judged her to be spirited and brave, fearless even. A young black woman speaking to minority audiences with truth and hope. She had founded a group called "Black Minds Prosper." It was a message of empowerment and optimism, a message that was pleasing to God. Wearing his black shirt and collar, Jack walked the five blocks to the community center and grabbed a seat near the back.

Kaitlyn Rowlands took to the podium. "It's a great pleasure to be here tonight. I know a lot of you here. As many of you know, I grew up just a few blocks from here. I grew up black and in the hood. And like so many, my father was absent and most of my uncles were in jail. I know what it's like. I'm not here to judge or talk down to anyone. I am one of you. However, I'm going to say some things you might not have heard before, especially from a young black woman. I'm going to ask you to keep an open mind. As you walk the streets of our community, clearly something is not working. The policies that were supposed to help us are not working. It is failing. The government told us all these programs would take care of us, would fix us. It's not working.

"Maybe it's time to have an open mind and consider other options, consider a different paradigm. In a way, what I am presenting is almost the opposite of what the narrative has been for years. The narrative has been that we can't make it on our own and we are oppressed by the white power structure. We can't make it without the government and racism is keeping us down. That is just ridiculous.

"Maybe it's time for us to open our minds to a new way of thinking. Some of the things I am going to say tonight might stir anger in you. That's okay. Just remember, it's nothing personal. You can agree or disagree, but maybe it's worth considering new approaches. Keep in mind, I love black people and this community. I offer my ideas with love and kindness in my heart, not anger or vitriol.

"First, I want you to consider this idea that society is against us. These are our neighborhoods and our schools. We have to stop looking to people outside for solutions and look inside, dig deep. The world is not going to change, but we can change the way we view it, the way we think. That's why I started an organization called Black Minds Prosper. We can stop being victims. Being victims is a sad pathetic state that puts others in charge of our destinies. There are no victims, only volunteers. You have the power within to change. There will always be racism in our country, but character is the real issue. That is a word we don't hear much about anymore, character. Racism is not the main problem. America is the least racist country on the planet. There are so many opportunities for our children who graduate high school and are educated. My brother just completed Army basic training. I am so proud of him, but I made sure he did his schoolwork, even though it wasn't cool among his friends. He was accused of 'acting white' which made me so angry.

"Parents, if your children don't know how to read, don't blame someone else. Is there a free library nearby? It's your responsibility to get them reading, no one else's. It starts in the home. Get books in the house and get them in their hands when they're young. How can our children in high school be reading at a fourth-grade level? You need to have reading skills to have a decent life in society.

"All this money going into educating our children and they're not being educated. Racism is not the problem. I'm sure there are some good teachers, but how come the children are not learning? The schools are failing our children. There are black and white teachers in these schools, so it has nothing to do with race. And some teachers have told me that liberal policies have undermined the discipline in the schools, so even the most dedicated teachers can't teach. And the unions protect the bad ones, so horrible apathetic teachers can't be fired. The real problem is idiotic leadership. Leadership that promotes flawed, devastating policies that harm our children. Again, the problem is not racism. It has more to do with foggy-headed, elitist, liberal policies, that, instead of empowering our children with discipline and character, mollycoddle them, leaving them inept and weak, unprepared for life.

"Something is clearly wrong. It's time for black minds to prosper. Every child in the neighborhood has a powerful mind that was given to them by the Creator, but if you don't exercise your mind it becomes weak. Their minds are underutilized. No wonder so many are angry and discontented. Do what you have to do to teach your children to read and employ their beautiful minds. Give them puzzle books and word games. It can be fun. You can buy them at the dollar store, so don't tell me you can't afford it. Sadly, we can't rely on the schools to do it. Maybe someday the schools will improve, but I'm not counting on it. Teach your children to read. Teach your children well. They are so worth it.

"The next thing I want to discuss is father absenteeism. There is not a white racist or Ku Klux Klan member who has ever forced a black father to leave his family. Yet, if you wanted to decimate the black community, that would be the most effective way to do it, leave a family fatherless, just devastating. We have thousands of young men growing up without a positive role model, without the love and security only a father can provide. It's wounding our community. And God bless all you moms that hold our families together, and in spite of the odds, still get your children on a good path. Like my mom, who raised me and made so many sacrifices. I love my mom, but there was not a day that went by that I didn't wish I had a dad. I wanted my dad, and so did my brother, but he did not want us. It still hurts."

Kaitlyn persisted saying more things that were rarely said. She encouraged young women in the audience to avoid pregnancy outside of a committed relationship, and especially before graduating high school. There were benefits upfront, but you would become trapped in the system. She went on in more detail about white supremacist movements. She acknowledged their existence but questioned their real impact. It was more of a media narrative. After all, how many white supremacist groups were there in Newark? It was a powerful talk delivered by a beautiful, positive woman, who had lived it.

She concluded her talk. "The two main issues are family and education. If young women here today would be more prudent it could have a very positive impact. Do not have a child until you have a family unit to provide proper care. And that means the young men here are going to have to step up and be fathers. We need mothers and fathers, but it's up to you to be there for your children, no matter what. And we need to teach our children to read. It's not hard. It's not complicated. There are other issues affecting us, like black on black crime, but if we strengthen the family unit and educate our children, I believe we will see a major improvement in other areas as well. Remember it begins with you. It's up to you. With some discipline and energy, we can turn it around so our children can flourish, so their wonderful black minds can prosper."

She sat down to polite applause.

Jack was impressed and went up to meet her. "That was some talk. I'm sorry you had to endure those catcalls."

"It's okay, Father, I'm used to it."

"Wow, you have the right attitude, Kaitlyn. You have a powerful message, but it takes guts to say those things. I haven't seen courage like that in a long time. We could use some of that in the church. Too many are running on fear."

"Yes, Father, a lot of cowards in positions of authority these days. A lot of them don't like me, but I don't care. I believe God wants me to say these things."

"I agree, Kaitlyn. Your talk was hopeful and edifying."

"Aren't you that priest I read about in the newspaper? You're edifying too."

Jack laughed. "I gotta go, Kaitlyn. Nice meeting you."

Cardinal Cesare and Alex were hosting the seminarians at the beach house. Alex had overseen the arrangements. He even managed the clambake. First, he had them gather up some fresh seaweed and driftwood for the fire. Then they dug the pit and lined the bottom with large rocks. The last step was to build a fire on top of the stones. Alex was most pleased with the result and thought the clams superb.

Prior to the clambake, there had been frolicking and horseplay in the ocean, a lot of frivolity, followed by a volleyball match on the beach. Alcohol flowed freely and by the time it came to eat the men were well-liquored.

Around nine o'clock that evening, the cardinal suddenly had a dizzy spell. He figured he had too much to drink and decided to go to bed early, alone.

The following morning, Bishop George woke up before dawn and noticed a voice mail message on his phone. It was from Cardinal Cesare. *Funny, I never heard it ring.* He listened and found it odd to say the least.

It was a bunch of dark voices, barely audible and grumbling profanity. It was followed by the sound of a freight train with an obnoxious whistle. The whistle would fade and then repeat over and over again, as would the voices. Then he would hear one loud curse word screamed among the grumbling. The whole episode repeated over and over. He listened for ten minutes. The message would not end. He started to feel cold. He thought maybe it was a pocket dial. He decided to stop, start over, and try listening again. There it was again, cursing and grumbling, a loud freight train with an obnoxious whistle, and then a gravelly voice abruptly and loudly screaming one curse word. He listened for another five minutes. It was like a loop and wouldn't end. He started to feel weak. He felt ice-cold chills. He abruptly hung up. Despite the time of morning, he called the cardinal.

A male voice answered. The bishop stammered, "Louie, Louie, is that you?"

"I'm sorry, the cardinal died in his sleep last night. May I ask who is calling?" The bishop fainted and collapsed to the floor.

A few days later, Marion Nicholson had breaking news. "The New Jersey State legislature has just passed a law making it a hate crime for any church or pastor to deny a same-sex couple the rights and privileges others have with respect to marriage in their churches. The governor has already said he would sign it. From what our legal consultants have told me, that would mean the Catholic Church would be legally obligated to marry a same-sex couple and include the Catholic mass as part of the ceremony if the couple requested it, under penalty of law. It is graded as a third-degree felony punishable by up to five years in prison and a $10,000 fine. Earlier I spoke to Bishop Paul George and here is what he had to say."

The film clip came on. "I might need a little time to pray about this, Marion, but my initial reaction is the legislature did us a favor. Over the years, the Catholic Church has lagged society in regard to accepting changes and adjusting to modern times. We want our LGBTQ brothers and sisters to feel welcome and accepted in our parishes. We do not want to be a church that promulgates hate. That was not the message of our Lord. It's time for the church to be more tolerant and compassionate. I can assure you, Marion, we will honor the law and the directive of the state legislature. I view it as the will of the people. Therefore, anyone who wishes will be able to have a full ceremony in our church, regardless of their sexual orientation."

Marion came back on holding her microphone and standing in front of the chancery. "There you have it, the bishop is onboard with the new law. Marion Nicholson Channel 17 Action News reporting."

It was Sunday morning and the church was packed. Everyone wanted to hear what Father McCreesh was going to say about the new law. He had previously mentioned "dark forces" at work in the church and many wondered if he would come out swinging. He would not disappoint. Jack had reached his limit and decided it was time for the unvarnished truth.

He began. "The smoke of Satan has entered the church, entered the church at the highest levels, including and especially our own diocese. The response by the bishop to this new law was outrageous and despicable. Where are our leaders? Where are the defenders of the faith? Some might think they're hiding under the desk, but that's not the case. Yes, they are cowards no doubt, but it's not their lack of action. They are taking vigorous action, action that undermines the teachings of Christ.

"It's time for bold truth. You see, there is a powerful group of subversives in the church, a gay cabal. They are known as the Lavender Mafia, and Cardinal Cesare was the local don. You could consider Bishop George as a high-ranking capo. They operate as a group of evil puppet masters and have many willing marionettes in the clergy. It's obvious why they did not speak out strongly against this new law. It's because they wholeheartedly support it. Behind the scenes they're celebrating their success. However, I, and my like-minded brethren, will never be bend to their will or be part of their gang. God is not pleased."

"Preach it, father."

"It says in the Bible that there will be a time where men will become lovers of themselves instead of lovers of God. It seems to be referring to end times. I don't know if this is the end times, but we certainly have a serious problem in the church.

"Many will want to deny the existence of this group, just like a former FBI director denied the existence of the Italian mafia for decades, but trust me, even though it may seem unbelievable, it's absolutely a fact. A friend of mine, a former Marine who left the seminary and started exposing them, died under very suspicious circumstances. They said it was random, drug-related, a robbery. I still have my doubts. And I believe they had a hand in destroying the career of a very fine reporter. These people are sinister and instruments of the dark side. Maybe some think I should just keep my mouth shut, but there has been way too much of that going on in the church for decades. I refuse to be muzzled. Let the truth begin, and let it begin with me. Let the chips fall where they may. God needs his servants to defend the faith. I refuse to stand down."

"You tell em,' Father."

"We need to take action. We need to fight. Pray and fast. Stay close to God and stay strong. Don't ever give up, don't ever yield."

"Amen, Father."

Chapter 25

Jack and Jakob were having dinner at Applebee's discussing their new assignments. "I have no idea why they're moving me, Jakob. I was only there a year. I was just settling in. Honestly, it's kind of annoying."

"They are moving you because they don't want to see you succeed," Jakob said. "And now they are sending me there because they think I'll have difficulty. They do not understand faith. I welcome the opportunity to be in the inner city, just like you did, Jack. The higher-ups are weak and spoiled. They think we are like them, that we want a cushy, soft life."

"You'll love it, Jakob. The people are so genuine and have an authentic faith. They have a great sense of humor. Every day I was reminded not to take life too seriously. I don't know much about this new parish, but I think it will be more dull."

"You'll do well wherever you go, Jack. Just take the Holy Spirit with you. Every parish needs a priest who respects the teachings of our Lord."

"Thanks, you're right, but I'm sure going to miss St. Bart's and Candace."

Meanwhile, across town at the mansion, Bishop George was dining with his father, Hermann. "So what do you think of the new The Religious Freedoms Act, Dad? It ensures all people have access to churches and services."

"I love it. Actually, it offers us the opportunity to move our agenda forward. This law may eventually be shot down by The Supreme Court, so we don't want to wait. I have some ideas."

"Like what, Dad?"

"I think we need to test this new law. I'm sure I could find a gay couple that would love to be married in a Catholic church with all the pageantry a Catholic mass offers, just need to find the right parish."

"Well that's not a problem, Dad. It's the law and I'm the bishop. I know some priests who would be happy to marry your couple."

"Yes, of course. But I want a stubborn one that will refuse."

"Refuse? Why would you want that?"

"Then we can protest and get publicity, raise some hell if you know what I mean."

"But the priest might get arrested."

"Yes, exactly. I'd love to see one of these fascist priests arrested. But, trust me, they will fold like a cheap suit when the handcuffs come out. Then I get to watch him have to say mass and marry a gay couple, priceless. It's called progress, Paul."

"Interesting, Dad."

"Yes, it will be epic. I want to use the new law to shove it down their throats. We just need to find the right priest."

Bishop George motioned for some more wine. "That will not be a problem. Leave it to me."

The server poured, filling each glass. "Dad, I need to talk to you about something. Do you believe in Hell?"

"No, not really. I don't know if I believe in an afterlife, but if there is one, I think we all go to a better place. Maybe really bad people should be concerned, but I think if you're a good person you don't need to worry." Hermann took a sip of wine and grinned, "Plus my son is a bishop, that should count for something."

"Yeah, Dad. I'm not much of the fire and brimstone type, but I had a very odd voicemail message the night the cardinal died. It was eerie."

"What do you mean?"

"It was an unending message from the cardinal, dark with strange voices and obnoxious train noises. Based on his time of death, I think it might have been made after he died. It was abnormal, like inhuman. It freaked me out."

"Paul, you're talking about a cell phone message. There is any number of reasons why a person could get a bizarre message. We have a lot of railroad workers in the area and it wouldn't surprise me if they use salty language. It was probably a wrong number or a pocket dial."

"Yeah, I thought of that, but it wouldn't end. It went for fifteen minutes. Honestly, I couldn't take it anymore. I felt icy cold."

"And it probably would have ended at twenty minutes if you just stayed on the line." Hermann chuckled, "You don't think the cardinal is in some dark netherworld, do you, Paul?"

"No, it was just the timing of it, and it was from the cardinal's personal phone."

"Anything can happen with technology. Maybe the lines got crossed. Plus, if it was after he died, maybe a worker or someone was messing with it. Who knows where that phone could have ended up? There could be any number of explanations that would be more reasonable than the cardinal calling you from Hades. After all, he was a cardinal in the church."

Paul smiled. "Yeah, you're right, Dad. I'm happy I talked to you."

Jack had finished packing his things and stopped to say goodbye to Candace. He took a seat in front of her desk.

"Thank you so much for everything, Candace. You helped me from day one. I was feeling some anxiety, being it was my first assignment. I don't know if I could've made it without you."

Candace smiled, "We were a great team, Father."

"I try and accept things as God's will," Jack said, "but I can't help but feel I was meant to be here longer."

"I still can't believe it, Father," Candace said. "We're all so sad. We loved having you, but somehow, we knew it wouldn't last. We'll miss you, but you've left your mark. All the programs you put in place will remain, so feel good about that, Father."

"Thanks, Candace. Most of all, I think I'm going to miss you and your positive spirit. I never once heard you complain. That's a rare thing. It's not exactly paradise here."

"St. Paul tells us to put our minds on things that are just and pure," she said. "So I stay in the positive, Father. It's always there. It's a choice, but I forever have hope in my heart thanks to the Lord. Don't feel bad, Father, you did more than you realize. You've brought the real faith back to our church." She beamed, her big smile on display, "And everyone loves the new music."

"Well, there is a bright side, Candace. Your new pastor, Father Kowalski, is a friend of mine. I think you'll like him. You might say he is cut from the same cloth."

"Really? What a blessing. I can't wait to meet him."

Jack stood up and opened his arms, "Goodbye, Candace. Thanks again."

While grinning widely, Candace said, "Could you let him know who is in charge of the music here?"

Jack laughed. "Sure, Candace. Consider it done. I'll make sure he understands."

Bishop Paul George rolled out of his king size canopy bed feeling tired and restless. It had been another disturbed sleep. The sleeping pills were not working, but he had to pull himself together. He was the homilist for Cardinal Cesare's funeral mass this morning. Hoping it would relieve the anxiety, he went into the bathroom and took two Xanax. As he showered and dressed, he felt swamped in a dull melancholy relentlessly nagging at him After a light breakfast, he slumped into the back of a black Lincoln Continental. "Good morning, Luther. Get me to the cathedral. Take it slow."

The Cathedral Basilica of the Sacred Heart, a magnificent edifice with mighty pillars supporting huge vaults, and delicate carvings, was the fifth largest cathedral in North America and the seat of the Roman Catholic Archdiocese of Newark. There was seating for almost two thousand, and today it would be filled to capacity. Fourteen hundred spots had been made available to the faithful through a lottery. The remainder were for various clergy, including hundreds of priests, a dozen bishops, and numerous cardinals. There were also other assorted noteworthy muckety-mucks, politicians and community leaders, who made it a point to never miss a chance to be associated with something noble and perhaps garner some cheap publicity. The first pew was reserved for two United States Senators, the governor, the mayor, several congressmen, and various other prominent state officials. Other choice seats had been reserved for prominent Protestant churchmen. The local television stations were there and would be providing wall-to-wall coverage. The Gateway City Men's Gay Chorus was seated to the right of the sanctuary and would be providing the music.

Bishop George arrived ninety minutes early and met with the sacristan. The bishop had been tasked with prepping things for the mass. He had delegated the responsibility to three priests, and everything was more or less ready by the time he got there.

The bishop walked out onto the altar and took a moment to admire the cathedral. The doors had not been opened yet and it was still quiet. He adjusted a small gold tray, known as a paten, on a table adjacent to the altar. As he began to turn away, he was shocked to see it fly off the table and almost hit him in the head. He put it back and glared at it. After a few seconds, it floated up and levitated.

Then it flew through the air and crashed into the wall. He turned pale and went into the sacristy looking for a priest.

"Bishop, are you okay?"

"Yes, I'm fine, Father. Here, take this paten, bless it with holy water and finish setting up. I need to dress for mass."

"Bless it with holy water?"

"Yes, just do it."

While fastidiously donning his vestments, the bishop could not shake a feeling of dread. Fortunately, a homily had been prepared, no need to feel so much anxiety, simply had to read what was on the paper. *I will be so relieved to get this over with.*

The doors opened and the faithful flowed in. After the local television station set up in the balcony for the live coverage, the reporter began in a low whisper. "The cathedral looks absolutely stunning. No expense has been spared preparing for the cardinal's service. All the princes of the church are here, and so many other dignitaries as well. It is a tribute to the life of Cardinal Cesare and the impact he had throughout our state during his many years of service to the church, a true pillar of the community."

The procession began, a long line led by cardinals and bishops who bowed and removed their miters after passing the cardinal's coffin, adorned with his scarlet red biretta. The pipe organ blared out the entrance hymn, *Praise to the Holiest.*

Bishop Rahmney greeted the congregation and especially welcomed each cardinal, bishop, and top-level politician, acknowledging each by name. "We welcome all these dignitaries and representatives of other faiths whose presence demonstrates the love we all had for our brother in Christ. Thank you for partaking in this celebration. It is with deep affection we celebrate the life of an outstanding son of our nation and of our church."

The service droned on at a slow pace with many long pauses filled with songs from the choir. In spite of feeling a bit wobbly, Bishop George was pleased to finally give his homily. Unsteadily, he made his way up the staircase to a marble pulpit suspended above the church, complete with a sounding board above.

"My friends, it is with a heavy heart that I take to this pulpit today. When I was a young priest, Cardinal Cesare, who was a bishop at the time, took me under his wing and guided me throughout my pastorate. It was his mentorship and example that led to my consecration as bishop. I will always be grateful to Cardinal

Cesare. He was a man of unique gifts and talents. His humility and dignity, his holiness and unflinching commitment, his firm leadership, such gifts made him a remarkable cleric. He was gentle with other people's mistakes and flaws but very conscious of his own.

"He assisted the church, and people of all beliefs, to face the challenges of these modern times. We will miss our dear friend who was so present to us and many others throughout the state. He was always bridge-building, even serving on the Anglican Catholic Dialogue advisory board, reaching out to our Protestant sisters and brothers. He continually found time for the less fortunate and embraced the texture, flavor, and color of the city, especially the inner city. During his many years of service as a diocesan bishop, he was known to visit homeless shelters and soup kitchens, soup kitchens where he would don an apron and humbly serve alongside the volunteers. He was not afraid to rub shoulders with those on the margins of society. Indeed, he seemed to relish it. He even made it a point to reach out to the LGTBQ community and was willing to withstand the predictable reproach he knew would result. He sought dialogue with them. He would stand up for what was right, regardless of the consequences, and never lost sight of the pastoral dimensions of his own vocation.

"He liked to be among the people. He even had an annual tradition of hosting clambakes for seminarians at the diocesan beach house. Actually, he did it more than annually, usually two or three times per year. He wanted to know them, to mentor them, to savor their youth and energy. Often, he would feel refreshed after these beach outings. He had a gift for relating to young seminarians, and youth in general, and always made time for them."

The bishop went on and on praising the cardinal with stories and anecdotes portraying him as an exemplary holy man, then he ended it. "We give thanks for all God has done through the pastorate of Cardinal Cesare, for the energy and gifts he has shared far and wide. He touched so many people in a remarkable way. We commend his soul to our Father's unfailing love while we say farewell to our humble brother in Christ. He who exalts himself shall be humbled, and he who humbles himself shall be exalted."

Later that day, Dusty Rodgers was reading the obituaries. "I lost another one, Gil. This one hurts. He was only twenty-five years old, such a gentle spirit."

"What was his name?"

"Fabio Alou, I knew he wouldn't make it. I could see he was carrying some kind of trauma. I was sure of it, but I couldn't get through to him."

"You can't let it get to you, Dusty. He's not the first and he won't be the last. I'm sure you did your best."

"I know. I tried to get him to open up, but I only had one session with him, and he wouldn't sign a release for me to talk to his counselor at the rehab. He was supposed to come back after but never made it. If I only had more time, but now we will never know. Whatever it was he took to the grave."

It was early on a Saturday morning and Bishop George sat in the hallway in a rumpled flannel shirt rubbing his neck waiting for the psychiatrist. He was relieved to see him coming off the elevator.

"Good morning, Paul. You got here early."

"Yes, thanks for meeting me on a Saturday. I didn't want anyone to see me."

"Okay, take it easy. Let's go in and talk, shall we?" The doctor took note of his rapid speech.

"I'm feeling so much anxiety. There's a committee that meets in my head every night just before bedtime. My appetite isn't good and I'm still having trouble sleeping. I think it's aggravating my anxiety."

"You mean the Seroquel isn't working? It was a hefty dosage."

"It helps me fall asleep for about two hours, but then I toss and turn all night."

"That's odd," said the doctor. "You should sleep through the night."

"I'm grinding my teeth and I'm still having nightmares."

"Maybe we should discuss the nightmares. Tell me more about them."

The bishop shifted in the oversized chair and glanced at the ceiling. "As you know Cardinal Cesare, who was my friend, passed away last week. He comes to me in my dreams. It's unnerving."

"What is he doing in the dreams?"

"All sorts of bizarre things, but the one thing he does every night is blow me kisses. He is dressed in his red cassock and has this dreadful grin on his face, and he keeps blowing kisses at me. And he is laughing, he keeps laughing but I can't hear it. It's not funny. I don't get it."

"What else?"

"He repeatedly does cartwheels and jumping jacks, tormenting me, so my sleep is not restful."

"Cartwheels and jumping jacks? That *is* odd. Did you have any unresolved issues with him when he died? Deep-seated resentments or perhaps guilt over unfinished business?"

"No. We always got along. Essentially, we were allies, and remember, I told you about the night he died and the phone call."

"Oh yes, I almost forgot. Hmm. Let me ask you something, Paul. Do you have a prayer life? Do you pray?"

"Not really."

The doctor looked down at his notes and paused. "I think we'll try a new medication."

Jack arrived at his new parish. It was much nicer in every way and included a housekeeper/cook and office staff. There were several paid ministry positions: religious education director, liturgy minister, music minister, and youth minister. Also on staff were a maintenance man, a sacristan, and a pastoral outreach coordinator.

Opening the door to the rectory, Jack was thankful it was a Saturday morning. He was not in the mood to meet all these people. The rectory was outstanding and had been recently remodeled. The kitchen and baths were lavish and squeaky clean. Everything seemed perfect, yet for some reason, it dispirited him. He couldn't quite put his finger on it, but there was something unsettling about this place.

He sat down in the living room on the cozy recliner and picked up a bulletin that was lying on the table. What's this on Wednesday nights? Gay dignity mass? I don't think so.

He took a deep sigh as he glanced at the shiny flat screen mounted on the wall. There was no sign of a crucifix. *I wish I could have just stayed at St. Bart's.*

Two days later Jack picked up the phone. "Father McCreesh."

"Jack, Jack is that you?"

"Yes, who is this please?"

"It's Nora. You are the new priest at Saint Agnes's, right, Jack?"

"Yes, I am. Hi, Nora. Nice to hear from you."

"I live right across the street. I'm having a really hard time since my husband left, Jack. I just need someone to talk to."

Jack noticed she was slurring her words.

"Could you come over and talk to me a little, Jack? I feel lost and so lonely. I'm sitting on my front porch. I'd love to talk to you for a few minutes. Could you come please, Jack? I'm depressed."

"Now, you want me to come now?"

"Yes, please, Jack."

"Okay, give me a few minutes."

Jack was not particularly busy, so he was happy to go see his old friend. As he put on his black jacket, he made a mental note about the slurring. It was only three o'clock in the afternoon, a little early to be drunk.

When he got there, she leaped into his arms right on the porch. "Oh Jack, it's so good to see you. I could just hug you forever."

She reeked of alcohol. He tried to release her, but she wouldn't let go. "Nora, Nora. Please, let's go inside."

There were empty beer cans all over. Dishes filled the sink and the refrigerator door was ajar. Jack listened to Nora's pity-filled rant for almost two hours. It took some patience and tactfulness, but he was ultimately able to get her to agree to go to rehab, after she had finally cracked, bawling out, "Jack, I'm an alcoholic, I'm an alcoholic." He consoled her and assured her it would be okay. He then arranged for the rehab to pick her up the following morning at 8:30 a.m. and agreed to sit with her for moral support just before they arrived.

Chapter 26

Father Kenneth had been on a good track. When he got to Honduras, he decided to try and live right, at least for a while, until he could get a feel for things. He had just achieved twelve months of sobriety but didn't bother going to the local AA meeting to get his one-year coin. His participation had been lax for the past several months. Sitting on the sand in a lounge chair, napping on the beach, had overtaken the mundane AA meetings.

While meeting with the parish council, he judged he had gained their confidence and it was time to make suggestions. They liked his idea of having pizza and movies on Friday nights for the youth of the parish. Father wanted to do more for the youth and interact with the young people. Everyone agreed.

He was pleased that after one full year in Honduras no one had ever brought up his past "troubles." At last, a clean slate, it was time to relax and sample the local beers and liquors he had been hearing so much about.

Father Kenneth had also taken note that the age of sexual consent in Honduras was fifteen. Fifteen! He decided that if he was discreet and smart about things, he could enjoy some drinks and maybe have some fun, while not having to worry about law enforcement. Things here were just better. He was happy with his new assignment.

The following week a notice appeared in the one-page bulletin: *Starting this Friday, Father Kenneth will be hosting a free weekly movie night for the youth of the parish. Pizza at 6:00 p.m. Movie at 7:00 p.m. This week's feature is the original "Star Wars."*

After getting a letter from a parishioner at Jack's parish, the bishop rubbed his eyes and summoned the secretary into the office. "Get me Father McCreesh on the phone immediately!" The secretary frowned and sashayed out of the room.

A few minutes later he buzzed. "He's on line two, Your Excellency."

The bishop took a big gulp of a Red Bull and cleared his throat. "Listen to me, Father. You are to reinstate the gay dignity mass. Do I make myself clear?"

"Yes, Your Excellency."

"The mass is to be brought back starting next Wednesday. And you will put an apology in the bulletin directed to the LGBTQ community. Do you understand, Father?"

"Yes, Your Excellency."

"So I can expect your cooperation in these matters?"

"No, Your Excellency."

"What do you mean, no? This is a directive from your bishop."

"It's a sacrilege and a heresy. I refuse to participate."

"You took a vow of obedience, Father."

"My loyalty is to our Lord, Your Excellency."

The bishop started stammering and stuttering, his voice becoming raspier. "Do as I say father, or I'll, I'll," he paused and was having trouble focusing, "reassign you to the state prison as the chaplain."

"Yes, Your Excellency."

"You – I – You." He slammed down the phone and called his father. With a clenched jaw, he said, "Dad, I've got that stubborn priest you've been looking for."

Jack had a transitional deacon assigned to him for the summer. Isaac had grown up in the inner city. He stood six-foot-three and weighed in at a brawny two hundred and seventy pounds. Jack was pleased. He knew Isaac from the seminary, tough physically and mentally, and truly orthodox. The bishop had assigned him with the old pastor in mind.

It was good to have one strong ally, as he was expecting conflict, especially after he canceled the gay dignity mass and replaced it with the traditional Latin Mass. He had heard some of the parishioners were going off the rails and planning a protest, but he didn't know what to expect. He soon found out.

As Jack was presiding over a noon weekday mass, a group came in during the consecration holding professionally printed signs, that read, "Homophobe Priest," and "Stop Hate." They kept shouting, "no justice, no peace."

Jack was stunned. He couldn't believe Catholic parishioners would interrupt a mass with protesting. He decided to persevere and in a low voice continued to say the offertory prayers. As he was handing out communion, they encircled him and continued to shout.

Jack ignored them, and when the mass ended, he thought about turning the other cheek, but his temper got the best of him.

He began shouting. "How dare you come in here like a pack of wolves and disrespect our Lord! How cowardly and shameful of you to come into God's house and disrupt the Holy Mass. You are all wicked tools of the dark side, fools all of you!"

They started chanting while bouncing around with their signs, "No justice, no peace!"

Jack felt himself balling his fists. A couple of male parishioners who were at the mass surrounded him as a sort of Swiss guard. Isaac also stepped up. They were outnumbered three to one.

"The next time you protest at mass the police will be called," Jack said, "and I'll have you removed. Or I might just do it myself. Satan is using all of you as a bunch of useful idiots!"

They started shouting louder. Jack began pacing, then went up and grabbed a sign out of a young man's hands and smashed it to pieces. The man, who had a ponytail, charged at Jack and was flipped to the ground. He hit his head on a pew leaving him with a small gash on his forehead. Others looked like they might jump in, but Isaac stepped forward and stood sturdy like a sycamore. No one moved.

The man with the gash got up, "I'm calling the police. You assaulted me!"

Jack said, "Out, get out right now!" He grabbed another protestor's sign, and while gritting his teeth, said, "If I'm getting charged with assault, I might as well get my money's worth."

Seeing this, the protestors were shaken and headed for the door. Isaac followed closely and made sure they continued their retreat. Jack trailed them outside and while shattering the second sign on the heavy cement steps, he barked, "There is a way that seems right to a man, but its end is the way of death."

Two of the protestors got in their car. "That priest is nuts."

After being contacted, the police declined to make an arrest. The bishop considered intervening with the chief but decided instead to just let his father's plan proceed. The protestors were advised to be patient and wait for further instruction. He assured them the priest would get his comeuppance.

A few days later a man approached Jack after the morning mass. Father, my name is Bruce Samuels. My fiancé and I are both members of this parish. We want to get married here at Saint Agnes's, just something simple. I was wondering if we could check the calendar."

"Certainly, let's go to the office," Jack said.

"We already did the Pre-Cana classes, Father, and it will be a very small party, so we don't need much planning. The sooner the better. We were hoping for a Saturday afternoon."

Jack looked down at the calendar. "I have an opening in two weeks. There's a funeral that morning, but if it's going to be something simple, we can do it in the afternoon, like three o'clock."

"Yes, Father. That would be great."

"I'd just like to meet with you and your wife," Jack said, "to go over the readings and make sure everything is in order. Could you stop by some evening this week, maybe Thursday, say around seven?"

"Yes, father. That will work."

The next day, Hermann George called his son. "Everything is in place. The protesters are being hired, the wedding date is set, and they're meeting with McCreesh on Thursday evening. When he sees they're a gay couple and denies them, that's when the fun starts. Are you sure he will refuse them?"

"Yes, I'm sure. I was going to say, 'Is the pope Catholic?' but I'm not sure that works anymore." They both laughed.

Thursday evening rolled around and Bruce Samuels knocked on the rectory door with his fiancé Jeffrey. Jack opened the door and welcomed them in.

Bruce said, "Father, I'd like you to meet Jeffery."

Jack was confused. "Is this your best man?"

"No, this is my fiancé. Jeffrey is to be my wife."

"Your wife? You want me to marry you two?"

"Yes, Father. I'm sure you're familiar with the new law."

"I am, but I won't do it. I'm sorry, it's nothing personal, but there is no way I'd ever marry a gay couple in this church, regardless of the law."

"You might as well do the ceremony, Father. We could just find another priest."

"I don't doubt that, but I won't be doing it."

"Father, it's only fair to warn you, we have a group backing us, Catholics for Social Justice. We will oppose you. And if you don't do it, I can assure you, we will insist that you be arrested and charged with a Third-Degree Felony. You might even go to jail. And trust me, this is going to garner media attention."

"Do what you have to do, Bruce, and I'll do what I have to do."

Bruce walked out of the rectory grinning and immediately called Hermann George.

"He refused, Hermann."

"He did? Awesome. Let me handle it from here. Just sit back and watch the show. I got this."

The following week articles started appearing in the local newspapers about a priest who refused to marry a gay couple. The story was heating up and many had strong opinions. A few days before the scheduled wedding, picketers started to appear out in front of the church, eventually being interviewed by the local news stations. A number identified themselves to the reporters as parishioners. Jack recognized some of them from the protest inside the church. He wished he had the authority to excommunicate them. The news media was loving it and were there every day.

Hermann George even had a news release issued under the veneer of "Catholics for Social Justice," supporting the gay couple and asking for an end to "all hate in any form."

After the Saturday morning funeral ended, a mob started to gather outside the church. Jack decided to lock the heavy doors. He went out the back and walked next door to the rectory. He called Jakob.

"You would not believe this Jakob, there are at least two hundred people out there protesting and chanting."

"Yeah, Jack. I heard about your problems. I wish I could be there. Stand strong, brother. Remember, 'blessed are you when they persecute you and say all manner of evil against you for My sake.'"

Jack smiled. "Perfect Bible quote, Jakob. Right now they're out there chanting, 'lock him up.' I'm pretty sure they're talking about me, so I think that counts as evil against me."

"Keep your sense of humor, Jack and I will try and keep mine because they will probably come for me next."

"Thanks, Jakob. I have to go. I'm not saying this is a good day, but I feel God's presence. When God is with you, who can be against you? Please pray for me, Jakob."

"I will Jack, and I think Candace is over there with a group from the church."

After ending the call, Jack looked out the window. There she was with a group of fifteen parishioners enthusiastically counter-protesting. They had homemade signs. He saw one that said, "We love you, Father." He felt a lump in his throat.

Down in the crowd, Candace went over to a street vendor to purchase a bottle of water. She overheard a woman talking to bystanders.

"That priest won't marry a gay couple, but I saw him messing around with a woman on the porch across from the church. He was cuddling her in broad daylight like there was no tomorrow. Next, he went inside for two hours. Then I saw him going back for more the next morning. And that woman is a drinker. Trust me, I know."

Candace darted over and got right in her face. "No, you don't know. You don't know Father McCreesh, so maybe you should just shut your pie hole."

The woman spun around, "Excuse me? Who are you?"

"Never mind who I am. Girl, you need to get your mind right. Don't you know gossip is a sin?"

"Well, I -"

Candace opened her water bottle and winked, "I'll pray for you, sista'." Feeling satisfied, she strutted back to her group.

Jack had no reservations. He looked at his mom's picture on the dresser. He knew what she would say. He spoke to the photo. "Thanks for raising me right, Mom." He went back to the church, knelt down in the first pew, and prayed for twenty minutes, offering up the present hardship for his mother's soul. He ended with, "God, Your will be done." Since it was nearing two-thirty, he unlocked the doors. He looked out and saw a wedding party pulling up in a limousine. Then he saw the police cars arriving. It was time.

The police approached the church and Jack met them on the steps. They were polite and professional. Jack recognized one as a former high school classmate.

Down on the street, Hermann was all smiles as the police appeared. "Get ready for the ceremony boys. This priest is going to fold like a lawn chair after the cops tell him he's going to the hoosegow. The first Catholic gay marriage ceremony and a conservative priest will be saying the mass. It doesn't get any better than this."

An officer spoke, "Father, are you refusing to do the ceremony?"

"I am."

"We're going to have to arrest you, Father. Chief's orders. Sorry, Father."

"No need to apologize, officer, you're just doing your job." Jack held his wrists out. "Do you need to cuff me in the front or the back?"

"The front will be fine, Father."

"Okay, men. Let's do it."

The crowds were chanting, and the television cameras were rolling, as he was loaded into the cruiser. Jack couldn't help but smile slightly when he recognized Candace's voice hollering in the background. She was putting up quite a fight.

As the cruiser drove off, Hermann George sat slumped in the front seat of a Cadillac Escalade gazing at the steering wheel.

Across town, Bishop George was meeting with a priest friend. "He has been preaching about the 'Lavender Mafia' and a gay cabal. It started at his old parish and he's still at it. And he has been raising questions about a murdered Marine."

"A murdered Marine? That was ages ago." The image of the Marine, who sometimes badgered him in his dreams, flashed through the bishop's head. "Hmm, it's worse than I thought. Thank you."

He picked up the phone. "Alex, the cardinal told me I could rely on you for special projects. There's a situation that needs to be addressed, a persistent abscess that keeps getting worse. Divine providence seems to have presented us with an opportunity. When can we meet?"

"I can meet you first thing tomorrow. Let's say 8:00 a.m."

The next morning, Alex arrived at the bishop's mansion. His eyes widened as the bishop entered the room unshaven and in an oversized, purple terrycloth bathrobe.

"Are you okay, Paul?"

"Just having a bit of trouble getting moving today but thank you for coming. Let me explain what I need."

Once he understood the specific request, Alex assured the bishop he could take care of it and a price was set. Just before leaving, Alex said, "Paul, you really ought to shower and shave. You'll feel better."

"Yes, I will after you leave. It's just that my insomnia has been acting up. I have no energy."

An hour later, the bishop exited the shower. His arms felt heavy as he gazed in the mirror and applied shaving cream. Suddenly, an image of a grotesque goat's head appeared. He closed his eyes and looked again. It was gone. His hand quivering, he reached for his Klonopin.

Jack was arraigned at the magistrate. Municipal Court Judge, Troy Lehman-James, who loathed conservatives, especially Catholic ones, set the bail at $100,000.

Jack used his one phone call. "Don't worry I'll be fine, Dad. If you can live in foxholes with Marines, you can live anywhere."

"That's a good attitude, Jack. I already talked to the bail bondsman. He thought you'd be released on your own recognizance but told me to call if you weren't. We have the money, Jack, it just might take a few days."

"Ok, thanks, Dad. Love you. Say 'hi' to Beth for me, send her my love."

Two Essex County guards were working the night shift.

"He's a priest, but he's not a sex offender, so we don't have to put him in protective custody."

"I was reading about this guy. He seems decent, standing up for his beliefs. Let's give him his own cell."

"I think the only single cell we have left is on C-block."

"That should be fine. It's the tamest block we have."

Jack had planned on keeping a low profile, but due to the publicity, everyone knew who he was. Over the next several days, he found many of the men respected his conviction and a few even asked to have Confessions heard. It was Friday afternoon and he expected to bail out on Monday. He settled in and accepted his plight with dignity and patience. Before bed, he kneeled and prayed. In spite of the lumpy old mattress, Jack felt serene as he laid down to sleep. A warm drowsiness covered him, and he fell into an exceptionally deep sleep.

The next evening, three men crept down the dingy, cement cellblock walkway. Two stood outside the door, while the other went in with a shank.

Jack, who was lying on his bunk reading, immediately perceived the dark, sinister look and rolled off taking a defensive stance. The man lunged and Jack was able to dodge it. He turned and rocked him with a classic left hook, knocking the man back. The two other men took note and soon it was three on one. Jack was managing but then he felt his shoulder, the old injury from the truck crash, give way. He lost all strength in his arm and in no time was being repeatedly stabbed. After the fourth stab, Jack's soul abruptly left his body and he watched from above as the men continued to stab him. There was a considerable amount of blood, and Jack felt relieved to be outside of the situation. More than relieved, he felt free and euphoric.

He took a moment and asked God to forgive the men. Suddenly, flaming wings of lightning flared before his eyes. He was jettisoned to a new setting. He found himself in a magnificent, dazzling meadow. The colors were phenomenal. Sheep, glistening and white as snow, wandered out onto the grass. They were talking to him telepathically and welcoming him. A mild scent of roses filled the air. He was experiencing great joy but had no idea where he was. He began walking and wanted to see more. He had never felt so alive.

Way off in the distance, he could see a group of people, moving in a column, walking towards him. He judged them to be a half-mile away. They were coming at a steady pace. He felt blissful watching and inherently knew they were there to greet him. At least he would be able to ask them what was happening. As the group got closer, he was comforted to see they were all smiling. Joy filled the air. The sheep were telling him to rejoice in the Lord.

A woman separated from the pack and started running. He was astounded. It looked like his mom, how she used to run, but he couldn't be sure. Plus, she was too young. She was getting closer. *No way, it can't be. It looks like Mom!*

"Jack, Jack," the woman was calling his name with a beautiful sounding version of his mom's voice, just richer and more melodic. When she was twenty yards away, he was sure. It was Mom! A younger version, but definitely Mom!

He ran to greet her. "Mom, Mom, you look great, I can't believe it!" He embraced her with a colossal hug. Indescribable joy filled his heart. "Mom, Mom, you're alive!"

As he was hugging her, he glanced at the approaching group still a ways off. It looked like his grandparents were in the front, and somehow, he knew others were relatives he'd never met.

"Jack, I love you, son. I missed you so much! I can't believe what you did. God is pleased. I'm so proud of you, Jack!" Her voice was angelic.

"Thanks, Mom. You raised me right. I missed you too, Mom! I'm so happy!"

The group was getting closer but not there yet. Mollie was still hugging him and said, "There is someone who wants to say hello."

Jack felt a tap on the shoulder. He turned around.

"Love you, brother. Semper fi."

REVIEW

A brief honest review is always appreciated. Or if you prefer, Amazon will allow just a rating (stars) without a written review.

OTHER BOOKS BY JOHNNIE BARLEYKORN:

FICTION

Annie's Dad is in Rehab

Sadie's Dad Smokes Crack

NON-FICTION

12 Step Survival Guide, Battling Addiction and Ornery Old-timers in Alcoholics Anonymous

Crushing Addiction. Spiritual Warfare in Alcoholics Anonymous.

Available on Amazon.

Printed in Great Britain
by Amazon